INHERITANCE

SINCLAIR MACLEOD

GW00726018

MARPLES
BOOKS

Published in 2013 by Marplesi

ISBN 978-0-9575566-3-8

A catalogue record for this book is available
from the British Library.

Dedication

To Robert and Jane with love and thanks.

As always, in memory of Calum,
my incredible son and constant inspiration.

Also available by Sinclair Macleod

The Reluctant Detective Series
The Reluctant Detective

The Good Girl

The Killer Performer

The Island Mystery (Short Story)

Russell and Menzies Series
Soulseeker

Acknowledgements

Thanks are due to Emma Hamilton, Geoff Fisher and my patient editor Andy Melvin.

As always my love and thanks also go to my wife of 25 years, Kim and my incredibly wise and gorgeous daughter, Kirsten. I could not write these books without their continued love, support and inspiration.

xx

CHAPTER 1

Thud!

"What the hell?" Bryan Nicholls exclaimed as he looked over the side of his little Byte sailing dinghy into the dark waters of Bardowie Loch. A black polythene bag, about the size of a small suitcase, floated close to the hull just below the surface.

Before it could drift out of his reach, he leaned over and grabbed it. He quickly calculated that there was too much weight in it to pull it aboard without risking capsizing the boat, so with his left hand on the rudder, he held the bag with his right and steered the dinghy back towards the quay in front of the sailing club building. He was at the far end of the loch and it proved to be a difficult operation to both control the boat and hold on to the bag. On a couple of occasions he nearly lost his catch back into the depths as he struggled to get a firm grip on it.

"Dirty so-and-so's," he said to himself. He was angry that someone thought it was acceptable to throw rubbish into the loch; he felt quite protective of the place. It was his haven, his escape from the stresses of life and a wife whose constant negativity wore him down. Retirement had meant him spending too much time with her, but buying the dinghy had offered him time away from her. The thought of someone defiling his little piece of paradise was horrific to him.

At the jetty, he nudged the bag into shallow water before securing the boat. He climbed out of the little craft and walked to where the bag had settled and reached down to lift it. It was heavier than he had imagined and he laboured to hoist it into his arms as his hands were so cold. Finally he had a firm hold on the slippery sides and waded towards the shore. As he came out of the water his foot slipped on an unseen large pebble and the package fell from his hands. It hit the ground and burst open to reveal a blue-white mass. Bryan cursed his stupidity and reached for the bag when he realised that he was staring at what looked like a nipple. He leaned over to peel away the rest of the polythene and was engulfed in an aura of putrefaction and decay as he revealed the torso of a man. His head reeled and the next thing he was aware of was a bank of low cloud rolling over him as he stared up at the heavens.

When he had recovered from his initial shock, he looked at the bag once again to confirm what he thought he had seen. When he was sure he hadn't imagined it, he searched frantically in his pockets for his mobile phone, removed it from its waterproof bag and called the police.

CHAPTER 2

A large group of people stood in silent reverence as a cloud of condensed breaths rose from them to coalesce and then dissipate in the morning mist. They were congregated around an open grave cut from black soil, where a dark brown coffin lay on wooden planks, while a minister read the funeral rites.

Slightly detached from the service, Detective Superintendent Tom Russell stood in contemplative mood. He had watched this process so often he could practically conduct the funeral rites for any of the major religions. No matter the weather, the burial of a murder victim was always a bleak occasion. Russell hoped his own funeral would be a celebration of a long life lived well, but it was difficult to celebrate when a life had been cut short by another human being. There was only despair and on a cold, bleak winter's day that sense of desolation was cast even deeper.

This was a large gathering but Russell had been to funerals where only three or four people had attended. The service may be different and the congregation may change but for that difficult period before the coffin was committed to the ground, the atmosphere was always exactly the same. Those who were close to the victim in life were closest to the grave at the service. There would be tears and sometimes wailing from friends and family who felt the loss most keenly. On the outer ring, those in attendance would be still, heads bowed and pensive. They were there to support their friend, colleague or neighbour who had suffered the agonising tragedy of murder.

Russell did all he could to ensure that he attended the funeral of the victim of every murder he worked. If the family involved had a difficult relationship with the police then he would remain at a respectful distance, avoiding any insults and the anger that might come his way.

This particular family were happy for him to be there and had been appreciative of his efforts in finding the killer, even though it had not been one of his most difficult cases.

The minister finished the service and called for the bearers to step forward. In Scotland, there is a tradition for male family members and friends to bear the weight of the coffin as it is lowered into the grave. Eight numbers were called, eight ends of four ropes were held and the load of the casket was taken by a group of men who ranged in age from early twenties to an elderly man in his seventies. The boards were removed, the bearers allowed the ropes to lengthen gradually and the coffin began its final journey. Around the grave the sound of sobs increased in volume and even Russell felt the tug of emotion.

When the coffin came to rest the ropes were cast on top of it. Members of the family stepped forward to throw a handful of soil or flowers into the grave, a symbolic act of finality and farewell. The service was over, and the rites were complete. The minister thanked everyone for their attendance and invited them on behalf of the family to share in a warming bite to eat.

The mourners began to drift towards the car park from where they would go to a restaurant where the food would be served, stories told and alcohol consumed as the process of life without the deceased began in earnest. The gravediggers, who had stood in deferential silence a discreet distance away, would finish the burial when the mourners had gone, their solemn task done in private isolation.

When the graveside was deserted, Russell walked towards it and picked up a handful of the earth. He bowed his head, thought a silent tribute and then cast the crumbling dirt down into the darkness. He wiped his hands with a paper handkerchief as he walked back to his car, contemplating the waste of a life that the case represented.

He looked up and was surprised to see Detective Inspector Alex Menzies standing by his Vauxhall Insignia, waiting patiently for him.

"Alex?"

"I'm afraid we've got a new case, sir."

"What's up?"

"A torso was found out at Bardowie Loch."

"Just a torso?"

"That's all that's been found so far. Divers are on their way to see if they can find the rest of the body."

"Here we go again. Do you ever wish you worked in a rural county of England?"

"Not if the TV dramas are a measure. The murder rate is worse than Glasgow and fifty times more complicated," she replied.

He smiled wearily. "Aye, true enough. Where's your car?"

"I got a Battenberg to drop me off, so I thought I would cadge a lift, if that's OK?" Through the years as the decals changed the nickname for UK police cars changed with them. First they were pandas, then jam sandwiches and now Battenbergs, due to the chequered luminous blue and yellow squares that adorned the sides of the vehicles.

"Your bucket playing up again?"

"Well, a little," Alex replied.

"When are you going to replace that piece of crap with something half decent?"

"I'll get round to it… sometime." Alex's shabby, aged VW Golf was the butt of jokes for the members of the Major Incident Team and she did intend to replace it, but she never quite found the time.

When the cars of the family and friends of the victim were gone the two detectives began their drive to the crime scene.

"Sir…" Alex began after they had been driving for five minutes, "can I ask you something?"

"Sure."

"Why do you go to every funeral?"

Russell glanced at her. "Why do you think?"

"You like steak pie?" she joked weakly.

"I'll turn it round and ask you what our job is?"

"To catch the bad guys and put them in jail."

"That's true, but it's only a part of it. The most important part is to get justice for the victim and their family. I've seen too many cops lose sight of that. It's great when we catch the culprit and secure a conviction; we have a few beers and move on to the next case. I understand the need to celebrate but we forget sometimes that the victim's family can only take a crumb of comfort from the killer going to jail. They still have to bury or cremate a loved one and then live their lives with a huge hole in them. I go to the funerals to remind me of that fact."

"What about the ones who die as a result of their own criminality? Why bother?"

"It doesn't matter what their background is, no one asks to be killed."

Alex wasn't sure she agreed with him but she couldn't help but respect his dedication to his principles. It was his way of keeping their job in perspective and it was one of the many things she admired about him.

***

The normally peaceful loch side was a picture of organised chaos when Russell drew up. There were police vehicles of every description parked in every available space, some of them even perched on grass verges. Inside the blue and white crime scene tape there was a milling swarm of people. A tent had been erected around the torso and the white-suited scene of crime officers were everywhere collecting evidence for a variety of different forensic disciplines. Alex could see the diving team out on the loch, already at work probing the murky depths in their usual methodical way from their rubber dinghy.

Once the two detectives had dressed for the scene, a ginger-haired man wearing a matching white paper coverall stepped confidently towards them.

"Detective Superintendent Russell and DI Menzies, MIT," Russell told him as they both displayed their warrant cards.

"DS Weaver, sir. I'm the crime scene manager."

Russell shook the detective sergeant's hand.

"Well, DS Weaver, what have we got?"

"Mr Bryan Nicholls discovered the torso at approximately ten twenty this morning while he was sailing on the loch. The witness has been interviewed and has agreed to make a statement but there is no indication that he was involved in any way. He's pretty shaken up to be honest, sir. Will you want to speak to him?"

"No, get him to the station for a statement and we'll keep his details handy, just in case."

"Will do, sir."

"Have the divers had any luck finding the rest of the body?"

"Not so far."

"Is the Procurator Fiscal here yet?"

"Not yet but she's on her way. The pathologist arrived about five minutes ago."

"Who is it?"

"Doctor Hogan."

"Thanks sergeant."

Alex joined her boss in signing the attendance sheet and ducked under the tape.

"Brilliant, the cheery Doctor Hogan. A great way to start the case," Russell said bitterly.

Matthew Hogan was a markedly surly Aberdonian who was not only uncommunicative but totally devoid of any ability to relate to his colleagues. In her previous dealings with him, Alex had thought him creepier than some of the villains they chased.

As they approached the tent the fog thinned out, replaced with high white clouds accompanied by tiny flakes of snow that fell intermittently.

Inside the forensic tent, Sean O'Reilly, the senior scene of crime officer, and Noel Hawthorn, the forensic photographer, joined the doctor as he inspected the body.

Greetings were exchanged and Alex was surprised to find that she was blushing at the sight of the handsome snapper. Noel grinned at her, amused at her predicament. The Christmas night out had ended with the two of them enjoying a slow, romantic dance, followed by a lingering goodbye kiss. Alex had felt a little guilty ever since and was uncomfortable at the thought of getting involved with a colleague. Noel had called and left a message on her phone indicating that he would like to take their relationship further but respected her right to choose the timing. She hadn't called back and this was their first meeting since that night.

"Tom, Alex," was all the photographer said before he turned his attention to his camera.

Russell was puzzled by Alex's reaction, as he knew nothing of his colleagues' brief dalliance. He ignored it and turned his attention to the doctor.

"Doctor Hogan, it's good to see you," he chimed in a forced, cheerful voice.

"Why?" was the doctor's response.

"It doesn't matter. What can you tell us?" Russell was resigned to the frosty atmosphere that existed between the pathologist and the police.

"I've been here five minutes. What are you expecting? A full post-mortem analysis and cause of death, maybe?" the doctor replied with heavy sarcasm.

Russell restrained himself from telling the doctor where he could stick his scalpel and forceps. "For example, approximate age, identifying marks or anything that might help me to start the identification process," he replied acerbically.

"The subject is male, anywhere between thirty five and fifty years of age judging by the muscle condition. Due to the water temperature it's hard to estimate time of death but I reckon at least seven days. All of this is entirely speculative and probably pointless."

"Thank you."

The pathologist moved his attention to the torso. He indicated the areas that he wanted Noel to photograph and when he was satisfied turned over the remains.

The broad back was peppered with tattoos and Russell was surprised to see he could identify whom they belonged to.

"Well, now we know who our victim is."

"Who?" Alex asked with surprise.

"Gregg Wright."

"Of *the* Wrights?"

"That's the one."

"How do you know?"

"The quote about going against the family is from the Godfather. Peter Wright junior has it carved into the fireplace in his house. Unless I'm mistaken, the two faces look like Peter Wright senior and junior. The victim's grandfather and father respectively."

"That's not good. We could be heading for some major trouble very quickly," Alex said.

"Why?" Jacqui Kerr asked as she walked into the tent.

"Our victim is Gregg Wright, son of Peter," Russell answered the Procurator Fiscal's question.

"Great. The last thing we need is another bout of gang warfare," she said, as if it was Russell's fault.

The Wrights were the leaders of one of the largest and most dangerous gangs in Glasgow. Much of the drug trade and prostitution in the city was divided between them and their bitter rivals, led by Malcolm McGavigan and his family. The rivalry had been close to open warfare at the end of the last decade but there had been a relative ceasefire in the past three years. A leading member of the Wright family being murdered was bound to raise tensions once again and the thought of a series of tit-for-tat killings was something that chilled the bones of both the detectives and the Fiscal.

"You'd better let the organised crime squad know," Kerr ordered.

"I will, ma'am." If Kerr recognised the sarcasm in Russell's voice she gave no indication of it. Tom Russell's relationship with the Fiscal was constantly tested by a combination of her air of superiority and his perception that she lacked competence.

"Well, doctor, what can you tell me?"

"The same as I told him, nothing at the moment," Hogan turned back to the body as if Kerr had ceased to exist.

"I think we'll go and see how the divers are getting on," Russell said as he gestured with his head to Alex.

When they reached the end of the jetty and were out of earshot of the tent, Russell said, "What a pair!"

"They're well suited; as ignorant and arrogant as each other," Alex agreed.

The crime scene technicians had been joined by a number of uniformed officers who were searching the banks of the loch for tyre tracks or other pieces of physical evidence that might prove vital in the case. Russell was impressed by the way DS Weaver had managed the initial phase of the investigation.

As they stood watching proceedings in the chill of the winter's day, on the loch a shout went up from the diver's boat. Another body part had been found. The diver who had found it went back below the surface while the boat brought the find to the jetty.

From the shape and length it looked like a limb wrapped in another black polythene bag. Two technicians carried it to the tent and Alex and her boss followed them. The doctor slashed the bag with a scalpel, and then peeled it away to reveal a left leg. It had been severed below the head of the thigh bone; the only other obvious damage was a circle of bite marks caused by fish that had managed to nibble through a hole in the bag.

"The wounds at the top of the femur appear to be consistent with those at the bottom of the torso but I will require further analysis to be sure."

Inwardly, Alex sighed. Why was he so scared of stating the bleeding obvious? How many bodies was he expecting to be found in the loch?

"Any idea what weapon was used?" Russell asked.

"Something sharp," was Hogan's reply.

Over the next two hours the team continued to work to retrieve the rest of the body. The secretary of the sailing club arrived and opened the little clubhouse. She served the detectives and technicians with cups of tea and coffee but seemed anxious to have them away from the loch as soon as possible.

"I'm sorry, Mrs Shannon, but I'm afraid we'll be here as long as it takes," Alex told her when she expressed her dismay at the negative publicity this would attract.

The media pack was already aware of what was going on and the usual suspects of the crime-reporting world had assembled on the periphery of the tape. Russell gave a short briefing confirming that a body had been found and that more details would be released when the police had more to report. The experienced reporters knew that there was more to it than a simple discovery of a body and the TV news began to report suspicions of there being more than one victim or that the corpse had been chopped into a number of pieces. In the modern era of twenty-four-hour news coverage there was little the police could do to combat speculation. News was no longer just the facts as the television stations had to fill their broadcasts with something, and the more sensational the better.

After three and a half hours the final shout was heard from the divers who brought the head of Gregg Wright to the shore. Alex and her boss joined a number of people in the tent to watch the final unwrapping. The parts had been laid out like a jigsaw and the skull was the final piece. Hogan gave it a cursory inspection and instructed Noel to record the details on video and with still photographs. They would be grisly images as Wright's face was bloated and grey, his blue eyes were clouded and the wound around his neck was ragged. His skin had begun to separate from his flesh and he looked worse than anything a cinematic make-up artist could ever have conjured from the darkest depths of their imagination.

"Any idea about the cause of death?" Jacqui Kerr asked.

Alex wasn't surprised to hear the derisive reply from the pathologist. "Well, I think we can rule out suicide, accidental death or natural causes. Beyond that the post mortem and the resulting analysis will tell us more."

Even Kerr bristled at the doctor's contemptuous attitude. "It was a civil question, Doctor Hogan. The least you can do is offer a civil answer."

Hogan ignored her as if she hadn't spoken. "Please arrange for the cadaver to be delivered to the mortuary. If you can secure an official identification of the remains, I will perform the PM this evening. Good day." He picked up his bag and walked out of the tent.

"Detective Superintendent, please make arrangements to meet the doctor's request. I will see you at the mortuary this evening if his conditions regarding the identification are met." She stormed out of the tent.

"Fuckin' happy day," Russell said with a weary sigh.

He ordered that the bags the body had been found in were entered into the evidence chain. Arrangements were made for the escort of the body as the search for evidence was wound up for the day. The light had begun to fade but the scene would be secured overnight and the search would resume at first light.

Russell said to Alex, "Let's get out to the Wright residence and let Mrs Wright know she's a rich widow."

CHAPTER 3

A call to their regular office in Helen Street secured Wright's address in Milngavie. Russell entered the details into his car's navigation system that would guide them to an exclusive road at the heart of one of Glasgow's most affluent suburbs.

As they set off, Alex said, "So what do you know about the victim?'

"He's allegedly the first in three generations of Wrights to have decided to make an honest living. He staged a very public falling out with his father and grandfather about fifteen years ago. He denounced their lifestyle and stated that he was keen to make a clean start based on a marketing degree from some university in England. There are plenty of coppers who think that was all bollocks and that he may be the best money launderer in Scotland."

"Those tattoos on his back aren't really the sign of someone breaking with the past."

"No, the 'family is everything' shite they spout is them mimicking their criminal heroes and it's hard to see Gregg breaking with that somehow. Nothing's ever been proved but we think the links are still as close as ever. Now they just have better accountants and lawyers to cover their tracks than they used to."

"Do you think the murder could be something to do with the McGavigans?"

"You can bet your life if we think it's possible, the Wrights will jump to that conclusion with both feet and both barrels. Then we'll be back to murders in broad daylight in public places and who knows what else. Personally, I'd be happy to allow the arseholes to shoot each other to extinction but the chances of innocent folk getting caught up in it is extremely high when there's revenge in the air."

"Do you think the gang squad will be able to help us?"

"They'll be monitoring them as much as they can but these things can come out of the blue. Maybe Wright accidentally ran over one of McGavigan's dogs and that's enough reason for all hell to break loose. It's just the way they think."

"You have reached your destination," the voice of the car interrupted their discussion.

"Wow," was Alex's response to the view that greeted her.

"And they say that crime doesn't pay," Russell replied, shaking his head.

They were at the bottom of a gated, cobbled drive lined with lights that led to a substantial brick villa. The gates were open and Russell drove in and pulled up in front of the house. The Wright home was built over two floors with a three-car garage attached to the side. As they stepped out on to the driveway a light came on, the front door opened, and a severe looking middle-aged woman stared at them. She was wearing a navy blue cardigan, a white blouse and a grey tweed skirt. Her low-heeled polished shoes and general air made her look like some old school head teacher from the fifties.

"Can I help you?'

Russell introduced himself and Alex before saying, "Mrs Wright?"

"No, Mr and *Doctor* Wright are in France on a skiing holiday, they're not due back until later this week. I'm Clarissa McAdam, their housekeeper."

"Can we come in?" Russell asked.

"Is there something wrong?"

"It's best if we do this inside," Alex encouraged gently.

The housekeeper led them through the stained-glass door into a square hall with a terracotta-tiled floor. There was a short stairway with a mahogany banister and turned balusters, which rose to the second floor hallway that was lined with a balustrade. To the right, a rich mahogany door opened on to a spacious living room with a cream carpet, white leather sofas, subtle lighting, a living flame fireplace and a huge TV. The walls were covered in large pieces of original art, brightly coloured images of Hebridean crofts and fishing boats. It all looked like it had been carefully designed to appear in a home interiors magazine.

When all three were seated Alex said, "Mrs McAdam…"

"It's Miss," the older woman corrected her.

"My apologies, Miss McAdam. We believe that we have found a body that may be that of Mr Wright.

The housekeeper gasped as her long thin hand went to her mouth. "What about Dr Wright?"

"As yet, we have found no indication that the doctor was involved. Can you tell us about this holiday they were supposed to be on?" Russell asked.

"They were due to fly out to Valmorel a week past Monday. Their flight was early in the morning, about four or five o'clock, I think it was."

"Do you know how they planned to get to the airport?"

"Mr Wright was taking the Range Rover and they were going to leave it in the airport car park."

"Were you expecting to hear from them while they were away?"

"No, they prefer to relax and forget about anything else while they're on holiday. It was a very strict rule that they weren't to be contacted."

"What was their relationship like? Did they fight?"

"They had their arguments like any couple but to be honest they seemed to live their own separate lives most of the time. They weren't a regular couple, if you know what I mean. The only time they ever spent any time in each other's company was when they went on holiday." As she was speaking, the implications of Russell's question dawned on her. "You don't think the doctor had anything to do with her husband's death, do you?"

"It's very early in the investigation and at the moment all we are trying to do is piece together what happened. You haven't heard from Dr Wright since they were due to go?"

"No, nothing, but as I said that's not unusual."

"As it appears that Dr Wright is missing would it be possible to have a look around the house to see if we can find anything that might help us discover what happened?"

"I suppose so but that should really be young Mr Wright's decision."

"Their son?"

"Yes, Calvin, he's at university in Edinburgh. They bought him a flat there and he lives in it during term and even during the majority of the holidays. They're not a close family."

"We'll need his contact details to speak to him, but for the sake of expediency it would be better if we began our investigation as soon as possible."

"All right, if you think it will help."

"DI Menzies, can you give the forensic team a ring and then we'll have a look round?"

Alex asked Miss McAdam for Calvin Wright's address in Edinburgh before she walked out into the hall to make the call. Alex understood from Russell's formal tone that he wanted her to let the team know that Dr Wright could be their prime suspect or possibly a second victim; all without upsetting further the already distressed housekeeper.

"Sean O'Reilly," the Irishman said when he answered the phone.

"Sean, it's Alex." She proceeded to tell him what Miss McAdam had told them.

"So there's a chance either the doctor's been abducted or she's done him in," he summarised.

"It's one or the other and the boss wants you to start at the house."

"No problem, I'll get some of the guys to come over. Where are you?"

She gave him the address before finishing the call. Then she rang one of her colleagues on the Major Incident Team and asked them to call the Lothian and Borders force in Edinburgh to ask them to visit Calvin Wright to let him know what had happened to his parents.

Russell walked out of the living room and said to Alex, "Let's have a look around. Miss McAdam doesn't live in and she wasn't here when they left, so they could have been taken from the house before they were due to leave on holiday. We'll see if there's anything that might help us."

"Right."

They began by crossing the hall to the door opposite the living room, which opened on to an expansive office or study. There was another living flame fire on the wall opposite the door and a large bay window to the left of it. The wall behind the door had floor-to-ceiling bookshelves that were populated with biochemistry, genetics and medical textbooks. The other wall had a line of beautifully crafted rosewood cabinets, which sat behind a desk that was constructed from the same wood. There were a couple of guest chairs on one side of the desk and on the other a luxurious leather office chair completed the look of an opulent, successful and very masculine room.

"Bloody hell, this room's bigger than my flat," Russell noted.

"You wouldn't think he was related to killers and drug-dealers."

"All show," Russell replied dismissively. "Not much chance of finding any trace evidence or fingerprints," he continued as he ran a gloved finger over the polished surfaces and cast a glance across the pristine floor. The smell of beeswax was a sign of the pride Miss McAdam took in doing her job properly.

The two detectives had a cursory look through the books but all the filing cabinets and the desk were firmly locked.

"Miss McAdam," Russell shouted.

Her shoes clacked across the tile floor of the hall and her head appeared around the door.

"Can I help you?" Some of her stiff demeanour seemed to have reasserted itself.

"Do you have the keys to these cabinets?'

"No, those are business related. Mr Wright has a set and his assistant, Jason Garner, has the other set. I believe Mr Wright may have given master Calvin a set as well."

"That's fine, thank you."

"Is there anything else?"

"Not at the moment, thanks."

When she had gone, the two police officers followed her out of the room. They climbed the stairs to the small balcony on the second floor. Each of the rooms they entered was immaculately clean and tidy with little sense that anyone actually lived in them. The only exception was the master bedroom, which was dominated by an oil painting of the family above the bed. It must have been painted about ten years previously as Calvin Wright looked to be around eight years of age. His mother was a little older than his father, a willowy woman with fiery red hair and a stern countenance. Gregg Wright had the narrow head that was characteristic of his family, and although he was thicker set than his father or grandfather, it was easy to see the family resemblance to the tattoos on his back. In the portrait, the members of the family were dressed in the kind of casual clothes that could be seen around any golf course in the country.

"I don't know anything about art but I know what I hate. That's as pretentious a piece of crap as you'll ever see," Russell said sharply as he looked at the picture.

"The 'nouveau riche' relaxing at the country club," Alex replied with a grin.

"Well I doubt the motive was robbery."

"I don't think anyone would want to steal the painting, sir."

"Not the bloody painting, the watches. There must be sixty grand worth here." He indicated a case that was sitting on a set of drawers. Inside there were five watches from TAG Heuer, Rolex and Omega with a space for another.

"It doesn't look like they were taken from the house," Alex suggested.

"If she was taken at all. Maybe she decided to end the marriage without waiting for the lawyers to bleed her dry. She just bled him dry and buggered off," Russell said with a grim smile.

They went back downstairs and into the kitchen. The unit doors were the same rich rosewood colour as the furniture in the study. They were complemented by green tiles on the walls and floor, as well as an array of matching chrome appliances on the worktops. Miss McAdam sat at the breakfast bar with a hot beverage of some description.

"Did you find anything?" she asked.

"Not yet but the forensic people will be able to take a closer look when they get here," Alex replied.

Tom Russell was opening cupboard doors and sliding drawers to peer inside. He stopped and indicated that Alex should join him. When she looked in the drawer she saw a substantial meat cleaver as well as a selection of sharp-bladed knives. No words were exchanged but it was obvious what he was thinking.

The final room they visited was an enormous conservatory attached to the back of the kitchen. It contained another television and high-end hi-fi separates as well as a couple of two-seater sofas. Along a shelf that ran the width of the glass stood a variety of orchids in a wide gamut of colours. The plants connected the floodlit garden to the house in a way that showed a keen sense of design, giving coherence between the home and the outdoors. Alex reckoned the overall design aesthetic was the result of either Dr Wright's influence or that of a professional designer.

They walked back into the kitchen when the doorbell rang. Sean O'Reilly and three other forensic technicians had arrived with a van's worth of equipment to begin their more detailed look at the Wrights' home.

Russell and Alex thanked Miss McAdam for her help and asked her to attend the station to give a statement. They left the house and walked to the crime scene tech's van.

"Hello again," O'Reilly said with a weary grin.

"Hi Sean. I don't know if there's much to go on but we need to start somewhere. Check the knives in the kitchen drawer, and see if you can get anything from the computer. We could have another victim or she could be in the wind but we need to find Wright's wife. Sorry, I know I'm teaching my grannie to suck eggs here, aren't I?" Russell finished apologetically.

Sean's smile widened as he said, "You are a bit but I've worked with our feckin' Fiscal for three years, so I'm used to it and you're forgiven."

"I think we'll work out of Milngavie station, so I'll see you there in the morning."

"No bother, I'll give you a bell if we find anything."

He led his team in their protective suits towards the house while the two detectives headed to the home of the victim's father. They both knew that the next hour or two could have far reaching consequences for them and the city of Glasgow.

**

Both the younger Peter Wright and his father lived in Park-house, a respectable little working class enclave between the social desolation of the Possilpark and Milton areas of the city. The family home had been in Milton and the Wrights felt comfortable within easy travelling distance of their old haunts.

Peter Wright junior was the leader of the organisation; his father had taken a back seat about five years previously. It was he who had purchased all four flats in the building and turned them into two separate houses. One for his father, who lived alone, and the other for him and his formidable wife Jessie.

Russell stopped the car in front of a black Hyundai SUV outside their house. A marked police car was sitting a short distance away after Russell had called for uniformed back-up, just in case.

"Get ready, Alex. This could get rough. Knowing them they might want to shoot the messenger first and think about the consequences later."

"I know," Alex replied confidently. She believed that she was experienced and trained well enough to deal with anything that might occur in the Wright house.

The winter sun was gone and starlight twinkled as the first frost began to form on car windows. They climbed a steep set of stairs to the front door on the left of the building. The doorbell chimed to the tune of the national anthem.

"Very patriotic," Alex said with raised eyebrows.

The door was opened by a stout woman with a head of scarlet hair that showed white at the roots. She was dressed in a blue velour leisure suit that did nothing to hide the cascading tubes of fat that formed around her body. She held the door open with her right hand, showing a line of gold rings on her fingers and a collection of bracelets and bangles on her wrist. A cigarette drooped from her lips like a plant long starved of light and water.

"Whit dae ye want?" she growled.

Russell did the introductions and completed the formality of displaying their warrant cards.

"Ah know who ye ur. D'ye think ah'm stupid or somethin'? Ah asked ye whit ye wanted, no' whit yir name is."

"We would like to come in."

"Yir never done pesterin' us, ur ye?"

"Can we just come in, please?" Russell kept his temper in check, as he knew things were bound to get difficult when he broke the news and he didn't want to do it at the front door.

"Ah suppose so. Wipe yir feet," she said before leading them through an immaculate hall into the living room. The decor was a combination of pale gold floral wallpaper and brilliant white gloss paint. Above the fireplace a print of Ibrox stadium shared the chimney breast with a Rangers Football Club crest. Below them, carved into the fireplace mantel, was the quote from the Godfather that Russell had recognised on Gregg Wright's torso. A large display cabinet was filled with ceramic statues of idealised Victorian country folk doing idyllic rural tasks. There were two large chairs and a sofa, all of which were covered in white leather with gold piping.

In one of the armchairs sat the once terrifying figure of Peter Wright senior. Russell got a shock to see his old adversary reduced to an emaciated, pain-wracked old man. He had an oxygen mask on his grey face and his legs were wrapped in a tartan blanket.

"Mr Russell… to what… do we owe… this pleasure?" Every word he spoke was weakened by his struggle to fill his lungs despite the aid of the breathing apparatus.

"Pete, you're not looking too good," Russell said with a degree of sympathy.

"Em... physema. Aw they... Senior Service... ah smoked. Caught... up wi'... me. No... like the... weak shit fags... ye get noo." He seemed to take pride that the cigarettes had poisoned him, like they were an honourable foe that he had taken on but failed to defeat.

His son rose from the other armchair. Alex was surprised to see how small the notorious man was. Around five seven, he had thin red hair that was flecked with grey. He wore large square glasses, a patterned sweater and brown Farah trousers. He looked as threatening as an off-duty accountant but Alex knew the truth behind the look. Peter Wright's violent tendencies made his father look like a member of the Salvation Army. His reputation was built on legendary torture sessions and the rapid removal of anyone perceived to be a threat. He had never been in prison but the police knew exactly what he was capable of, though they had never been able to prove it.

He stood between the detectives and his father in a protective role as if they were threat to the old man.

"I'm sorry but I'm afraid we've got some bad news."

'Whit? Whit news?" Jessie Wright said from the doorway.

"A body was discovered in Bardowie Loch that we believe to be your son Gregg."

"Naw, ye're wrang, Gregg's in France wi' that wife o' his." Jessie said.

"I've seen the body. His face and the tattoos on his back make it pretty conclusive."

"Was he murdered? He must've been. They don't send MIT fur an accident or suicide. Who did it?" Wright junior asked as he ran through his thought processes audibly.

"Mr Wright, we're at the very early stages of the investigation."

Jessie Wright pushed passed Alex to flop down on the settee where she began roaring loudly with grief. "Peter, ye need tae get that bastard McGavigan. If ah get ma hauns on him, ah'll wring his fat neck maself."

"Don't worry, pet. Ah'll sort this." Wright betrayed little emotion but there was a granite-like resolve in his words.

"Before you go off on a revenge-fuelled spree, we don't have a clue who might be involved, we've only just started the investigation. You can't take the law into your own hands." Russell was trying to placate them with his tone but it was clear that he was giving them a warning.

"We look efter oor ain and naebody will get in ma way." Suddenly the sheep's clothing was cast aside and the wolf appeared. Alex could understand the fear that Wright engendered in large parts of Glasgow as she watched him transform in front of her into the gang leader.

The old man was very quiet, only the sound of his hard-won breaths came from him while Jessie Wright's wailing had quietened to sombre sobs.

"Ur ye done?" the younger of the two Wright males asked.

"Do you have any questions?"

"Naw."

"A family liaison officer will be in touch."

"Ye cin stick yir family liaison up yir arse. Noo fuck off."

Alex and Tom Russell turned and left them to their anger. It was their substitute for the grieving process that most people experienced; it would sustain them until it could be turned into their interpretation of justice: revenge.

Outside, Alex walked to the marked car, thanked the uniformed constables and told them they were free to return to normal duties.

Back in the car, Russell was finishing a phone call as Alex fixed her seatbelt.

"That was Hogan. They've decided to use Wright's dental records for the identification due to the condition of the body, so at least we're spared taking the Addams family to the mortuary."

"That's a relief. I don't think they were listening to what you were saying. If they decide to take things into their own hands, it'll descend into anarchy."

"Aye, they're nutcases without a shadow of a doubt. We need to get to McGavigan's crew quickly, find out if they're behind the murder and defuse this time bomb before it blows up in our faces."

"Any word on the PM?"

"We've to go at eight, it's going to be busy. There'll be more braid than a South American dictator's birthday party."

"Lots of opinions, none of them helpful."

"So cynical, DI Menzies."

"I'm learning from the best, sir," she said with a straight face.

"Touché, Alex," Russell replied with humour in his voice.

"Fancy a bite to eat before we go?"

"I could do with something."

"My treat. Chinese sound good?"

"Perfect."

CHAPTER 4

When they arrived at the mortuary just before eight, the viewing room was already a hive of activity. Alex quickly noted an Assistant Chief Constable, two Chief Superintendents, Detective Superintendent Lindsay Morton from the organised crime squad along with one of his DIs, and a DS. Jacqui Kerr was holding court and apparently lecturing the ACC.

Lindsay Morton approached Russell. "Tom, how the hell are you?" he said with genuine warmth.

"Apart from a dismembered corpse, I'm good. You know DI Menzies?"

"Alex, of course. Good to see you."

"And you, sir."

She had worked with Morton's team during a particularly nasty sex-trafficking case two years previously. He was a fiercely intelligent man with a calm demeanour who had led the investigation with a steady hand, never letting his passion for the job get in the way of good police work and was always willing to listen to those around him. He was a lithe, athletic man who enjoyed cross-country running, orienteering and mountain walking when he wasn't heading up the squad that monitored and tried to counter the large crime organisations in the city.

"What's your feeling about this, Lindsay?"

"From what we hear there's no reason for McGavigan's lot to be involved but with these lunatics you can never be sure."

"Was Gregg still involved with his father's real business?"

"We're pretty sure that he was using some of the property and financial companies he owned to wash his father's dirty cash but it's all done through layers of accounts in offshore banks. It'll take a full forensic accountancy team to pick it apart."

"If it's the McGavigan crew we're going to be cleaning up bodies for months."

"I know. Even if it's not them, we still might be," Morton replied with resignation.

Inside the post-mortem suite, Hogan arrived with Noel Hawthorn, as well as a female technician and his assistant for the day Dr Gupta. Gupta was an effusive little Glaswegian who Alex had found to be friendly and helpful. Normally, the younger man was the perfect antidote to Hogan's sullen, unaccommodating attitude, but it looked like Hogan had already given him a hard time and he seemed more reserved than he usually was. With the exception of Professor McIllvanney, who was the senior pathologist in the team, Hogan tended to treat the other pathologists as his subordinates despite them being officially at the same level on the organisational pyramid.

"I'm ready to start," Hogan announced over the noise of the people in the viewing room.

He began the initial inspection of the body, speaking his findings for the recording that would form the basis of his report. Everything was delivered in a monotone that rarely included plain English. Some of the officers asked him to clarify certain phrases he used, which seemed to annoy the pathologist as it interrupted the flow of his narrative. His voice betrayed his infamous contempt for those he felt weren't on his intellectual level. There was little in his first inspection of the pieces of the body that added anything to what they already knew.

His examination of the dismemberment wounds produced little, other than the pathologists' belief that Wright was already dead when the cuts were made due to the lack of blood in the wounds. Small traces of minerals were swabbed and would be part of the collection of evidence that was sent upstairs to the forensics lab. He was reluctant to state a weapon but when pressed by ACC Muldoon eventually suggested that due to the weight and thickness of the various wounds, something like an axe had been used to remove Gregg Wright's head and limbs.

When everyone was satisfied that the visual inspection was complete, the technician washed the remains.

"The cause of death is exsanguination due to the victim's throat being cut with a sharp knife or scalpel. The cut mark is above where the skull was separated from the torso. Judging by the wound the killer was behind the victim, pulled his head up and sliced through the carotid artery and across the larynx," Hogan reported.

"So that makes it a right-handed killer?" Russell asked for confirmation.

"Unless you know another way to slice open a throat from behind in that manner," Hogan responded sarcastically.

"It was simply to clarify your statement, doctor." Russell was raging at Hogan's inability to answer a simple question without resorting to derision.

"I thought my statement was all the clarification required."

Russell muttered a swear word under his breath and Hogan went back to work. Within the remainder of the procedure there was little else of value to the police and it would be up to the forensic laboratory to offer any further evidence to aid the enquiry.

In the aftermath, as everyone was getting ready to leave, ACC Muldoon approached Alex and her boss.

"I think you know how sensitive this is, Tom. I want this tucked away before we're knee deep in blood and bodies. The press would have a field day, what with the new Police Scotland organisation coming in April."

"Yes, sir," the detective superintendent replied neutrally, while feeling amazed that politics was at the forefront of the ACC's mind.

"I'd like to finish my career with no major loose ends. I finish up at the end of March, so no cock-ups."

"No, sir. We will treat it with the highest priority, sir. We will liaise with Detective Superintendent Morton and I'm sure we'll get to the bottom of it."

"Good man."

Muldoon walked away, apparently reassured by Russell's reply.

Russell spoke to Morton and confirmed that his colleague would attend the briefing the following morning at their temporary home in Milngavie police station.

When Russell and Alex were safely ensconced back in his car he said, "No cock-ups! As if his retirement is the only fuckin' thing we're worried about. Management!"

"Yes, sir." Alex always found it easier to agree with him when higher ranks irritated him but this time she was genuinely sympathetic. So many of the senior members of the force seemed to be self obsessed or preoccupied by what the press or the politicians wanted. She understood the importance but surely if they put the public first everybody would benefit.

He drove her the short distance to their base at Helen Street station to pick up her car.

"I'll see you tomorrow, Alex. When the fun really begins." Russell waved as she drove off and then set off for his flat.

***

As Russell locked the car on the street outside his flat his head was already swimming in a tidal wave of possibilities. The killing of Gregg Wright brought to mind all too vividly the previous gang-related deaths he had seen in his career. Glasgow's reputation as one of the Europe's most violent cities came in part from the historic level of maiming and killing related to the struggle to control the city's underworld. The razor gangs that had once terrorised the streets had mutated into organised criminal empires in pursuit of money and power through prostitution, extortion, corruption and drugs.

He walked up the stairs to his first-floor flat and opened the entrance to his landing. Standing outside his door was a dishevelled figure with a straggly beard and a haunted expression. A stranger would realise the similarity between the two men if they looked closely at them for long enough, but certainly not initially.

"What the hell do you want?" Tom Russell asked his brother.

"Aw Tom, don't be like that."

"What are you doing here?"

"Can a guy no' visit his big brother?" he replied with his arms open in a pleading gesture.

"Not a word for four years and then you turn up on my doorstep without so much as a phone call. What have you done?" Russell wasn't going to let his sibling off the hook.

"Ye're always so suspicious."

"Forty-four years of experience wi' you has taught me a lot."

"Are ye gonnae invite me in?"

"I suppose so," the elder brother relented.

Tom Russell unlocked his front door while his brother lifted a battered suitcase and followed him into the tiny flat.

"Tidy wee place you've got here," Eddie Russell said as he walked into the living room.

"Aye, Karen and her lawyer made sure it was both tidy and wee. Do you want a cuppa?" Russell was still bitter at how his wife and her divorce lawyer had carved him up when he and Karen had separated.

"Aye, tea please."

While Tom was preparing the drinks, his brother settled himself into the sofa.

"So what do you want?"

"Can I crash here for a couple of days?"

"Only if you tell me what's up. You don't appear out of the blue unless you're in trouble."

As Tom put the cup down on the small table in front of Eddie, he could tell that his brother was uncomfortable. The detective flopped wearily into the armchair and sat in silence, the way he would sometimes when he was interviewing a suspect.

Finally, Eddie relented. "I got myself into a bit of bother in London."

"What kind of bother?"

"I kinda owe someone a lot a money."

"I take it we're not talking about the local credit union."

"No, more the kind of smash your kneecaps union."

Tom sighed, "Jesus, Eddie. How much?"

"Eight grand."

Tom Russell found it difficult to be patient with his brother at the best of times but he struggled to choke back his full level of disgust at this latest lunacy. Eddie was always chasing easy money through gambling or some crazy get-rich-quick scheme. The thought of applying himself to study or work had never occurred to him as a way of making a living. Even by Eddie's standards this was idiotically dangerous. "Eight fuckin' grand. How did you lose eight fuckin' grand?'

"Poker. I was sitting with a flush, I thought it was a certainty. I wrote an IOU to cover the bet but he was sitting with a full house. How was I supposed to know?" he pleaded.

"Who was it you were playing with?"

"A Serbian guy called Dragovic or something."

Tom shook his head. "Shit, you'll be lucky if it's just your kneecaps. You are an arsehole of the most brainless kind."

"So can I stay for a few days until I get some cash together?" Eddie asked pathetically.

"Where are you going to get eight grand?"

"There's a guy ah know that owes me a couple of thousand. I was going to give that to the Serb and then try work something out from there."

"I don't think these guys operate a deposit and twenty-four-month payment scheme."

"Ah know, ah know. I'll work something oot.'

"You can stay but if these Serbs turn up at this door, you're on your own. You'll need to sleep on the couch, I've only got one bed."

"That's fine, Tam. Thanks."

Tom Russell kept his furious thoughts to himself as he prepared a dinner for them both. The atmosphere was strained as they ate and Tom was glad when he threw Eddie some blankets and then went to bed, with a heart heavy with worry for his idiotic brother.

***

"Ye'll never walk alone, Davie," Paddy Niven waved to his drinking buddy as he staggered towards the door of the Astral bar.

"Fuck off ya wee tim," Davie slurred with a good-natured humour.

Paddy laughed; he loved to wind up Davie about football and Davie was normally good at giving as good as he got in return. There were odd times when the banter got out of hand and they came close to blows, usually around an Old Firm game, but thankfully they were few and far between; Paddy preferred the quiet life.

It had been a good day as his estranged son Dermot had phoned to tell him that he had got an apprenticeship to become a plumber. Dermot had left with his mother and his two sisters when he was very young. Paddy hadn't been the most attentive father but both he and the boy were making strides towards building some kind of relationship as Dermot approached manhood. Paddy admitted to himself that Mary had done a good job raising the kids and that she was probably right to have left him when she did; not that he would ever give her the satisfaction of hearing it from him.

The day had got even better when he had won fifty pounds in the bookies; a rare achievement that he savoured by emphasising the fact to Jimmy Collins, his local bookmaker. Jimmy had laughed, knowing that he would regain the money plus plenty more from his customer within the month. He didn't begrudge Paddy the odd celebration.

Paddy walked the half mile to the Astral with a spring in his step. That had been four hours ago and he had spent the intervening time buying a drink for everyone in the pub and whittling down his winnings so that there was only ten pounds left. Five half pints of lager and five measures of Whyte & Mackay whisky had left him with a warm glow and he hardly noticed the freezing air as he began his journey home. He hummed the tune of a Celtic anthem as he made his way unsteadily towards his flat. On the way he stopped at his local chip shop where he bought himself a fish supper; a rare treat that his winnings allowed him.

He blew on the food to cool it as he continued his walk. His route took him through a quiet street that housed a couple of factories and a warehouse. The buildings were in darkness and the streetlights did little to illuminate the icy pavement. Half way along the street a figure stepped out of the doorway of the warehouse.

"Paddy Niven?" a male voice asked.

"Aye, who's asking?"

"We ur," another man said from behind him and he felt a blow to the back of his head. It knocked the power from his legs, causing him to drop the fish supper as the two men grabbed him. A car pulled up beside them and they bundled Paddy roughly into the back before driving off.

Maybe it's not going to be such a good day after all, Paddy thought.

CHAPTER 5

Milngavie Police Station was relatively small and rarely at the centre of an investigation on the scale that was required by a category 'A' murder. The senior officer in the station was Detective Inspector Mackie and he was happy to step into the background as the Major Incident Team and all their supplementary officers descended on his little fiefdom. Mackie was heading for retirement and the last thing he needed was to be involved in the murder of a gangster's son.

Overnight the I.T. team had turned the station into a major incident room with extra computers and telephones packed into every available space including the break room. By the time Alex, Russell and Detective Superintendent Morton arrived to begin the briefing around forty officers of various ranks and experience had assembled in an office designed to accommodate fifteen people.

"Good morning ladies and gentlemen," Russell announced with a voice loud enough to silence the chatter.

"As you know the body of Gregg Wright was found in Bardowie Loch yesterday morning. I will give you a full briefing in a minute but first Detective Superintendent Morton from the Organised Crime Squad will give you the background about why this is a murder we need to solve very quickly."

Morton stepped forward. "Good morning all. I know most, if not all, of you will know at least some of this but it's worth reiterating. Gregg Wright is the son of Peter Wright who is himself the son of Pete 'Razor' Wright.

"Razor Wright was an enforcer for the Wilsons back in the late fifties and early sixties. He eventually took control of the gang by allegedly slitting the throat of Stevie Wilson sometime in the late sixties. Although Wilson's body was never found and it was claimed he had run to Spain, Wright's legend was born. When he assumed control, the gang was running protection and prostitution rackets but he had an eye for more. He set up a loan-sharking business in the seventies around the same time as heroin began to be the drug of choice in the city. He was quick to realise the potential in the drugs scene and was ruthless in his exploitation of that situation. During the same period, with the help of his son Peter junior, many of the rival gangs were forced out or absorbed through a concerted campaign of violence and intimidation. If anything Peter junior is an even more sadistically vicious little bastard than his father and is feared by his peers for an alleged talent for torture, among other things.

"Since the mid-eighties when the second big wave of drugs began, the Wrights have fought to protect and expand their empire. The chief rivals for the crown of biggest scumbags are the McGavigans, led by Malky McGavigan, or Malcolm as he likes to call himself these days. Three years ago we had eight murders in the space of three months as these two psychos went after each other. Although officially there is no link between Gregg and his family's organisation, there is still a possibility that McGavigan is responsible. We need to find the killer quickly and hope we can prevent this escalating into a full-scale war. Last time we were lucky that there were no members of the general public killed, but I don't fancy putting that luck to the test a second time."

A ripple of muttered conversation ran through the room.

Russell interrupted before the discussion could expand, "OK, thanks. Let's go through what we know of this case so far."

He proceeded to tell the gathered officers the details of the crime scene, the discovery of the body and the findings from the post mortem using as a visual aid Noel Hawthorn's photographs, which were pinned on the incident board. He also told them what they had learned from the Wrights' housekeeper about the couple's holiday plans. He explained that Dr Jennifer Wright was a suspect in her husband's murder but equally she could be another victim and that finding her was the single most important task they faced. He told them that her whereabouts could help to establish a motive other than a gangland feud.

When he was finished the briefing he turned to the crime scene manager who was standing at the front of the group. "DS Weaver, what have you got?"

"Sir, uniforms are continuing a sweep of the area surrounding the loch and canvassing the Wrights' neighbours to see if they saw anything. We checked with the airline but neither Wright nor his wife reached the airport for their flight that morning, so they were either taken from the house or en route."

"Forensics?"

"No sign that they were abducted from the house. The knives all checked out as clean for blood, so we've not got a lot to go on so far."

"Thanks Frank. We need to speak to Dr Wright's friends and family, check if anybody's heard from her. She may be running scared and has reached out to someone."

"I'll get a team on it."

"I also want a team checking CCTV, traffic cameras or anything that might give us a clue where she's gone. Check railway and bus stations for any sign of her travelling out of the city. Same for car hire agencies. Another team should be allocated to get a hold of mobile phone records for both parties. DI Menzies and myself are going to have a look at Wright's business dealings. DS Weaver, can you organise those teams please?"

"Yes sir, will do."

"Get to it folks and let me know of any significant developments immediately."

The briefing broke up and the investigation began in earnest.

***

Gregg Wright's business empire was controlled from a modern, spacious office in Strathclyde Business Park, situated to the east of the city close to the town of Bellshill. The buildings were set in a campus that hosted a diverse range of different companies. The G. Wright Group had a building to itself, set in a garden with a little stream and waterfall. Alex imagined that it would be a great place to work during the summer but in the winter it was probably not so different from anywhere in the centre of the city, just more difficult to get to.

A curmudgeonly security guard asked them to sign in and used the phone to request that someone come to collect them and take them to a senior member of the management team.

A couple of minutes later an attractive woman in her early twenties arrived.

"I'm Carla, I'll take you up to see Mr Garner." As they walked to the lift she said, "It's terrible what happened to Mr Wright." It seemed to Alex that there was little real feeling behind the statement. It was a bland platitude.

The news reports had been sketchy and Alex thought that it was just as well that the young woman didn't know just how horrific it really was or she might have reacted differently.

They alighted on the third floor and the two detectives were led to a brightly lit corner office that offered a spectacular view over the gardens.

The young woman knocked on the glass door and was invited in by a sandy-haired man.

"This is Mr Garner," Carla informed them.

Russell and Alex completed the formalities of the introduction and Garner invited them to sit.

"Can we get you a tea or coffee?" she asked politely. When the detectives declined, she closed the door.

"Mr Garner, I take it you know why we're here."

"Gregg, yes, it's a terrible thing." Alex judged that Garner was in his mid-thirties. He was dressed in an immaculate navy blue pin-striped suit with a dazzling white shirt and subdued grey silk tie. Everything he wore looked a little big for him, as if he had recently lost some weight. His pale face looked drawn and the dark circles gave him the unhealthy look of a man who was operating under a weight of stress.

"What's your position here, Mr Garner?" Russell asked.

"I'm a director of the company, my title is chief operating officer but basically I'm Mr Wright's second-in-command."

"So you're now in charge?"

"For the moment, at least until the board of directors say otherwise."

"How long have you worked for Mr Wright?"

"About five years now."

"Can you tell me a little of what you do here?"

"The group is the umbrella company for a number of other companies. We have a call centre, a property business, a finance company and a car dealership. We employ a total of about three hundred people across the city and beyond. My job is to ensure that all parts of the business are functioning smoothly." It sounded like he was reciting from a company brochure.

"I take it you know of Mr Wright's background."

Garner paused before saying carefully, "I think everyone is aware of his background, as you put it."

"Was he still involved with his family's business dealings?"

"If he was, it wasn't through the G. Wright Group and I don't know how he could have found time for anything beyond this company, he was always a very busy man."

"I hope you're not holding anything back, Mr Garner. You can understand our concerns that if he was still involved with those enterprises, there may be some people who would be very glad to see him dead."

"I understand that, superintendent, but I've told you what I know," Garner replied indignantly.

"Was he a popular boss?" Alex asked.

"I wouldn't say that, no. He didn't deal with the staff directly. He wasn't what you would call a people person, at least with his employees."

"Did he have any problems with disgruntled ex-employees?" she continued.

"No more than anyone else I don't think."

"Did he receive any threats of any kind?" Russell asked.

He considered his answer and then said, "I'm sure it was nothing but there was one man. He was a customer of our finance company. He had problems repaying a loan and he sent some e-mails directly to Mr Wright. They were full of threats, we reported it to the police but they decided that he was just a crank and didn't pose any genuine threat."

"What do you mean by problems?" Alex arrowed in on his comment.

"We offer thirty-day loans, if a customer doesn't pay within the thirty days we are legally allowed to take the money from their bank account when their wages or benefits are paid in. The gentleman in question didn't seem to be aware of that and he was unable to pay another bill that led to further difficulties for him, I'm not sure of all the details. Whatever it was, he blamed Mr Wright and responded with the threats."

"We'll need the man's name and address."

"Of course."

Russell sat back and let Alex continue. "What about business rivals? Did Mr Wright make enemies?"

"I think everyone makes enemies in business, don't you?"

"The kind of enemies who would kill?" Alex pressed.

"I wouldn't like to think so but there is a former partner. Mr Wright gained complete control of the property business when Mr Briar financed a development that went wrong. There was a lot of acrimony with lawyers' letters flying everywhere but I doubt Mr Briar would be the type to kill anyone."

"We will also need the details of that disagreement," Alex said.

"Of course."

Russell saw an opportunity and stepped in to take over the conversation. "Mr Garner, I hope you will continue to be as cooperative. We will need access to as much company information as possible to check out the possibility that the motive for Mr Wright's murder is related to his business life. I hope that will be possible without the need for a warrant."

Garner suddenly looked uncomfortable. "I would like to help as much as possible, obviously, but there are certain commercial considerations to be taken into account. I think you will have to liaise with our solicitors."

"If we must," Russell said with evident disappointment, but Garner didn't seem to be swayed.

"Was it customary for Mr Wright to avoid contact with the business when he went on holiday?" Russell asked.

"Oh yes. It was the only time he insisted on no phone calls or e-mails."

"So everyone knew that he was due to be on holiday?"

"Yes, as I said it was a very strict rule. Breaking it was a sacking offence."

"Well, thanks for all your help, Mr Garner. Our forensic I.T. team will need access to Mr Garner's computer and other officers will probably visit this afternoon. We'll also need access to the files that Mr Wright kept at home."

"I'll call the lawyers and get them to help you as much as we possibly can."

"Thanks."

Garner picked up the phone and said, "Carla, will you escort the detectives to the reception please?" He then pressed a few keys on his computer keyboard and wrote a short note with the details of the man who had threatened Wright and handed it to Russell.

A short time later Carla arrived and walked them back to the front door.

When they were back in Russell's car he asked Alex, "Well, what do you think?"

"I'm not sure, boss. He's nervous about us digging into the business files but it's hard to say whether that's commercial concerns or the fact that we might expose the connections to the Wrights' less legal businesses."

"In his position, I think he knows there are connections but he's hoping that if we get limited access with his legal eagles peering over our shoulders that we'll go away happy. I'll speak to the Fiscal but I'm sure she'll take the softly, softly approach, at least initially. What about the two possible suspects?"

"The payday loan customer would certainly be a possibility. People can be dangerous when they are that desperate."

"Ironic that Wright was up to the same dodges as his grand-father only this time it's legally sanctioned."

"Parasites with lawyers' letters rather than baseball bats," Alex said with revulsion.

"What about the former partner?"

"If there's enough money involved, anyone's capable of kill-ing, we know that from experience."

"I think I'll concentrate on the Wrights and the McGavi-gans while you look at this business stuff. Paddy Niven has got contacts within the McGavigan organisation, if there's anybody who knows if they're involved, it'll be Paddy. We'll go back to the station and take it from there."

CHAPTER 6

After a quick lunch, Alex looked for an officer who could accompany her on her visit to Ben Allinson, the man who had sent the threatening e-mails to Wright. She found a young man sitting peering at a computer screen.

"Hello, what are you up to?"

He looked startled. "Ma'am, I'm doing some data entry, ma'am."

"What's your name?"

"Detective Constable Kelly, ma'am. Paul Kelly, ma'am."

"Well, Paul, how would you like to accompany me as I interview a suspect?"

"Really, me ma'am?"

"Why not?"

"Sorry, ma'am, this is my first murder investigation as a detective."

"Well, I need somebody to chum me and if you're going to know what detective work is all about you need to get out and meet people. You'll not learn much sitting on your backside in front of a computer."

"Yes ma'am," the baby-faced DC replied enthusiastically.

She led him to her car and was a little embarrassed when she noticed the coffee cup on the centre console that had been there for a week and the fast-food wrapper in the foot well of the passenger side that had become an almost permanent resident.

"Sorry about the mess," she said.

"It's fine," he replied.

"Tell me about yourself, Paul," Alex said when they were on their way.

"I served three years as a constable before completing my detective training at the end of last year. I've worked a few break-ins since then but this is my first major incident, ma'am."

"Paul, you don't need to add the ma'am. It makes me feel ancient and that's something you don't want to do to me, or any other woman for that matter."

"OK, eh…"

"Anyway, I didn't ask for your CV, I wanted to know about you."

He seemed puzzled by her request.

"Why did you become a copper?" she asked, trying to help him understand that she would like to know more about him as a person.

"My dad was a firefighter, I didn't fancy running into a burning building but I wanted to help people."

She continued to gently probe him for snippets of his life as they drove to the suspect's house in Darnley. She discovered that he was gay and lived with his partner in a flat in the West End. He was a keen archer and loved to read. He asked little in return, which wasn't great for a detective. She felt that he would have to gain more confidence if he was going to succeed in his chosen career. Criminals could smell fear and sense hesitancy as easily as any predator.

As they parked outside the block that housed the man's flat she said to Kelly, "The guy we're going to see threatened Gregg Wright after some problems relating to a loan. He's likely to be very emotional and it's our job to keep him calm and get the information we need. If he becomes too difficult we might have to take him back to the station. OK?"

"Yip, I know the drill." The nervous quiver in his voice unmasked his confident words.

The street was typical of many of the large housing estates in the city. Rows of tenement blocks that had been renovated recently were fronted by small patches of green, but the renovation had little effect. There were still broken glass shards on the tarmac, litter blew erratically in the chill breeze and there was an air of general malaise that permeated the area and its people like an infection. The snow that had threatened the day before didn't amount to anything and the fog had rolled back in, which only added to the feeling of despondency.

Alex pressed the button on the intercom with Ben Allinson's name on it. There was no reply and after another couple of tries she decided to use the button for the neighbour who lived on the same floor.

"Aye, who is it?" an elderly male voice shouted from the intercom in response.

"Mr Smith, it's Detective Inspector Alex Menzies and Detective Constable Paul Kelly. We'd like to come in and speak to Mr Allinson, your neighbour, please."

"Aye, whatever hen. In ye come."

The two detectives climbed the stairs to the second floor where Mr Smith was peering out of his door. He was a small man with a shock of white hair, which was yellowed from the cigarette that hung from his lips and the many packets that had preceded it. His faced was creased and thick-lensed spectacles magnified his eyes. He wore a dirty grey sweatshirt and ragged blue trousers.

Alex showed her warrant card. "Thanks Mr Smith."

"Nae problem hen. Could ye no' get a haud o' him?" he asked indicating his neighbour's door with a movement of his head.

"He didn't answer, no."

Above the smell of the tobacco and fried food that was emanating from Mr Smith's door, Alex caught an ominous odour exuding from the direction of Allinson's flat.

"Mr Allinson! Mr Allinson!" Alex roared as she battered the door. There was still no reply and she turned to DC Kelly, "Do you think you could kick this in?" Normally she would have done it herself, but it would be difficult as she was wearing high heels.

"Sure." It took three full-blooded bangs with the sole of his boot before the door gave way in a shower of wood splinters. Alex rushed in, checking each door as she went until she arrived at the living room. In the centre of the room, Ben Allinson was hanging from a short piece of rope attached to a hook in the ceiling. His eyes and blue tongue bulged from his face, which was itself a horrible shade of greyish purple. Below him a puddle had formed on the laminate flooring and there was a chair kicked to one side.

"Shit," Alex said. She knew that there was nothing she could do as the smell of decay and urine filled her nose.

Paul Kelly stood in the doorway, his mouth open in a state of shock that seemed to paralyse him.

"Paul, Paul," Alex shouted. He was suddenly aware of her again and looked at her but she could still see the trauma in his eyes.

"Paul, I need you to go back to the landing and call the station, get the police surgeon and some uniforms out. I'll have a look around. Do you understand?"

He nodded weakly, "Police surgeon, yes." Alex directed him back out into the close where he could make the call. Mr Smith was still standing in his doorway, curious to see what was happening. "What's goin' oan, hen?"

"Mr Smith, I'd appreciate it if you could go into your flat and we'll have someone come to speak to you soon," Alex suggested firmly.

"Is he deid?"

"Mr Smith, please."

"Aye, awright hen." He retreated into his home, chastened by the detective's urgent tone.

Inside the flat, Alex began to check for more information. It looked like Ben Allinson had been struggling with life for some time as every room was in a state of chaotic disorder. His dirty clothes were scattered across the floor of his bedroom, the surfaces hadn't been dusted in a while and the carpet was covered in a grim pattern of stains and crumbs. In the kitchen, there was a pile of fast-food containers on the worktop, dirty dishes in the sink and, on a small table, a single piece of A4 paper with a hand-written note. It was a simple letter that conveyed a tragic amount of pain.

Benjamin and Caroline,

I'm sorry but I can't do this any more. I've let you both down and I can't give you the life you deserve. I hope some day you'll be able to forgive me for all I've done.

With love,

Dad

xx

There would be a cursory investigation but it looked like Ben Allinson had taken his own life. Whether the letter amounted to a confession of murder was less clear.

Alex walked back in to the living room where his body hung, the empty husk of a soul now departed. She paused to look at the family photographs on the wall featuring happy kids and smiling parents. There were a couple of posed studio pictures as well as the usual scenes of holidays and Christmas, first day at school and sports days. All of them were the history of a once complete and solid family that was now torn apart with no chance of reunion. Judging by the pictures, the Allinson children weren't even in their teens. Alex sighed as she turned away.

She went back out to the close to await the arrival of her colleagues where Paul Kelly seemed to have regained his composure.

"Do you think he committed suicide?" he asked.

"Looks that way. The locked door and a hand-written note would indicate it."

"Do you think he was the murderer?"

"I don't know, Paul. I hope he isn't, his family will have enough to cope with in the next few weeks."

It was another ten minutes before the first of the crime scene team arrived. They were followed five minutes later by the police surgeon.

"I'll go and talk to Mr Smith while you go in with the surgeon, if you're up to it," Alex said to Paul.

"Of course," he replied. Alex was impressed at the young detective's powers of recovery.

As he disappeared into the Allinson house she knocked on the door of the neighbour's flat.

"Come in, hen," the elderly man said when he saw who it was.

He led her into a tidy living room, furnished with a floral three-piece suite, a smoked glass topped coffee table and the kind of wall unit that had once been a feature of every home in the seventies and eighties. There were ornaments and holiday souvenirs decorating every flat surface.

"D'ye want a cuppa, hen?"

"No, I'm fine, thanks."

"Ah'm jist here masel' noo. Loast ma Lizzie tae cancer a couple o' years back. Ma weans ur good tae me though, come roon' and keep the place tidy, know?"

"It's good to have a supportive family," she replied kindly.

"Whit's up o'er at Ben's?" he asked.

"I'm afraid it looks like he's committed suicide."

A tear formed in the elderly man's eye. "Ach poor bugger. He hud some time o' it."

"Can you tell me a little about what happened?"

"He worked fur wan o' they big high street shoaps, in their warehoose, know? They shut doon and he loast his joab aboot nine months back. He tried like a madman tae get a new joab but naebody's hirin' thanks tae they bastards in Westminster. He goat intae financial bother and then Tracy, his wife, she took the weans and left him a couple o' weeks back. They weans wur everythin' tae him," he exhaled sadly as he completed the story.

"Was he ever a violent man?"

"Naw hen, no really. He became angrier, shouted mair efter he loast his joab but ah never seen or heard o' 'im hurtin' anybody."

"He had some problems with a loans company," Alex prompted.

"Aye, Tracy tellt me aboot that. They took his giro money straight oot his account an' he goat his electric cut aff. That wis the final straw fur her, ah think."

"Did she say anything about Mr Allinson issuing threats to the loans people?"

"Naw hen, nothin' like that."

"Thanks Mr Smith, you've been a big help."

"Nae bother hen. Ah've loast a good neighbour, poor Ben."

Alex said goodbye and walked back to the Allinson flat. Dr Gupta had replaced the police surgeon and he was poised over Ben Allinson's body -which had been cut down and laid on a tarpaulin. The small team of officers and technicians looked on.

"Hi doc, what do you think?"

"Need the PM to be sure Alex, but it looks like suicide. There's no sign of any ligature marks other than the rope and it all looks consistent with a hanging."

"How long?"

"No less than thirty-six hours, maybe as much as seventy two. I'll know more later."

Noel Hawthorn was standing awaiting instructions, his camera poised in his hand.

"Hi Noel," Alex said.

"DI Menzies," he replied.

She indicated with her head that she wanted him to join her in the hall.

"I think we need to talk," she said, determined to over-come her embarrassment.

"Sure, when you're ready," he replied. His dark brown eyes smiled and Alex found herself remembering the kiss.

"I'll give you a bell tonight."

"I'll look forward to it."

They stepped towards the living room again and Noel said as they walked in, "Do you think this is the man for Wright's murder? It would save a lot of grief if it was."

"It would but I doubt it, we'll need to do a full check but I don't think this man would have been capable of cutting up anyone."

When everyone was finished, a uniformed officer was left to wait for the housing association, which would organise a joiner to secure the flat. Alex and Paul Kelly drove back to Milngavie station. Alex told him of Allinson's troubles and by the time they completed the journey, they both felt the poor man's pain.

***

It was late afternoon when they arrived back and Superintendent Russell was sitting waiting for Alex. She detailed all that they had discovered at Allinson's flat while Russell sat in distracted silence.

"Doesn't really sound like our killer," Russell said. "Pity, we could have done with an easy win."

"I'll get DC Kelly to check him out, just in case. How did you get on?"

"I'm worried about Paddy, he hasn't been in the pub or his usual bookies today and there's no sign of him in his house. Apart from the post office and the shops that's the limit of his life really."

"Do you think the Wrights have got to him?"

"If we know he's got contacts among the McGavigans, you can bet the Wrights do as well. The big worry is they'll not be so polite about asking him what he knows."

"What are you going to do?"

"We'll leave it until tomorrow, we've got one last visit to go before the day's out."

"Where?"

"Calvin Wright's back at his parents' house. I'd like a word with him."

"I'm ready to go if you are."

"Grab a coffee and then we'll head."

Half an hour later they were pulling up outside the gates of the Wright villa. The gates were now locked and Russell had to buzz the intercom to gain entry. On the driveway in front of the house a brand new black Audi TT shone like an advertiser's dream.

Miss McAdam was waiting at the door and she invited them into the house and then escorted them to Gregg Wright's study. Calvin Wright was sitting behind the desk, which was covered in a bundle of papers and a laptop. They knew he was eighteen years old but he held himself with the confidence of someone much older. He had blonde floppy hair and striking bright blue eyes; neither of his parents' genes were obvious in his looks. He was dressed in expensive but casual clothes that projected exactly what he was, a wealthy student with exquisite taste.

"Master Calvin, these are the people from the police I told you about."

"Thanks Clarissa," he replied.

He turned his attention to his visitors. "Sorry, I'm just going through some of my father's things, there is a lot to do." He came from behind the desk, offered the detectives his hand and invited them to sit on the chairs facing his own seat. Alex was amazed to see how calm he was; there was no sign of the distressed teenager she was expecting.

"Is there any word about my mother?" By his tone he could have been asking about the weather.

"We're still looking for her," Russell replied.

"I'm sure she'll turn up." Alex caught Russell giving her a look that told the story of his reaction to what was happening.

"We'd like to know a little bit more about your parents."

"I don't know what I'll be able to tell you to be honest. I've been at university for the past four months and before that I was at boarding school. You could say that they weren't the most hands-on parents."

"Why was that?"

"They were both very wrapped up in their work. Father was always at the office, and my mother had her lab. I was an accident that they were happy to farm out to other people to look after."

The icy impression he gave of his family life and the details of his parents' indifference would hurt most people but seemed to be an irrelevance to him.

"What does your mother do at her lab?"

"She's a geneticist, like my noted grandfather, Sir Nigel Hayworth. She's obsessed by how genetics influences behaviour. She shouldn't have to go any further than her relationship with her father and her son. He is as warm as a glacier, just like she is with me."

"You don't seem to be worried about her or concerned by what happened to your father," Russell said.

"I have learned not to worry about things I have no control over. What did happen to my father?"

"We can't give you too many details but he was definitely murdered. Can you think of anyone who would want to harm your father?"

For the first time the peculiar teenager showed emotion. He laughed. "Did you ever meet my father? He could make enemies easier than friends, that's for sure. His only motivation in life was money and he didn't care who he crapped on to get it."

"Anyone in particular come to mind?"

"Grant Briar must be high on that list. My father crushed him to get complete control of the property business. They had been partners for ten years and my father manoeuvred Briar into a position where he decided to invest in a project on his own. Little did he know that my other grandfather - the less renowned one - controlled the security on the site. There was a fire just as the interior of the building was close to completion. Of course, it was ruled as accidental but Briar was in too deep. He had so much money tied up in it and he was relying on selling the flats on at a substantial profit. The delay cost him a fortune and my father offered to buy out his half of the partnership and Briar had to agree. My father planned to hold on to the property until the market picked up. The whole thing nearly tipped Briar into bankruptcy but my father wasn't too worried about that, he had achieved exactly what he wanted: Briar out and a property for a steal. He boasted about how he had done it."

"So your father wasn't as isolated from his family as he portrayed."

"My father was nothing if not clever, superintendent. You won't find any direct business connections between them but it didn't stop him using the leverage my grandfather could provide in other ways."

"Do you think your father could have been killed because of that leverage?"

"The McGavigans you mean?"

"Yes."

"Possibly."

"You're very well-informed about your father's business."

"It was the only thing he would talk to me about; I was the heir apparent, you see. He envisioned me taking over his empire and that's why I'm at university studying business rather than art or biology. My future was mapped out from the minute my unplanned conception was confirmed." The calm mask had fallen away to be replaced with an undisguised anger at his place in the world. A little of the petulant child had crept through the adult's defensive wall.

"And will you now inherit everything?"

"Yes, when I'm twenty one. Until then it will be my mother's responsibility, if she's not in jail or worse."

"Do you think your mother could have killed your father?" Alex asked.

"I would be surprised if she could generate enough passion to do it but I have to be honest and say they had nothing in common. I don't know why they got married. She was a step up for him on the social ladder and he was a subject for her to study at close range, I think that's all there was to it. Maybe she finally got tired of it and got someone else to get rid of him, I don't know."

"Can you tell me where you were the day your mother and father were due to go on holiday?"

"In Edinburgh, probably."

"We'll need a little more than that but I'll give you time to get over the shock and remember the details of where you were and who you were with. Thanks for your help and we'll be in touch."

When Russell's car had pulled out of the gates of the Wright residence he said to Alex, "What the hell was that all about?"

"I was going to say he was weird but that doesn't begin to describe it. I think he's a sociopath; there was just so little emotion."

"I wonder if he's capable of organising someone to kill both his parents. He's certainly got plenty of motive."

"Resentment against them and a big pile of money definitely amounts to a lot of motive. If it is genetic, lunatics on one side and anal-retentive blocks of stone on the other, it's a bad combination."

"I think there's more to him than meets the eye. We'll have a look at his bank accounts; see if there have been any large payments made recently. That's for tomorrow, I'll drop you back at the station and you can drive your heap home."

"Yes, sir," Alex said with a weary grimace.

***

After a dinner of chicken and potatoes, Alex spent two hours cleaning her flat - since she had thrown Andrew out it took a lot less time than it used to. She put on some athletic clothes and went for a thirty-minute run followed by a quick shower.

When all that was over she knew she could not prevaricate any longer and that she had to speak to Noel. Her biggest problem was that she didn't know what she was going to say; she didn't know what she wanted out of a relationship - in truth she didn't even know if she wanted one. Noel was handsome, funny and kind but there was still a part of her too hurt by the betrayal of finding her ex-fiancé in bed with another woman. It had scarred her and left her doubting that any man was capable of truly loving her and giving her what she needed.

She lifted her mobile and found Noel's number. He answered within two rings, as if he had been poised waiting for her call.

"Alex, how are you?" She could hear the smile in his voice and could imagine the gleam in his eye.

"Hi Noel, I'm fine. Man this is awkward."

"Really? Am I that bad?"

She rushed her answer. "No, no, it's not that, it's me."

"Ah ze old it's not you, it's me ploy," he replied in an Inspector Clouseau-style French accent.

Alex beamed despite her stomach doing cartwheels. "You know what I went through with Andrew. I'm not saying you're the same but I've just about managed to put him behind me and I don't know if I'm ready to trust a man again."

"Alex, I know I'm a catch but I'm not saying you'll fall for me so hard that you'll want to marry me within a week. What about we go out and have a good time and let things take their natural course?" he asked as if it was the easiest thing in the world.

"It's difficult. We see each other at work. What if it doesn't work out?" she asked apprehensively.

"I'd rather we take the more positive approach and say that we're two mature people who could still be friends, even if it doesn't work out between us. I would rather give it a go and know what happens, rather than wonder at what might have happened."

He made it all seem so reasonable and in many ways she knew he was right.

He continued, "Why don't we start with the cinema or go for a meal?"

"Cinema or a meal? Am I not worth both?" she said, teasing him.

"Absolutely, but I'm just a poor photographer, so don't set your expectations too high."

She laughed. "At least you're honest."

"So what about a trip to the flicks on Saturday, job allowing of course?"

"OK, the pictures it is."

"I'll give you a bell later in the week."

"Noel, thank you for understanding."

"No problem. Believe me, it's my pleasure."

The call ended and Alex headed for bed feeling both more excited and apprehensive than she had been in a long time.

CHAPTER 7

Assistant Chief Constable Muldoon walked in just as Tom Russell was about to begin the Wednesday morning briefing to the team of detectives who were crowded into the room like penguins on an ice floe.

"Morning, ladies and gentlemen. I'm here to see what progress we're making. Carry on, Tom."

Mutters of reluctant greeting came from the assembly.

"You timed it well, sir. We're just about to get started," Russell replied with as much fake enthusiasm as he could muster. He began by quizzing the team that had been assigned to find Mrs Wright and the missing Range Rover.

"We checked the CCTV recordings from the cameras going intae the toon that night but there was no sign o' the car on either o' them, boss." This came from Detective Sergeant Rankine, a twenty-two-year veteran with a bushy moustache, pot belly and grumpy attitude.

"Thoughts?" Russell asked.

"They must have been taken close to home and the car driven out into the country maybe."

"Good, where could they have gone?"

"Eh…"

"Sergeant, I'm not asking you to tell me this minute but we need to think where he might have taken them. You need to think of ways to find that bloody car."

"Yes, sir." The DS looked annoyed and abashed by Russell's mild rebuke.

"Phone records?"

"Sir, both Gregg Wright and his wife's mobile phones went dead on the day they were supposed to leave and haven't pinged a tower since," DS Weaver offered.

"What about their phone records?"

"Nothing out of the ordinary from what I could see. Wright used his phone a lot. The majority of calls were to and from his business, in particular with Jason Garner. They were exchanging calls and texts until midnight before Wright was due to go on holiday. Dr Wright hardly uses the phone for either texts or calls. There were a few to her father but she didn't receive or make a single call on the day before they disappeared."

"Did you find any sign that Wright was in contact with his father?"

"Not on either his mobile or the home phone but I suppose he could have had a non-contract handset or SIM card."

"Has Dr Wright's father been contacted?"

"Yes, sir. We tracked him down in the States. He was in San Francisco for a conference and is now spending some time with a friend who is a professor at the University Of California, Sacramento. He's due to be there for another few days. He hasn't spoken to his daughter for about three weeks. It was strange because he didn't seem too worried about her and there was no indication that he would cut his trip short."

"It's a family trait, apparently. What about personal computers?"

"The I.T. guys are still checking them out."

"Did you make any progress getting access to the business records?"

"The Procurator Fiscal negotiated access but it'll have to be on their premises with one of Wright's lawyers looking over our shoulder; they're worried about commercially sensitive material."

"Commercially sensitive! This is a fuckin' murder investigation. That's the best she could do?" Russell knew that there had been little hope of anything more but he was still angry at the Fiscal's capitulation.

"I'm sure the Fiscal has secured the access we need, superintendent," Muldoon said in admonition of Russell's gripe. He didn't want any wedges being driven between the Fiscal's office and the investigating team.

"I'm sure," Russell replied with no conviction.

"I've got a couple of forensic accountants and I.T. guys to come with us when the briefing is over," Weaver said.

"Thanks DS Weaver. I need to be informed as soon as you find anything suspicious or helpful."

"Yes, sir."

"Ben Allinson, DC Kelly?"

"He had no record and he didn't own a car, so it would have been difficult for him to get to Milngavie. I spoke to his old boss and he said that he was a nice guy, never caused any problems."

"We'll keep him in mind but unless forensics turn up anything connecting him to the scene, we'll leave him on the back burner. Talking of forensics, anything from their magic machines yet?"

"Yes, sir," a short woman with a flame of red hair and a broad Belfast accent replied.

"Sorry, I don't know all your names yet. You are?"

"DS Ann-Marie Craigan, sir."

"What have you got for me DS Craigan?"

"The lab found traces of pine wood in either side of the dismembered pieces. They confirmed the pathologist's theory that the victim was chopped up with an axe and they reckon it had been used to cut firewood. It further indicates a rural location."

"It definitely looks that way. It has to be somewhere in the Campsie Fells, relatively close to the city and Bardowie Loch."

"Sir, do you think we're looking for more than one killer?" Alex asked.

"It's possible. What do you think folks?" Russell threw the question out to the team.

"It would be difficult for a single person to subdue both Wright and his wife," DS Craigan replied.

"One man could have done it wi' a gun," Mac Rankine countered.

"Why not just shoot them?" Weaver asked.

"There's something very personal about it, or the killer is trying to send a message," Alex theorised.

"Which brings us back to McGavigan and his merry men," Russell said.

"I think we need to go right to the source," Alex suggested.

"That's our first task today, Alex. Not that it'll do much good, even if he is involved, all he'll tell us is that he's just a poor put-upon businessman, but we still need to ruffle his feathers a bit to see how he reacts."

"Yes, sir."

"Anybody got anything else before we allocate the workload for today?"

There was no further information, so Russell continued, "I want some uniforms out in the villages around the bottom of the Campsies. That Range Rover must be somewhere out there and somebody must have seen it. Get the media team to brief the press with the details of the car and get a team ready to take the calls."

He continued with a change of tack. "We also need to take a look at Calvin Wright, the son. Having met him, we think he's definitely capable of arranging this. DS Weaver, assign some officers to check his financials and phone records."

"Yes, sir."

"OK, anything I've missed?"

"I don't know why we're bothering for a member of the Wright family," Rankine mumbled.

"DS Rankine, we aren't here to judge the victims," Muldoon intervened before Russell could reply. Although Russell had some sympathy with Rankine, there was still the bigger picture of innocent lives being put at risk. That was why a gangland murder always attracted huge resources and attention.

"Let's get to it," Russell said.

Some of the detectives drifted off to their various tasks while DS Weaver organised the new work details.

"Ready to face Mr McGavigan, Alex?"

"Always."

***

Malcolm McGavigan ran his varied legitimate businesses from a room above a snooker hall in Govan, within walking distance of the Major Incident Team headquarters in Helen Street. As they entered the building Alex could hear the click of the balls as they collided on the baize. A flash of their warrant cards brought a sullen response from a female receptionist who indicated a stairway with a flick of her head, while she continued to chew on her gum and then turned her attention back to the copy of Heat magazine that lay open in front of her.

"That's what I love about this country, the quality of customer service," Russell said in a loud voice as they walked to the stairs.

When they reached the first floor a rotund man in his early twenties opened the door to the office as Russell and Menzies approached. They both knew that he was Malcolm's son, Alan, a thug with few brains and little subtlety. The feeling among the city's police was that if Malky let go of the reins, he wouldn't be able to entrust his legacy to the idiot son. Many thought that there would be an unsightly scramble for power within the organisation and that they may be mopping up the blood for months in the wake of McGavigan's death.

"In here," the charming doorman said gruffly.

McGavigan's office was a dark, wood-panelled room that hadn't been decorated in about thirty years. Malcolm McGavigan sat in a plush leather desk chair, his meaty palms rested on the arms; he appeared to be completely at ease with the world. Every time Russell had met him, the crime boss gave the impression that he was a feudal lord granting his serfs an audience. He was a thickset man but there was little fat on him and there was no doubting that he had presence. Unlike Peter Wright, there were no scary legends of personal violence. He seemed to use an aura of invincibility and threat to keep his troops in line.

"Detective Superintendent Russell and DI Menzies, what an honour," McGavigan said with a grin.

"Malky," was Russell's simple reply.

"I'd prefer Malcolm, it sounds a little more mature don't ye think? Take a seat, take a seat. Tell me Mr Russell, are ye still drinkin' in the Station Bar?"

"When I can, Malky." An involuntary shudder ran down Alex's back. She hated how much the crime lords of the city knew about the senior police officers. That simple question had been McGavigan's way of letting Russell know that he was keeping an eye on the detective, as much as the police kept an eye on him and his people. Initially, she had been surprised that McGavigan knew who she was but now she realised why: she had moved into the radar of the gangs with her promotion to the Major Incident Team.

"So what brings you to my humble establishment, as if I couldnae guess?"

"Gregg Wright, Malky. Just Gregg Wright." Alex could see her boss warming to the task. This was his arena, this was combat and he was in a gladiatorial mood.

"As I said, I would appreciate Malcolm," McGavigan bristled and Alex did well not to smile. One-nil to her boss.

"What do you know about the death of Gregg Wright?"

"Except what I've seen in the press, absolutely nothing." He beamed again but it was hard to gauge the meaning behind it, it was all just a game to him.

"We know that you and Mr Wright's father haven't always seen eye to eye, shall we say. We're a little concerned that you've decided to reignite your disagreement."

McGavigan laughed. "What would I have to gain by that? Stability is good for business."

"You didn't think that a couple of years ago."

"Some misunderstandings that had nothing to do with me."

It was Russell's turn to laugh heartily. "Somehow I thought you would say that."

"Maybe you should be havin' a closer look at some of Wright's lieutenants. From what I hear not everything is rosy within their ranks. Mutterings of internal fights and that there are a few concerned that Peter junior may have been about to hand over control to Gregg."

"Why would he do that? He and his son were estranged, allegedly."

"Oh yes, that little pantomime. I'm sure if you look closely enough at Gregg Wright's business dealings you will find more connections than they would have you believe."

"Like what?"

"Just between ourselves, I'm pretty sure that there's money going through his books that is covered in illegal substances and by the time it comes back out again it is squeaky clean, then it rests comfortably out of reach of the taxman in an off-shore account."

"You know this for sure?"

"Let's say I have my sources."

"And this so-called split in the Wright gang?"

"Some of his senior lieutenants think that he's gone soft and would like him to take more aggressive action. Maybe they decided that he needed an extra push in the right direction. Killing his son and setting me up as the patsy would be perfect for their plan, d'ye no think?"

"You think that someone within the Wright gang killed Gregg Wright?" Russell asked incredulously.

"Well, I know it wasn't me."

"I only have your word for that and you'll need to forgive me if I don't think that's much of a guarantee."

For the first time since they entered the room McGavigan's attitude changed and anger flared. "Think what ye like Russell but I had nothin' tae dae wi' that bastard's death. If they decide to go after wan o' mine as a result, I'll be ready, but I didn't start this."

"What about one of your lot? I mean Alan here isnae exactly the brain of Britain, is he?"

"Hey…" Alan reacted, but before he could finish his father said, "He might be as thick as two short planks but even he wouldn't be that stupid."

"Give me a name then."

"I wish I could, superintendent, but I honestly don't have a clue."

"I think you might be full of shit and if I find that you are behind this or know who is, I swear I'll make your life a fuckin' misery."

McGavigan brushed away the threat. "It's the truth, I swear. If that's all, I need to get back to work."

Russell had nothing else to say and the two detectives left without another word.

As always, Russell waited until they were safely back in the car before asking Alex if she believed what McGavigan had said.

"McGavigan's a thug but he's not a psycho. From what I've read, everything he does is calculated; he doesn't do anything that won't profit him somehow. He didn't start the killings last time although his lot were as bad once it got going. He controls half the city and I think he believes that's enough until the Wrights do something stupid. Maybe this is the something stupid."

"Do you think anybody connected with the Wrights would kill Gregg just to start a war?"

"I think that some of them might be unhappy at the thought of the business going completely legit and spoiling all their fun. In many ways Gregg Wright was the perfect target to provoke his father without affecting how the illegal business is being conducted."

"I don't know. You're right, as these bastards go McGavigan is intelligent, but trying to provoke internal strife in the Wrights would be an effective way of crippling them and allow him to move in on their territory."

"Do you think Paddy will know?"

"I think he's the best chance we have of knowing what's really going on inside this nest of rats."

"So what next?"

"Fancy a visit to a former property tycoon?"

"I'm going to need a bath by the end of this day," Alex joked.

CHAPTER 8

Grant Briar's penthouse flat overlooked the Clyde, close to the new performance venue that was rising next to the S.E.C.C. He greeted the detectives at the door and showed them through to a living room that had a panoramic view of the river. The floor was a beautiful expanse of real oak and the furniture was both minimal and chic. A large abstract oil painting dominated one wall, while two sides of the room were glass, which opened up the vista to include the Finnieston crane and down the river. Briar indicated a two-seater sofa while he dropped down on another and stretched his arms along the back in a way that appeared to be an attempt at casual indifference.

Briar looked to be older than Gregg Wright by five to ten years. His hair was in the process of changing from black to grey and the goatee beard he sported was nearly white. His tan was fading and rings of distress circled his eyes. He wore a dark blue sweater over a white polo shirt with grey trousers. Alex noticed a pale band where a wedding ring used to be. Despite his attempt at casual indifference it was obvious that life was not going well for Grant Briar.

"You have a lovely home Mr Briar," Alex said.

"Thanks but it's not mine, I'm only renting. I guess you are here because Gregg Wright finally got his just desserts."

"We're here about Mr Wright's death, yes," Russell replied.

"I didn't kill him but I'm delighted that someone did," he said honestly.

"Because of your business dealings?"

"We were partners for ten years and yet I was still too stupid to see what the spiteful little prick was up to," he said acidly.

"Can you give us some details?"

"There was a former warehouse that became available in the Merchant City. It had been renovated back in the eighties as an office but they couldn't fill it any more. It was a prime property to convert to flats and make some real money. Wright and I had worked together on every property since we became a partnership but he said that he didn't like the look of it due to the economic situation. I thought he was wrong because no matter the state of the country there's always money at the top end and the flats I was planning were going to be in the half a million quid range. I tried hard to persuade him but he wasn't interested. I should have known he was up to something. Anyway, the flats were just about ready to be sold last October when there was an *accidental* fire." He emphasised the word by indicating quotes with his fingers.

"You don't think it was an accident?"

"I didn't find out until later that Wright's father owned the security company the builders had hired. I know what happened but can't prove it; the fire did enough damage to stop me being able to sell the flats. I had put everything I had into it and I would have made a couple of million but the bank wouldn't give me any more time."

"And Mr Wright offered to buy you out of your partnership?"

"That bastard knew exactly what he was doing. He bought me out and it kept the bank off my back but I've made absolutely nothing out of the flats and I'll need to start again."

"Did your financial problems affect your relationship with your wife?" Alex asked.

"That was my other little surprise. Wright dissolved the partnership and then told me, 'Oh by the way I've been shagging your wife.' While I was working every bloody hour that God sends he was making sure my wife was getting looked after." His face lost its pallor as his anger began to build.

"Where is your wife now?"

"She buggered off down south with the kids. She'll go dig gold from some other rich sucker. The bitch was only ever interested in money," he said with a bitter resignation that signalled he wasn't too bothered about losing her.

"Gregg Wright ruined your life," Tom Russell said.

"He did but now he's dead, it's definitely become a little better." He tried a smile but it didn't have the energy to reach his eyes.

"How did you become partners in the first place?"

"A friend of mine knew Wright and that he had money that he needed to invest. I had a lot of experience in property and Wright wanted to make some money while the market was booming. When we met it was obvious that his cash and my knowledge were a pretty good fit. We went in on a deal together, we both made a bit of cash and then Wright offered me a partnership.

"Did you know Mr Wright's background before you went into business with him?"

He looked coy before saying, "I knew enough. I actually thought that having a partner with a gangster for a father would be a good thing. Huh, a brilliant piece of judgement." He laughed at his own naïveté.

"You thought the Wright clan would add extra influence?"

"Yes, exactly."

"Tell me about Wright."

"You mean apart from the fact that he was a lying, cheating, swindling bastard?"

"Yes," Russell replied, ignoring Briar's sarcasm.

"Wright was interested in one thing. Money. No, make that two: money and power. I know I was the same in some ways but he took it to a different level. He loved buying companies and asset stripping them. He didn't give a shit if someone had built an incredible business, he would swoop on anything that was even slightly vulnerable and strip it of everything that was worthwhile. Machinery, property or stock, it didn't matter to him; it was like playing Monopoly."

"Is there anyone in particular who suffered from these kinds of business practices?"

"The list is almost endless. It got worse when the recession hit. He was the ultimate financial vulture, gobbling up companies in administration and spitting out the bones."

"Have you ever heard of anyone making direct threats?"

"I couldn't give names but I'm sure there were e-mails and letters telling him he would be killed. But when you are Peter Wright's son it's easy to take direct action to nullify any threat."

"So Wright and his father were still close?"

"All that fall-out crap was for the press and potential investors. If he needed anything done, like a councillor bought or a target frightened, he'd meet with his father and suddenly the problems would just melt away."

"Was he in the habit of having affairs?"

"You've got to be kidding me. That was part of the power trip he loved. It's like asking does a fish swim. He shagged anything and everything he could; money's an amazing aphrodisiac and he was always happy to oblige any woman stupid enough to cast her eye in the direction of his wallet. His wife didn't give a damn what he did. I should have guessed that he would go after my Samantha. As I said, I was blindly stupid."

"From what we've heard, the Wrights had a strange relationship," Alex remarked.

He nodded. "She's a weird one. Very intelligent but I have no idea why she got married. She certainly wasn't passionate about him or even the creepy kid they produced. She only had a passion for the work she did."

"Dr Wright is missing, do you have any idea where she might have gone, say if she was scared?" Russell asked.

"If she's not with her father, she might have gone to one of the other houses they owned, but if she's scared she could have gone anywhere. She didn't have a huge number of friends I know that much, so I can't imagine that anyone took her in."

"I think that's all for now Mr Briar, but please don't leave the country, we may need to talk to you again."

"Fine, I've got nowhere to go."

Russell left his card with a request for Briar to contact him if anything else came to mind.

"He's a shifty bastard with a whole load of motive," Russell said on the drive to the station.

Alex voiced her thought process. "He knew what he was getting into when he went into business with Wright. He would turn a blind eye to the crimes of Wright's family as long as it benefitted him. That points to someone who isn't that troubled by consulting a moral compass."

"Is he a killer?"

"Possibly, but Wright wasn't exactly Mr Popularity, was he? We could even be looking at a jealous lover or husband."

"Most people go through life without making enemies; Wright collected them like football stickers." Despite his attempt at humour, Alex could see the strain on Russell's face. With every day that the killer went unidentified they got nearer to Wright being just the first in a series of murders.

Russell's phone rang just as they arrived back.

"Detective Superintendent Russell."

"Sir, it's DS Craigan. The car's been found," she told him.

"Great, we're just outside the station, I'll see you in a minute."

DS Craigan was waiting in the incident room.

"Tell me what you've got, sergeant."

"A cyclist spotted a burnt-out Range Rover in Peathill Wood, not far from Lennoxtown. Uniforms are in attendance and have confirmed that it is Wright's car."

"Any detectives on site?"

"No, sir. I was about to go after calling you."

"Why don't you and DI Menzies go and have a look?"

"There must have been another vehicle. It looks like we've got two assailants, sir," Alex said.

"Looks like it and suddenly the gangland scenario is looking more likely. Go check it out, let me know what you find."

**

Alex found the detective sergeant to be pleasant company on the drive to the car dump site. Although born and raised in Belfast, she had come to Scotland ten years previously to study at Stirling University. She was direct, intelligent and had managed to keep her femininity intact as she rose through the ranks of the Strathclyde force. Alex felt they had a lot in common and Ann-Marie was a distinct improvement on many of her female colleagues who, rather than forming bonds, were ultra-competitive with other women.

The satellite navigation on Alex's phone directed them to the edge of the wood where a uniformed officer was waiting to guide them to where the car had been abandoned.

He led them to a narrow track off the main path that was overhung with branches from the trees. They had to leave the car on the main route as the track was only suitable for something with four-wheel drive due to the thick, cloying mud. Alex and DS Craigan suited up in their forensic suits, as much to stop their clothes getting dirty as to protect the evidence at the scene. There was a single set of distinct tyre tracks on the marsh-like path.

"There was probably a second vehicle parked back where we are," Craigan said as she gestured to the evidence.

"Looks like it."

After a walk of about two hundred yards they found the Range Rover in a small clearing. It had already begun to rust where the paint had been burned away from the metal and puddles of rainwater had formed inside. All of the internal fittings had been consumed by the intensity of the flames and all that was left of the seats were exposed springs and their metal skeleton.

"They have certainly done a number on it. I doubt the forensic guys and girls will get much from this," Alex said as she shone a torch into the interior.

"Look at the position of the driver's seat," Craigan replied.

"That's quite close to the steering wheel for a man of Wright's size," Alex noted.

"She was driving. How could this have panned out?"

"The killers could have stopped the car and forced Wright out. Killed him and then made Dr Wright drive the car here."

"Where is she?"

"Maybe she killed him and her accomplice followed her out here. They chopped up the body, dumped it in the loch, burned the car and then she disappeared."

"What if the killer was in the back seat of the car? He slits Wright's throat while he was sitting in the passenger seat and then Dr Wright would be so scared he could have made her drive here. His accomplice meets them here and then they take her somewhere else to sexually assault her and then kill her."

"A grim thought, but it would explain her disappearance. We won't know for sure until we find her. We'll get the forensics team to check around here for blood or even her body; they could have chopped up Wright around here. They can have a look at the car back in the compound. Give them a ring, please, and ask for a team and some dogs while I have a look round."

DS Craigan lifted her phone from her pocket and began the process of bringing the scientists to the scene. In the fading light it was difficult to search the surrounding area and Alex concentrated on the environs of the car. There was no obvious sign of blood or other evidence in the immediate vicinity of the Range Rover. With the help of one of the uniformed officers, she popped open the boot of the car, concerned by what she might find. She was relieved to see that Jennifer Wright hadn't been left to die in the flames. Inside were the melted remnants of three suitcases. Their wheels and some of the metal had survived the flames, but little else.

"Well, we know they did set off on holiday," she said to Craigan as she joined her when the call was finished.

"Helps us with the timeline," the other woman commented.

"True. We'll see what else forensics come up with but at least it helps a little."

They tramped back through the sticky mud to the car and placed their coveralls in a bag to be dumped when they got back to the station.

***

While Alex and DS Craigan had gone off to check out the car, Tom Russell had a personal problem he had to take care of. In the crowded station it was difficult to find a space where he could make a private phone call, so he decided to take a walk so he could conduct the conversation without anyone eavesdropping.

The number he had stored was for a former colleague, Detective Inspector Jonny Holt. He had come to Glasgow to work in the anti-terrorist squad on secondment from the Metropolitan Police in the wake of the attempted bombing of Glasgow Airport in 2007. He had been pulled in as an advisor at the same time that Russell was a DI in the organisation. A bond formed between them and they could often be seen in the pub after a tough week, chewing the fat while solving the force's and the world's problems. Holt was confident without being cocky and Russell felt he had learned a lot from the Londoner.

"DI Russell, you old bastard, 'ow are you?" Holt said when he answered the call.

"That's detective superintendent to you," Russell said with mock seriousness.

"Christ, they must be struggling if they promoted you to super," Holt joked.

"It's a quota system, they've got to have at least one grouchy old man at that level."

The Englishman laughed, "Good on you, Tom. Congratulations. What can I do for you?"

"I'm hoping you'll be able to do some sniffing on the quiet about a visiting nutcase."

"One of yours?" Holt's professional curiosity was piqued.

"No, a Serb who goes by the name of Dragovic."

"Oh fuck, those Eastern European bastards are vicious. Why do you want to know?"

"Let's just say that there's someone I know that owes this guy some cash. I want to know how bad it might be."

"I'd order a plot and a coffin for your friend if he's into serious money with someone like that but I'll run a check."

"Thanks Jonny, I appreciate it. How are things in the capital?"

"Worse than usual. Cuts and Leveson have pushed morale to a fuckin' all-time low. Jockland?" Lord Leveson's inquiry into the press in the wake of the hacking scandal had exposed corruption among some members of the Metropolitan Police and the image of the force had taken a battering.

Russell was equally downbeat. "Merging us into a single force plus the cuts but still as much work to get through, so we're feeling much the same."

"I'll do some poking around and see what I can stir up. If you get down this far, you owe me a pint."

"You bet. Thanks again, Jonny."

They ended the call and Russell was left to wonder just how he was going to extricate his brother from this latest mess.

When Alex and DS Craigan arrived back at the station they briefed him on what they had found.

When they were finished Russell said, "I wish we knew where this woman fits in. Is she a victim or the one who initiated this?"

"We need to expand the search and look at her work colleagues, maybe they'll have a better idea of what she was thinking and what kind of relationship she had with her husband. I don't care how indifferent you are, if your husband is sleeping around it must get to you at some point," Alex observed.

"Put it on the list of things we need to do tomorrow. Go home and get some rest. Thanks for your work today, Ann-Marie."

"A pleasure, sir."

The two women said goodnight and headed home while Russell sat down at a computer to catch up with his e-mail. It would be another three hours before he eventually made his way to his flat.

CHAPTER 9

Eddie Russell uttered a disgruntled, throaty groan as his brother shook him roughly and switched on the light above his temporary bed.

"Whit ye daein'?" he grumbled.

"Welcome to my world. I've got a call, there's been a murder that I need to attend."

"Cin folk no' get murdered at a decent time o' day?"

"I'll let the press know and get them to post a bulletin. Maybe they can persuade the public to get murdered at a time that suits you," Tom Russell replied with sarcastic sharpness.

Eddie rolled over and pulled the blanket above his head to protect his eyes from the brightness while his brother continued his preparations to begin his working day.

He had been woken twenty minutes previously by the trilling sound of his phone. A familiar voice said, "Sir, it's Rick Johnstone."

"Rick, what can I do for you at this ungodly hour?"

"We've found a body in Bath Lane. I thought you might like to know that we think it's Paddy Niven."

Russell had shot out of bed and told Johnstone that he would be there as soon as he could.

His concern for his informant had proved to be all too valid. He wouldn't admit it to many people but in the time he had been his eyes and ears in the Glasgow underground, Niven had grown on the detective. He was an amiable rogue, a harmless old chancer who wouldn't have hurt anyone. He might dip their pocket or tap them for a cigarette but there wasn't a violent bone in his body.

Russell had dressed quickly but with his usual attention to detail. Well-tailored suit, immaculate white shirt, blue and grey striped tie and polished shoes.

Now he was collecting his wallet, phone and car keys, much to his brother's annoyance.

"Get this mess cleared up before I get back," was his parting shot to Eddie before he left the flat. In reply, Eddie moaned a vaguely positive response.

***

Bath Lane runs parallel to Bath Street, connecting Hope Street and Renfield Street at the heart of the city centre. It's too narrow for anything other than a single vehicle as the buildings on either side block the light and creates a claustrophobic atmosphere. The limited pavement space hosts the occasional commercial waste bin and the walls are decorated with graffiti tags.

Crime scene tape fluttered in the chilling breeze at either end of the lane, which was now brightly lit by a couple of large floodlights. The high-visibility jackets of the uniformed officers added extra illumination as the light bounced from the reflective panels. White-suited detectives and scene of crime technicians busied themselves around a single point in the middle of the lane. At the centre of the huddle of interested parties lay the corpse of Paddy Niven.

Tom Russell stood looking down on the battered body of the unfortunate man, DC Richard Johnstone by his side.

"I thought you might like DI Menzies to be here too, she'll be along soon," Johnstone said when the senior officer had arrived.

"Thanks Rick. How's Georgia?" Rick's wife had been caught up in a case the two detectives had worked together the previous year.

"On the mend, sir. There's nothing like a near-death experience at the hand of a serial killer to put your life in perspective," he said with dark humour. "She was a bit traumatised at first but then she seemed to find an inner strength and she became determined to prove that he wasn't going to ruin her life."

"And the baby?"

"She's grand, sir. Starting to crawl and get into mischief."

"Glad to hear it." The polite discourse over, Russell turned his attention to the corpse. It looked like Niven had been pretty badly beaten by someone who knew exactly what they were doing. His face was a collection of bruises with the occasional isolated island of undamaged skin. His eyes were narrow slits trapped in bloody mounds of swollen flesh. His clothes were even dirtier than usual and in places were ripped due to the beating or maybe as a result of rough treatment when he was dumped. There was little blood around the body, so the consensus was that he had been killed somewhere else and left in the lane. Russell's gut told him that Paddy Niven had been left as a warning to the McGavigans that Peter Wright was not going to be messed with.

"Here's the doc," Johnstone said.

Russell was relieved to see that Dr MacNeil was the on-call pathologist. The Hebridean Islander was a much more pleasant and cooperative personality than her Aberdonian colleague. She strode to the middle of the gathering, acknowledging the faces she recognised as she went. She set her case down beside the body and began her assessment.

"We don't normally see you at these kinds of scenes, detective superintendent," she said to Russell.

"I believe this one might be a bit different but I'll let you examine the evidence and tell me if I'm right."

First, she checked the bruising on Paddy Niven's face and asked a forensic technician to swab for potential foreign DNA on his skin. As she worked, Alex arrived to join Russell just as the doctor was lifting the bony arm of the victim. Paddy's sleeve slid down to reveal a pattern of round red circles.

"Cigarette burns; it appears that this man may have been tortured. Is that what you were expecting to find?"

"Let's just say I thought it was a possibility."

The doctor continued her investigation, turning Niven over to look at the back of his head. She noted the wound that had occurred when Niven had been subdued but it didn't look severe enough to be the cause of death. "Despite the damage I can't give you a definitive wound that would have killed him. None of these wounds should have been fatal, at least not to a healthy man."

Russell shook his head sadly. "That's not how anybody would describe Paddy. Too many fags, too much fatty food, too little exercise and let's say he was fond of a drink or two."

"I can smell alcohol and salt and vinegar.

"That sounds about right," Russell said with a melancholy smile.

"I'll be able to tell you more after the PM but it could've been the shock or a heart attack that killed him."

"No matter. The beating was what brought it on and that will amount to a charge for whoever did this. Not that it's going to take Sherlock Holmes to work out who that might be."

"You think this is Wright?" Alex asked.

"I'm positive. Paddy was known to have connections with McGavigan, he used to be involved with some of his crew back in the nineties. Wright thought that he could get Paddy to tell him who killed Gregg and when he died he thought he would use him as a warning. He was left here so he would be found quickly and serve as a shot across McGavigan's bows to let him know that Wright isn't going to be messed around. It's the typical macho posturing you get from these dicks all the time." Russell's mood was dark with a dangerous cocktail of anger and disgust.

"What do we do now? You know it's unlikely that Wright was involved directly and even if he was he'll have his people lining up to give him an alibi," Alex said, trying to placate his temper by getting him to think about the problem rationally.

"I think I'll pay him a little visit."

"Is that wise, sir?"

"Alex, to be honest I don't give a shit whether it's wise or not. They've killed a harmless old man as part of something that could fast turn the streets of this city into a battleground. They don't own this city and I'm going to make sure they know it."

"Rick, make sure Paddy's movements are traced over the past couple of days, on the outside chance that I'm wrong."

"Yes, sir."

Russell turned and walked quickly back to where he had left his car with Alex trailing behind.

"I think I'll come with you," she said when she caught up with him.

"Fine, but we handle it my way."

***

As they drove towards Peter Wright's house, Russell's phone rang. He activated the speaker through controls on the car's steering wheel.

"Detective Superintendent Russell," he growled.

"Did I catch you at a bad time, Tom?" Lindsay Morton asked.

"Sorry, Lindsay. It's been another shitty start to a day. What can I do for you?"

"It's what I can do for you. My man inside Wright's organisation has discovered that an old friend is back in town. Lennie Warner, one of Wright's old enforcers. He served six years in prison in Ulster for some creative use of knives - and I don't mean as a chef - but he was also known to be one of Wright's team back in the late nineties. Apart from his love of knives he was quite fond of an axe every now and again."

"Interesting. What are your thoughts?"

"This guy is a real psycho; the kind that would be quite happy if there was a war to fight, no matter the enemy. We know there are some hardline elements within Wright's lot that want the McGavigans wiped out; I'd imagine that if they were looking for someone to get a conflict started, Warner would be the go-to bam."

"Cheers Lindsay."

"Do you want me to pick him up?"

"No, we'll pay him a visit. Where is he?"

"Possilpark, living with his mother, apparently."

"Text me the details and we'll have a friendly chat with him."

The call ended and was shortly followed by a ding from the phone as the text arrived.

"Sounds like a possible," Alex said.

"I'm still finding the thought of one of Wright's own starting a fight by killing Gregg highly unlikely," Russell replied.

"Maybe it's the beginning of an attempt to snatch power."

"We'll see."

They arrived outside the home of the Wrights as children were walking to school to begin their day. Russell banged on the front door but it took another couple of hard knocks before there was a response. A furious Jessie Wright swung open the door and shouted, "Whit's your fuckin' problem?"

"Get out of ma face, Jessie. Ah've got an appointment wi' yir man," Russell moved to step into the house but the woman moved her considerable bulk into the doorway. She was dressed in a nylon nightdress that did not flatter her in any way. Her scarlet hair was sticking out in every direction and she had not yet applied any make-up, which meant she managed to look even uglier than normal.

"Ye've goat nae fuckin' appointment. Ye need a warrant if ye want tae come in," she said defiantly.

"Fuckin' move or I will do you for pervertin' the course of justice and assaulting an officer of the law. Understand?" Alex had seen Russell's performance as a Glasgow hard man before but she was pretty sure that this time he wasn't acting.

Something in Russell's eye told Jessie that this wasn't the time to try to obstruct him from his goal. As she stood back, she glared at Alex as if it was her fault.

Alex followed Russell into the living room where Peter Wright was sitting with a tray, on which rested a plate with a large fried breakfast.

"Whit the fuck is goin' oan, Jessie?" Wright shouted.

Russell walked towards Wright, flipped the tray and scattered its contents across the floor before lifting the gang boss by the collar. "Paddy Niven. You just couldnae help yirsel could ye? Whit did that auld man dae tae you?"

"Whit's...up?" Pete Wright senior looked up from his own breakfast, the oxygen mask resting on his chest.

"Yir son hud an auld man killed, that's whit's up."

"Ah hud nothin' tae dae wi' some bastard getting killed. Ah don't even know this Niven. You've gone too far Russell," Wright junior asserted as he was dropped back on to the couch.

"Ye know who did it and if ye don't hand them tae me oan a plate, your life is no' goin' tae be worth livin'." He turned and walked towards the door with a confused and concerned Alex close behind.

"You better watch yir back, Russell," Wright shouted to the detective's back.

"Fuck off, Wright."

"Sir, you were out of order," Alex said to him as they walked down the path towards the car.

"Sometimes, Alex, we've got to stop fannying about and sticking to the rules. These people don't have any rules but we're expected to treat them with kid gloves. This guy arranged the torture of an inoffensive, silly old duffer just to satisfy some part of his ego that he thinks has been insulted. He believes he can do whatever he likes but I'm here to let him know that there's a line that even he can't cross. If I had my way I'd throw him, his cronies and McGavigan's lot on to an island and let them kill each other to extinction but we've got to do something to protect the non-combatants. If we can't, what's the point?"

"This could affect any case we can prepare. I understand your anger but if Wright decides to complain what am I supposed to do?"

"Whatever your conscience decides," was his curt reply.

CHAPTER 10

By the time Alex had retrieved her car from the city centre and driven to Milngavie, the briefing team had assembled in the confined space. There was a buzz of anticipation that indicated somebody believed they had a breakthrough.

She joined Russell at the incident board, which was now covered in pictures of the possible suspects, as well as the original images of the crime scene. Beside each was a note with their name and their connection to the victim.

"Settle down everyone, let's hear what you've got. DS Weaver?"

"Sir, as requested we did a check on Calvin Wright. He stands to inherit his father's business and assets, which their lawyer's conservative estimate puts at a value of roughly thirty million pounds. That doesn't include what he may gain from his mother's personal inheritance – that might add another five million to that total."

"That's a chunk of change and a bloody good motive for murder."

"There's more. Three weeks ago he lifted ten grand in cash from his bank account in Edinburgh and around the same time made a number of calls to a non-contract phone that has since gone dead."

"Very interesting, I think we need to have another, less friendly little chat with young master Wright and maybe we should make it on our turf rather than his. Alex and DS Craigan, I want you to bring him in and sweat him a little."

"It'll be a pleasure, sir." Alex wasn't sure how things stood between her and her boss but she was glad to have something to do that might move the case forward.

"OK, what else have you got for me?" Russell asked.

"Forensics sweep of Peathill Wood didn't turn up anything worthwhile, I'm afraid," Craigan said.

"So he or they probably weren't killed there. What about the car?"

"Sean O'Reilly looked especially grumpy when he saw it, he's definitely not optimistic."

"That's just Sean's default look, he can't help it," Russell said, glad to introduce a little levity into the proceedings.

"Where are we with Wright's company records?"

DS Frank Weaver was the man in charge of the investigation of the business records. "It's really slow going. The lawyers are checking everything we ask for and generally making the search as difficult as possible. We'll hopefully do better today."

"DS Rankine, I'd like you to liaise with Stewart Street station over the murder of a man named Paddy Niven. He was killed sometime last night and I think it might be linked to the Wright case. Can you arrange to attend the PM and let me know the results?"

"Aye, nae problem," the older detective responded.

"I thought you might want to go yourself, sir," Alex said.

Russell shook his head vehemently. "No, I couldn't watch the docs cut up someone I know personally. It's too creepy. We also need to have a look at Dr Wright's workplace, speak to colleagues and get some idea of their thoughts on the doctor and her husband. DC Kelly?"

"Sir," Kelly's voice piped up from the back of the room.

"You can be my chauffeur."

"Yes, sir."

"Anything from the TV broadcast?"

"Some nutters claiming responsibility, some trying to be helpful and some seeking attention," Weaver said with resignation. The only problem with asking the public for help was interviewing everyone who volunteered information and hoping that one of them would have something useful to say. Ninety nine per cent of the information given was either irrelevant or deliberately misleading.

Russell wasn't surprised; he had been down this road many times. "The usual then. OK, those of you working the stuff coming in from the phones and the reports from the uniformed staff keep it up and let me know if anything turns up. I also need someone to look at who Gregg Wright was sleeping with. Anyone up for it?"

"Ah'll take a run at it, sir," Rankine offered.

"Cheers Mac. I'll give the ACC a quick call to update him, then DC Kelly, you and I can get going. The rest of you, back to work."

***

Alex wasn't too surprised that Calvin Wright insisted on the presence of a lawyer when she went to his home to bring him in for questioning. In her experience there were two classes of people who insisted immediately on the comforting presence of a solicitor: the very rich and the habitual criminals. With Wright's family history, he fitted both categories and he was always going to be accompanied.

The tiny interview room was very warm when the detectives sat down with the suspect and his lawyer. Everything about the station was small and this room felt like the most cramped of all.

Alex performed the introductions for the sake of the tape recorder and the video camera that was mounted in the ceiling.

"Mr Wright, thank you for coming in. We've got a few questions that have arisen as a result of our investigations."

"I am more than willing to help, inspector," replied the fresh-faced man with polite calm.

Alex pulled a piece of paper from a file and pushed it across the table. "The first comes from this particular withdrawal from a branch of the Bank Of Scotland in Leith. According to this, you withdrew ten thousand pounds in cash three weeks ago. We would like to know what it was for."

"You don't need to answer that, Calvin," Mr Jenkins, Wright's solicitor, interrupted.

Wright looked at the lawyer and when he turned back to look at the detectives he was grinning like he had just won the lottery. "It appears I don't have to answer that."

"Mr Wright, I would have thought that you would be keen to help us get to the bottom of your father's murder and your mother's disappearance."

"That's unless I killed them," he laughed and his solicitor squirmed.

"I would advise against saying something like that, even in jest," Jenkins said firmly.

"You stand to inherit a considerable amount of money, don't you?" Alex continued patiently.

"I suppose so."

"Well, that's a motive that we can't ignore and we were hoping to clear things up today so that we can eliminate you from our enquiries," Alex said, unruffled by Wright's curious behaviour.

"I don't see the relevance in what my client does with his own money," said Jenkins. "His family has been the victim of a truly heinous crime and all you can do is harass him."

Alex turned her gaze on Jenkins and gave him a steely look. "Mr Jenkins, you should understand that as the family lawyer you may find yourself with a conflict of interest before long, so I would appreciate it if you let me do my job."

Before he could answer, she reached into the folder again and placed another document on to the table. "Now, Mr Wright, in conjunction with this large cash withdrawal we have the fact that you made several calls to a phone number that you hadn't used before or haven't contacted since. That number is no longer active and was obviously a pay-as-you-go phone. Would you like to explain that?"

"Inspector, I must protest," Jenkins whined.

"Giving us nothing isn't going to stop us being suspicious. Isn't that right, DS Craigan?'

"Absolutely, inspector."

The chilling, emotionless grin crept across Wright's face like a shadow. "This is only about my parents, right?"

"Yes," Alex replied cautiously.

"What if I told you that my family reputation goes before me and that some folk in Edinburgh expect me to behave in a certain way?"

"Go on," Alex encouraged.

"I would caution you against saying something you might later regret," Jenkins warned his client.

"It'll put the inspector's mind at rest, won't it, Alex?"

Alex was close to letting loose on the arrogant little sod but instead she said coolly, "That's detective inspector, if you don't mind."

Wright was now enjoying himself. "I provide a service for members of the student body."

"What kind of service?"

"One of my family's historic businesses, shall we say?"

"Drugs, then?"

"A little relaxing herb to get them through the tough times, when studying gets too much for their poor little brains."

"Marijuana?"

"That's the one," he beamed with untouchable confidence.

"Ten grand would get you a lot of grass, Mr Wright. That could get you a lengthy spell in jail."

"Is it really worth it, Alex? To put the already strained public purse to any more expense than is really necessary for a little harmless recreational smoke?" he said reasonably.

"Mr Jenkins, I don't appreciate your client's familiarity. He's just confessed to the supply of a Class B controlled substance, it's not a good idea to antagonise me. I suggest that you tell him that he's not in a position to provoke me into taking action."

Jenkins leaned over and whispered in Wright's ear.

"My apologies, detective inspector, I meant no disrespect." Despite his words there was little contrition in his tone.

"I'll do a deal with you, Mr Wright. If you tell me where we can find your stash, you can surrender it to us as a public-spirited citizen. Then we'll know that you are telling the truth."

"Fine. No skin off my nose. What's ten grand when you're about to inherit thirty million?"

"Just to be clear, Mr Wright, can you give us the details of your movements on the evening before your parents were due to leave for their holiday?"

"I don't know. Screwing some tart or getting hammered. Maybe both." His grin fixed itself to his face once again.

"Can you supply names?"

"Probably not but I was in Edinburgh, honest, Alex."

Alex's patience was being worn very thin and she felt like slapping him but professionalism won out and she sat back.

"Can we stop playing games? Where are the drugs?"

Wright told the detectives.

"Are we done here?" Jenkins asked.

"Take him out of my sight, please," Alex said with a weary sigh.

"That little shite," Ann-Marie Craigan said when the lawyer had led his client away.

"I still think he could have done it. Never mind hiring a hit man, he's capable of killing them himself. He thinks his connections and money will get him out of every hole he digs for himself," Alex replied.

"Did ye see his face when he said he was inheritin' thirty million? That's one cold little bastard." The detective sergeant's broad Belfast brogue was as effective as any Glaswegian accent when it came to adding force to a swear word.

"I'll let the super know but I think we need to try and track his movements the day his parents were due to go on holiday."

"We could check CCTV. See if we catch him on the M8 on that night."

"That's worth a try. It would be good to slap the cuffs on him and wipe that supercilious smile off his ferrety wee face."

"I agree. I would love to put him in Barlinnie. I'm sure some of the bears would like a new girlfriend to cuddle up to."

Alex laughed at the image Craigan had created.

***

Paul Kelly wondered if he was really cut out for detective work as he drove the head of the Major Incident Team to the West Of Scotland Science Park off Maryhill Road. Russell's confidence and insights were intimidating to the young man; he could never imagine doing what Russell did with such apparent ease. He decided that this trip gave him the chance to study the super at close range and that he would try to learn as much as he could. They chatted amiably but for his part Tom Russell was worried that the young DC's lack of confidence would limit his career.

Hayworth Genetic Solutions was the company formed by Jennifer Wright's father, Sir Nigel Hayworth. It existed to further the understanding of human DNA and from that knowledge, the production of genetic solutions to medical problems that would lead to large profits. The company was founded in 1992 and had grown to employ over one hundred scientists and technicians.

It was housed in a smart, modern building close to the River Kelvin at the south-west corner of the science park. A charming receptionist, who according to her name tag was called Harriet, welcomed the two detectives. She asked them to take a seat while she arranged for someone to speak to them.

Five minutes later a short, balding, bespectacled man arrived. "Hello, I'm Dr Leo McDougall. I'm Dr Wright's colleague. This isn't really convenient, we're very busy."

"This is a murder investigation and we're kind of busy too. What do you think is more important?"

The scientist looked abashed and said, "Sorry. Would you like to come up?" He led the detectives to a stairway, which took them to the first floor.

Russell guessed the doctor to be in his early thirties despite his mature looks. He was dressed in a casual check shirt with a loose polka dot tie as well as a pair of royal blue casual trousers. His ID was on a cord around his neck and in the picture he looked stiff and surprised. He had a high, almost squeaky voice, which combined with his nervous habit of pushing up his glasses on his nose made him appear worried that something was about to attack him.

The two detectives were led past a series of laboratories and offices to a small room that overlooked the river.

"It's terrible what's happened," Dr McDougall said when they were all seated.

"Doctor, we're hoping you might be able to tell us about your colleague."

McDougall reached for his glasses, took them off and polished them on the end of his tie.

"What would you like to know?"

"Can you tell us what kind of person she is?"

"No."

"Sorry?"

The cleaning became more frantic. "I can't because she's not the kind of person anyone gets to know."

"What do you mean?" Russell was puzzled by his answers.

"She talks about the work we do and that's it. Literally. She tells you nothing about herself or life away from work and she never asks or shows any interest in what is happening in anyone else's life."

"That must make her a difficult person to work with."

"You have no idea." He peered through the lenses of his spectacles, decided that they weren't clean enough and then breathed on them before resuming the motion with the tie. "We try to leave her to her research as much as we can. I have to work with her, as technically she's my boss but it is very challenging. She thinks she has free rein as her father's a director. Those things combined mean she isn't the best team player or leader for that matter. She thinks she's on a different intellectual level from the rest of us. My apologies, that was unprofessional, but I think she rates somewhere on the Asperger's scale. She just doesn't connect with people in any meaningful way."

"What kind of work does she do?"

"Her area of expertise is genetic markers that are passed from a parent to offspring which relate to behaviour. For example, is there a genetic predisposition to depression or addiction?"

"So her work is more theoretical?"

"Not pure theory, no, because a lot of the DNA markers can only be traced using volunteers." He looked through the glasses again and decided they were clean enough to resume their position on the bridge of his nose.

"What kind of volunteers?"

"We get them from a variety of sources. Some have come to us from support groups, we use students and some members of the public who are interested in the subject."

"What is the method of study?"

"Well, our methodology is always the same whether it be medical or psychological. We ask the subjects to complete an extensive survey covering their family history, lifestyle, medical history and their moods. Depending on the research area, we may ask for multiple generations of the same family to take part in the study. DNA samples are taken and comparisons are made to find where the similarities exist. There has been a lot of success in medical discoveries but the discovery of character traits has been a slower process." At the end of his speech his spectacles received another nudge up his nose.

"And what happens with the results of these studies?"

"When we find a genetic link, the results are passed across to our solutions team who will then try to design drugs to cure the genetic problems."

"It's a lengthy process?"

"Lengthy and expensive. Companies like ours couldn't exist without venture capital that takes a long-term view on making a profit."

"But potentially very profitable."

"It can be, yes."

"Who supplied that capital?"

"I believe some of it came through Dr Wright's husband as well as friends of Sir Nigel and a big VC company in the States."

Russell filed that piece of information away. Could Jennifer Wright have married purely as a way of accessing her husband's money? It might be nothing but it was another small piece of the jigsaw. He decided that it was time to get closer to the heart of the matter at hand. "Are there areas of your research that would be regarded as controversial, maybe with those in the religious community?"

"We have had some crank e-mails, letters and calls but nothing the police have felt is a real threat. We don't use stem cell research here although we do work with other organisations that do."

"What about those you study? Ever have any problems with them?"

He removed his glasses and began the manic cleaning once again. He hesitated before he replied, "There's been nothing while I've been here but I believe there was something before I joined the company. I don't know the details. You would have to ask Sir Nigel about that."

"Is Sir Nigel still in California?"

"As far as I know. We don't see him too often these days, even when he's in the country. He isn't involved with the day-to-day research. He keeps a guiding hand on the strategic tiller but he's really in semi-retirement."

"Is there anything you could tell us that might help in the search for Dr Wright?"

"There is so little I know about Jennifer the person, that I would be guessing. I think it's more likely that she got caught up in something her husband was involved in, don't you?'

"It is more likely, Dr McDougall, but we need to be thorough. It's important we find her, so if she gets in contact with anyone associated with the company, you have to let us know straight away."

"Of course, I'll let the staff know."

Russell deposited his card on the little man's desk and asked him to call if he could think of anything that might help. McDougall nodded an enthusiastic affirmative while at the same time ushering them politely but quickly out the door.

CHAPTER 11

When he got back to the incident room, Tom Russell was already feeling exhausted and it was only midday. Alex and DS Craigan had finished interviewing Calvin Wright and they were both sitting staring at computer screens when he arrived.

Alex told him what had been said by the youngest member of the Wright family and the way he had behaved.

"He's a Wright, what else can we expect?" was his response. He shared a review of what he had been told by Dr McDougall.

"I wonder what the problems were before McDougall arrived?" Alex pondered.

"I think he knows something but he's too scared to say. DC Kelly, maybe you could do a check on the history of the company. Interview anyone who might be able to give us the lowdown." Russell thought that he needed to instil some self-belief in the DC and hoped that these interviews might help.

"Now, sir?"

"Well you can have a bite of lunch first," he smiled to reassure the younger man that he wasn't the ogre that he might appear.

"Do you want to go and check out this Lennie Warner with me?" Russell asked Alex.

"Sure."

"Grab a bite to eat and then we'll head."

As Alex walked away, Russell's phone rang. He could tell from the display that it was Jonny Holt. He answered it and asked Holt if he could call him back.

"I'm going for a breath of air, I'll not be long," he told Alex.

Outside the station he rang the London detective's number. "Sorry about that Jonny, but I'd rather keep this conversation private."

"Understood. Well, Dragovic is not someone you want to cross, I can tell you that. He was one of Arkan's tigers during the Balkans war. He was just seventeen when he signed up and served in Croatia and Bosnia during the conflict. You can imagine the kind of atrocities that he was accused of. After the war was over he spent some time in Belgrade running the Serbian end of a sex-trafficking racket. He left there in 1999 and finally reached London in 2002, by which time, according to Interpol, he had graduated to racketeering, drugs and illegal gambling. Since he arrived here he's been suspected of involvement in at least three murders and numerous torture sessions including an Albanian gang in Hackney. He left them with all their major joints smashed beyond repair, incapable of controlling their limbs and guaranteed never to walk properly ever again. The rumour mill says Dragovic personally oversaw each of those sessions finding ever more inventive ways of disabling them including nail guns, bayonets and a baseball bat. Unfortunately, like Interpol, we've been unable to pin him down as yet. He's as bad as they get, so if your friend's got any sense, he'll get the hell out of Dodge."

Russell's stomach performed a somersault as Holt ran through Dragovic's litany of criminal activity. How was he supposed to liberate his stupid little brother from the clutches of this madman?

"Thanks Jonny, I owe you."

"Not a problem. Cheers." Holt hung up the phone and Russell leaned his back against the station wall and stared into the white clouds that hung pregnant with the possibility of snow. He stood still for so long that an elderly lady approached him and asked, "Are you all right, son? You look like you've had a shock."

"I'm fine, thank you," He reassured her and rushed back to the warmth of the station.

Alex noticed the look on Russell's face when he returned but she decided it was best to leave it be. He made no mention of what he'd been up to and she thought that if he wanted to talk, he would do so in his own time.

When lunch was complete they drove in Russell's car to Possilpark, an area with one of the toughest reputations in the city. It had once been an area of working-class people and the centre for over ten thousand engineering jobs, but a three-year spell of closures in the eighties had seen the jobs disappear and ripped the heart out of the place. When the jobs had gone, the drug dealers moved in and a long cycle of decay began. Recent attempts to renovate the housing had halted the decline but there were still precious few places to work and there was an air of gloom and anger about the people who lived there. They often turned that resentment on each other and it was not a place that inspired much hope.

The address Morton had given Russell was in one of the last surviving blocks of high flats in the city. Warner's mother's flat overlooked the Forth and Clyde Canal across to Firhill Stadium – home of Partick Thistle Football Club – and then beyond over the north west of Glasgow.

When the police officers reached the door of the apartment it was opened by a tiny woman not more than five feet three inches tall. Her white hair had been permed and styled with plenty of body and as a result added about three inches to her natural height. She wore a thick green cardigan, a heavy tweed skirt, brown wool tights and fluffy pink slippers. She looked over her pink-framed glasses as she inspected her visitors.

"Can ah help ye?"

"Mrs Warner, we'd like to speak to your son. My name is Detective Superintendent Russell, this is Detective Inspector Menzies."

"Well ye can come in if ye want but whatever ye think he's done, ah can tell ye it wisnae him," she said confidently.

She ushered them through a short, narrow hall and into a beige and brown living room that was little warmer than the air outside. Hopes of an early resolution to the case disappeared as the two detectives were introduced to Lennie Warner. He sat in a wheelchair, a skeletal form with clothes that may have fitted him once upon a time but were now two or three sizes too big. Alex could see at least three layers; the man was struggling to keep warm in the freezing house. He wore a pair of gloves with the fingertips removed. She reckoned he was in his mid to late forties. His thin, sandy-coloured hair was limp and his green eyes were racked with pain. She doubted that he could lift an axe, never mind wield it to cut a body into pieces.

"Ah tellt ye, it couldnae be him. He got hit by a car in Ireland. Left him paralysed so it did. Sorry it's so cauld but we cin only afford tae heat the place at night," the old woman said.

"I'm sorry we've bothered you, Mrs Warner," Russell turned to leave.

"Whit ye wantin'?" Lennie's voice grated.

"Sorry, we didn't mean to disturb you. We had a tip and it's proved to be false," Russell said.

"Maybe you can help us, Mr Warner. What do you know about the Wrights?" Alex said. She reckoned there was no harm in asking.

"Peter Wright and that lot?"

"Yes."

"Cin ye gie's a minute, maw?" he said to his mother, who walked into the kitchen and shut the door.

"Ah don't want her hearin' any o' this, know?"

"I understand."

"Is this cause Gregg Wright got murdered?" he asked.

"Yes," Alex replied as Russell decided to let her run with it to see where it got them.

"Somebody tell ye ah wis back and thought maybe ah did it?"

"Something like that."

"That wis a bum steer, wisn't it?" he laughed with a cackle but it was cut short as it appeared to be causing him pain. "It only hurts when ah laugh, try to walk or take a piss," he said.

"We heard that there might be some conflict among the Wrights, have you heard anything?"

He held Alex's gaze, considering his answer.

"Normally, ah widnae talk tae the likes o' you, but Wright wisnae too keen tae help me oot wi' ma troubles when ah goat back. Ah did a lot fur that bastard but when ah came back it wis like ah didnae exist, so it's nae skin aff ma nose. Ah've been oot the country fur a while but that disnae mean ah wisnae kept informed. Billy McCarron – Wright's second in command ye could caw him – he thinks that they should wipe McGavigan aff the map and grab his business. Wright slapped him doon last year but fae whit ah've heard, McCarron's still keen oan the idea."

"Could he have killed Gregg Wright or at least arranged it to provoke Peter Wright into a reaction?"

"Fuck naw, at least ah don't think so. That wid be like startin' a revolution an' probably committin' suicide and McCarron's lots o' things but he's no' fuckin' stupid."

"Are there others in the gang who think the same way that McCarron does?"

"A few, but killing Wright's boy, that's a whole different thing, know?"

"What about McGavigan? Do you think he's got the balls to make a grab for Wright's territory?"

"No' fae whit ah've heard. Last time he was worried that if it goat oot o' haun they wid be so weak that the Triads or the Albanians wid move in an' wipe out baith lots."

"Would you be willing to help us out with some more information if you hear anything?"

"That wid depend, widn't it? Ah still hear whit's goin' oan but ah widnae like ye tae think that ah'm a mug and that it wid always be free."

"What kind of price were you thinking of?" Alex asked, happy to play his game.

"At least twenty knicker fur each wee tidbit," he said with a smirk.

"Call it fifteen and maybe a bit more for the good stuff, how's that?"

"Ye're a hard wummin but ye've goat a deal." He offered a trembling, emaciated hand, which Alex shook before passing him her card along with a twenty-pound note. She had just secured her first confidential informant.

"Ta. Ye're awright… fur a polis," Warner said.

He shouted to his mother to invite her back into the living room. She offered Alex and Russell a cup of tea, which they declined politely before saying goodbye to the despondent pair.

Mrs Warner walked them to the door. Just as they were walking away she said, "He's payin' fur his sins noo." She closed her door before the lift arrived.

"He would have settled for a tenner," Russell said.

"I know, but the two of them could die from hypothermia. I don't imagine I'll get much from him but you never know. It's hard to think of him as the vicious bastard that Superintendent Morton described."

"Don't let his disability fool you, he'd still turn on you if he could. Just watch yourself if you're dealing with the likes of him."

"Yes, sir."

"You know, Alex, the more I look at this case, the more I find it unlikely that this is gang related. I think Gregg Wright was more than capable of getting himself into bother without the help of his father or his connections," Russell said.

"Possibly, or there's an angle we're not seeing at the moment. McCarron is worth a look."

"Aye, I suppose so. Let's get back and see if Rankine's back from the mortuary yet. I would like to know what killed Paddy Niven and if there's any way I can nail Peter Wright for it."

***

DS Rankine was sitting at his desk when they returned to the incident room.

"Mac, what have you got for me?" Russell asked eagerly.

"It wis a heart attack, Super. The doc reckons that his heart couldnae take the strain o' the torture. They gave him a real workin' o'er, poor bastard."

"Why, what did they do?"

"As well as cigarette burns, there were signs that they hud been giein' his baw… I mean his testicles a right good bootin'. There wis signs of bruisin' on baith his knees, the doc reckoned it wis caused by a metal pipe. He was struck in the back o' the heid, the doc reckons that was tae subdue him. He wis some mess."

"Poor Paddy, he didn't deserve that. Any trace or DNA evidence?"

"They've been sent to the lab; the doc found some hairs that might prove useful but they could be fae his dug for aw we know."

"Interesting."

"They'd normally be more careful than that," Alex voiced the same thought that Russell was having.

"Knowing our luck, it's probably nothing. Anything else, Mac?"

"Nothin' else of note although she did say that Niven widnae have lived much longer anyway. He had stage 4 liver cancer."

"OK, Mac. Thanks." The detective team could see that Russell had been affected badly by Niven's death.

"I better get some of the paper work done and check what shite we've been sent about Police Scotland now," Russell said as he dropped down at his temporary desk and retreated from interaction for a short while.

There was a period of relative calm as the team continued to process the huge amount of information that the murder inquiry had already generated. Russell had a mail from the media team asking for an update and he obliged by calling the press officer responsible. It was quicker to speak to her directly rather than him trying to type an answer, his typing skills being of the one-fingered variety. DC Kelly reported that he had been unsuccessful in his attempts to find out what had happened at Hayworth. When the young detective had completed his report, Russell called ACC Muldoon and gave him the same update that he had sent the press officer. Muldoon was happy to stand in front of the cameras and field the questions from the press in his shiny uniform. It was always the same when the brass were worried at the public perception of the force, particularly when they were dealing with a gang-related killing. Russell hated dealing with the journalists and was happy for his boss to do the interviews and press conference routine.

As he was finishing the briefing of his senior officer, he noticed Alex gesticulating frantically.

"What's up?"

"DS Weaver's been trying to get a hold of you."

She handed her mobile phone over and Russell said, "Frank, what have you got?"

"Sir, one of the forensic accountants discovered something interesting. Wright was making regular donations of around five thousand pounds a month into an account he recognised. It's a company that is acting as a front for The Council for the Defence of Scottish Family Life, the right-wing organisation."

"That shower of shite run by Shuggie Evans?"

"The very one. Those payments stopped two months ago and a similar amount has been transferred to another political organisation that is campaigning for a 'Yes' vote in the referendum."

"I knew there had to be money going to that bastard from somewhere. What the hell would Wright want with that lot?"

"I'm not sure, sir, but considering who's in charge and the type that are involved, I thought I'd better let you know."

"Thanks Frank, anything else among the pile?"

"Nothing obvious so far. We're still trying to sort the wheat from the chaff as it were."

"Good, DS Weaver. Pass on my thanks and tell the team to keep up the good work."

"Thanks sir, I will do."

When the call was over, as he handed back the phone he asked Alex, "Did he tell you?"

"Yes."

"What do you make of it?"

Alex stared at her computer screen. "According to their website, Evans and his mob are promising a business nirvana of no taxes for Scottish businesses when they've completed their version of ethnic cleansing. Probably to try to attract funding from people like Wright."

"Why would anyone want to align themselves with pond scum like Evans?"

"That's what the shell company is for, a buffer between respectability and scum. If the forensic accountant hadn't already done some work on the SCDFL, we probably would have been none the wiser."

"True, but what does it mean in terms of the murder?"

"Evans wouldn't appreciate the loss of revenue, particularly if he's not persuaded too many others to sign up for his vision of Valhalla."

"I'd love to put that wee prick away for good. That lassie's face still haunts me."

In the early part of the last decade Russell had put Evans in prison for a serious assault on a young Asian woman. Evans had carved a swastika into the woman's cheek and it took a number of operations performed by a top plastic surgeon to remove the terrible scar. The image was forever etched into Russell's memory and as far as he was concerned the only way to expunge it would be to ensure that Evans wasn't allowed to walk the streets. During an investigation the previous summer, Evans had reappeared in his new guise as the leader of a far right-wing organisation. There was nothing to connect him to that crime but Russell had flagged up his organisation to Special Branch as he was concerned by the extremity of the politics as well as the violent reputation of its members.

"We'll need to try and tie Evans with Wright a bit more before we can move on him."

"Don't worry, we will," Alex said confidently.

"Maybe we should put a shot across his bows anyway, just for the hell of it." Alex could see the gleam in Russell's eye at chance of getting something on Evans.

"DS Craigan," Russell shouted.

"Sir?"

"Grab a DC and go to Shuggie Evans' place and have a wee discussion about his whereabouts on the night of the murder."

"Yes, sir." Craigan was delighted to get away from staring at the endless witness statements on her computer screen. She found Kelly and then went in search of a uniformed officer to accompany them on their task.

When they were gone, Russell's fatigue overtook him again. "I'm getting too old for this, Alex. I keep waiting on the call that says Wright's retaliated and we'll be off down a long and dangerous road."

"If McGavigan isn't involved, would Paddy have been able to convince Wright's thugs that there was nothing to tell?"

"I don't know. Judging by what Mac said they were at him for a long time before he died."

"Let's hope he convinced them that it wasn't worth going to war over."

"You know what torture brings; whatever answer the torturer wants. I wouldn't be surprised if wee Paddy told them that McGavigan was involved just to get them to stop beating him. He wasn't the strongest either physically or mentally."

"If that's the case we can expect the bodies to begin mounting up."

"I know. Fancy a visit to another scumbag?"

"Which one?"

"McCarron."

"You take me to all the best places," she replied.

After a short laugh he said, "Let's go."

They were just about to leave when a female uniformed officer rushed into the office.

"Sir, there's been a shooting. One of the McGavigan gang was shot at a car wash in Kinning Park. A masked man stepped out of a car and shot him four times before driving away."

"Fuck!" Russell shouted.

"Sorry, PC…"

"McWilliams, sir."

"PC McWilliams, contact DS Weaver and tell him to meet us at the scene as soon as possible. I want him to manage the scene to give us some consistency. Does the ACC know?"

"I'm not sure, sir."

"OK, I'll contact him. Alex." He was walking out the door and indicated that his DI should follow him.

He was reaching into his pocket for his mobile when it rang; when he looked at the screen it was obvious that ACC Muldoon had already been informed of the shooting.

"Sir."

"Tom, I take it you've heard."

"Yes sir, we're just leaving."

"Get this sorted Tom. We can't afford this getting any fucking worse. Get a grip on these bastards and quickly." Russell had never heard the ACC swear before and in another situation it would have been comical due to Muldoon's refined accent.

"We're doing our best, sir."

"What is wrong with these people?"

"I know, sir. I'll update you as soon as I can."

"No need, I'll be there." He hung up abruptly.

"Great, that's just made my day. Muldoon will be joining us at the scene."

"His arse is in the fire now and he'll not be keen to be the only one getting roasted," Alex observed.

"That's for sure but all he'll be is a bloody nuisance."

Russell was so anxious to get to the scene of the murder that he put on the lights and used the siren to make progress as quickly as they could. They sped across the Kingston Bridge and down on to Paisley Road West and arrived within fifteen minutes of leaving the station.

The car wash was housed in the forecourt of an old petrol station in a rundown industrial estate. A cordon had already been set around the whole area and there were people everywhere. As Alex and Russell suited up, Frank Weaver drew up and parked behind them on the road outside the locus.

"What have we got, sir?" Weaver asked as he approached.

"One of McGavigan's crew. Shot four times. That's all I know. I need you to run the scene, Frank. I just want it to be consistent."

"No problem."

The two senior officers waited until the DS was also suitably garbed for the scene before all three approached the cordon. A female detective sergeant from Govan station was running the scene when they arrived.

"Good afternoon, Shona."

"Good afternoon, sir."

"If you don't mind, DS Miller, I would like DS Weaver to take over the crime scene management. He's part of our investigation into the murder of Gregg Wright and there's a more than even chance that this will be related."

She looked a little disgruntled but said, "Yes, sir. I understand."

"Give him a full briefing of what's been done so far and then come and join us. I'll get you assigned to the joint investigation." That seemed to assuage some of Miller's annoyance and once again Alex noted how good her boss was at managing those under his control.

Within the cordon, the usual huddle of senior officers had assembled overlooking the body. As well as Muldoon there was Superintendent Morton, Sean O'Reilly looking even more crabbit than usual and, off to one side, looking like she had stepped in something she didn't like, the Procurator Fiscal. There was a team of five crime scene technicians on their knees peering at the tarmac looking for the smallest traces of evidence. Poised over the body was Dr Hogan, the pathologist, who managed to look bored.

Russell and Alex acknowledged each of the attendees.

"This is very bad news, Tom," Muldoon said.

"I know, sir." Russell had to bite back a sarcastic reply.

"What are you doing about this, superintendent?" Jacqui Kerr piped up.

"Sitting scratching my arse," he muttered under his breath.

"What was that?"

"We're doing all we can but it's very difficult with no concrete leads and little in the way of physical evidence. You know, that stuff that can actually secure a conviction."

"I don't like your tone."

"Well don't ask such stupid questions." Alex could see over the Fiscal's shoulder Lindsay Morton beam a smile when he heard Russell's statement.

"Tom." The warning shot came from Muldoon.

"I apologise, sir, but we are doing the best we can with the information we have, which isn't a lot."

"I'm not happy with you, superintendent. Maybe that rank of yours is weighing too heavily," Kerr said sharply.

"Sir, I don't think the Fiscal's attitude is particularly helpful in this situation either," Alex said to Muldoon before Russell could react in a way that would have him demoted and confined to a desk until retirement.

"You're quite right, DI Menzies. In-fighting isn't going to catch a murderer." Alex was pleased to hear her boss defend his team. As far as she was concerned there was always too much deference given to everything Kerr said.

Jacqui Kerr made no apology but walked away from the police group. Russell turned his attention to the body.

"What have you got for us Dr Hogan?'

"Shot four times in the chest. Closely grouped. Death would have been instantaneous." He stood up and moved around the body and it was only then that Russell could see the identity of the victim. Alan McGavigan's face was now slack, his eyes glazed and his skin the colour of old lace. His blue sweatshirt had four blossoms of violet staining where his blood had saturated around the black bullet holes. A river of pink drained from below the body where the blood had mixed with the soap suds from the car.

"Aw hell, could this get any fuckin' worse?" Russell sighed.

"I doubt it," Lindsay Morton said. "Sorry, Tom, I thought you knew."

"Sean, what have you got?"

"The four shell casings were found. Shells are .38 calibre, maybe from a Glock. We'll need to get ballistic tests done to be sure. We're still searching for anything else but unless he left a fingerprint on the shells it's going to be tough finding the shooter."

"Cheers, Sean. Keep your fingers crossed but the chances are the gun will be unregistered, untraceable and already at the bottom of the river. Lindsay, any ideas? We've been hearing about a rift in the Wright gang and that Billy McCarron might be looking to stir up the hornet's nest again."

"My intel was that Wright had slapped McCarron down in no uncertain terms but as always it's a volatile situation. There are never any guarantees about how they're going to react at any given moment. Gregg Wright's murder is a circumstance we've never really faced before," Morton said honestly.

"I despair of this fuckin' city sometimes, I really do," Russell moaned.

There was a loud commotion at the edge of the cordon and suddenly Malky McGavigan broke away from a couple of uniformed PCs who were desperately trying to prevent him approaching his son's body. He ran across the garage forecourt and Tom Russell stepped out to prevent him reaching the bloodied body of his son. McGavigan swung a punch at the detective, Russell saw it coming but the force of the connection was still enough to knock him backwards and on to his backside. Of the others, only Alex reacted quickly enough and she flicked a swift kick, which connected with McGavigan's knee, causing him to crumple to the ground. Alex pounced and forced him onto his stomach before calling for a pair of handcuffs. They were supplied and she clamped them on to McGavigan's wrists. He continued to struggle but slowly the energy dissipated as anger was replaced by resigned grief.

"Are ye calm now, Malcolm?" Russell said.

"They killed ma boy," was the reply, the gang lord's voice crackling with the pain of loss.

"I know, but you need to let us handle it. Get off him, Alex."

She did as she was ordered and then helped McGavigan to his feet. The fight had gone from him, at least for the moment.

"Can ah see him?"

"I don't think that's a good idea right this minute. We'll get him cleaned up and then you can see him. We'll go back to the station and have a wee chat first."

"What ur ye gonnae dae aboot Wright? Ah didnae huv anythin' tae dae wi' his boy's murder, ah swear."

"I think even Wright knows that."

"So whit's he want tae start a war fur?"

"I think Wright might have a few discipline problems. We're going to have a word with him as soon as we've sorted you out."

"Ah'll need ma brief," he said as the father disappeared to be replaced by the gangster.

"No, you won't. I just want to talk, no lawyers required. Now if you're willing to come with me, we'll remove these cuffs and go as civilised people."

"Aye, OK. You promise ah'll get to see him?"

"I promise."

McGavigan nodded his agreement and Alex removed the cuffs, then returned them to the PC who had supplied them.

"Alex, can you deal with the rest of the formalities here, while I chat to Mr McGavigan?"

"Sure, sir. I'll see you back at the station." Alex wasn't sure what her boss had planned but she hoped he knew what he was doing.

McGavigan ordered his driver to go back to their office and Russell escorted the distraught father to the police car.

CHAPTER 12

The Scottish Council For The Defence Of Family Life had new headquarters in a city centre office. They had moved from less salubrious accommodation in the Gorbals only the week before. When Craigan and Kelly arrived there were still boxes and crates waiting to be unpacked.

"I'm Detective Sergeant Craigan, this is Detective Constable Kelly. We'd like to speak to Hugh Evans," Craigan told a pretty, youthful-looking woman who was sitting at a desk close to the main door.

"If you would like to take a seat, I'll see if he's available." She indicated a couple of chairs opposite her.

Craigan and Kelly followed her suggestion. Craigan could see a series of leaflets with wholesome pictures of white families and titles like 'How gay marriage corrupts your children' and 'The Islamist threat to Christianity'. Kelly turned to Craigan who just shook her head; she could already understand why Russell hated Evans with the passion he did.

The woman returned and said, "I'm afraid Mr Evans is very busy at the moment. He suggested you make an appointment."

"Oh he did, did he? Well, this is a murder investigation and our time is a little more precious than his." Craigan was on her feet and through the connecting door before the receptionist could move; DC Kelly hurried to catch up.

"I'm sorry, Mr Evans, she wouldn't listen," the woman shouted through the door as Craigan made her entrance.

Inside the office, Evans was sitting in a leather executive chair behind a desk constructed of dark wood. He was wearing a charcoal grey suit that looked well cut from an expensive material. He also sported a white shirt and a blue silk tie. Someone meeting him for the first time would think he was a respectable, successful businessman. That image was betrayed by the gold sovereign ring on his left hand and the trace of a home tattoo on his right.

"That's OK Vicky, I'll deal with this," he said. His pudgy features were set in an annoyed grimace as he turned to Craigan and asked, "What do you want?"

"We're here to talk to you about your relationship with Gregg Wright," Craigan replied.

"Oh look, Daniel, Belfast ham," Evans said when Craigan had finished speaking.

The other man in the office smiled broadly at his boss's insulting pun.

"What did you say?" the Irish woman was in no mood for Evans's attempts at wit.

"Nothing. Gregg Wright, who's that?"

"He's a man who until recently was paying you a substantial amount of money to support your cause. Not long after the money stopped, Mr Wright turned up dead. I'm sure you must have read the reports in the press."

"I don't read the press, it's full of left-wing, anti-Christian, pro-Jewish propaganda."

Craigan's anger was beginning to grow. "I'm not here for one of your bigoted lectures, you little prick. You also attended a party held in Mr Wright's honour. Do you remember that?"

"Vaguely, but I get invited to so many things these days. There are a lot of people who are coming round to my way of thinking."

"Where were you a fortnight past Tuesday night into Wednesday morning?"

"I have no idea, I would need to check my diary, but I wasn't anywhere near this Gregg Wright, I know that much."

"Losing the kind of cash that he was putting in, you might not be able to afford this fancy office for much longer."

"I have many people who are happy to support our cause."

"I'm sure you have, all of them brain-dead morons, but five grand a month, that's going to hurt."

She had touched a nerve. "If you've got nothing else, I'd ask you to leave me to my legitimate business. There is such a thing as harassment." He stood up and walked around the desk to face her.

Craigan knew there was little point in continuing until they had more information. She was a little annoyed at Russell for sending her in with nothing to work with. "We'd like you to supply details of your movements on the night in question within twenty-four hours or we'll be back to take you in for further questioning," she told him forcefully and turned to leave.

"Whatever you say, darling," Evans said dismissively as he patted her rear.

With snake-like responses Craigan spun on her heels, grabbed his wrist, forced it up his back and pressed him on to the desk. She then manoeuvred his other arm into a position where she could place handcuffs on both wrists.

"What the fuck ye daein' ya Irish hoor?"

"Hugh Evans, I'm arresting you on suspicion of assaulting a police officer. You are not obliged to say anything but anything you do say will be noted down and may be used in evidence. Do you understand?"

"Assaulted ye? Ah tapped yir fat arse."

"Did you get that reply, DC Kelly?"

"Yes, sarge," Kelly replied as he wrote in his notebook.

The other man in the room said, "Aren't you being a little heavy handed, detective?"

"Sir, did you witness the suspect placing his hands on me?"

"Yes, but…"

"Then we'll need you to come with us to make a statement."

Craigan hauled Evans up from the desk and was subject to a string of curses as she escorted him out of the office followed by an amused Kelly and a sullen witness.

***

Instead of the police station, Russell decided to stop the car outside a greasy spoon café on Paisley Road West.

"Come on, we'll have a cuppa."

"OK…" McGavigan replied warily. Cops weren't supposed to be friendly; he didn't like it when the normal rules of engagement were changed so radically.

Russell ordered two mugs of strong tea and then two people who were traditional enemies sat at the table next to the window like old friends. There was no view of the busy road as the glass was fogged up with condensation. Russell thought that it was probably for the best, as any of McGavigan's crew might have jumped to the wrong conclusion if they saw the two of them together.

When they were settled, Russell said, "Things might not be what they appear. There's a chance that the same person killed both Alan and Gregg Wright."

"What d'ye mean?"

"You said yourself that things aren't all sweetness and light among Wright's lot. There may be a power struggle going on and someone may be out to provoke a war. There is a chance if you react to this attack you will be giving the rebels within Wright's organisation exactly what they want. I've been told that you were worried about outside parties being able to grab control of the drug trade in this city; this might be how they do it."

"I don't know whit ye're talking about."

"Malcolm, this conversation is off the record. I am trying to stop a bloodbath in this city and let's say, just for this moment in time, your business is not my concern. There's no point in denying any of it because it really doesn't matter. I don't want innocent people getting caught up in an ever increasing level of violence, so I am asking you to be honest with me and to listen to what I've got to say." Russell pressed his point as forcibly as he could.

McGavigan wasn't stupid and he realised that Russell was being sincere. "I wis worried that Wright and I would weaken each other so much that we would be ripe for the picking by other organisations, shall we say."

"What if one of those organisations promised one of Wright's lieutenants his own bigger slice of the new pie? Or even offered one of your own men the same thing?"

McGavigan looked sceptical as he asked, "Is that what you think happened?"

"I think it's a possibility. Alternatively, it could be, as I said earlier, that someone is making a grab for power within Wright's gang. At the moment I don't know but what I don't need is you rising to the bait. You need to trust me."

"What if ye're wrong?"

"Then you, me, Wright and the whole city are screwed."

"Whit will I say tae ma lot if ah do nothing about Alan's murder?"

"You think they'll want immediate reprisals?"

"Aye, ah wid if ah wis them and I've got a position to protect."

"You need to control them, you need to spin some line about taking your time. You're worried about the attention we're giving you, whatever it takes to stop this blowing up into something even worse. You do this and we'll forget about the assault charge; I could throw the book at you for the punch you swung at me. You don't want to be in the cells unable to control what's going on out here, do you?"

Russell stared into McGavigan's eyes trying to get a measure of what he was thinking; what he saw was an intelligent predator staring back at him. "Ah'll give ye a week but if ye've got nothing then ah'll need to react or I'll be the one who'll need to worry about discipline and that's not going to happen. It's the best ah can do."

It was an olive branch and Russell realised that there was little negotiating room. Even this agreement was better than nothing. He only hoped that he could get to the killer or killers before Glasgow became a combat zone once again.

"I'll do my best."

The two men supped their tea and after a short period of silence, McGavigan said, "Ah didn't want this life for ma Alan, know?"

"No, what happened?" Russell asked, curious as to where this was going to lead.

"Ah thought that I could give him a better life. I tried to encourage him to stick in at school but he wis never very academic. He just looked up to me and it didn't matter that ah tried to tell him that I wisnae a good example, he just wanted to be like me. As he became a teenager, he grew into this big brute of a boy that could terrify the hell oot o' folk and that's what he did. He caused all kinds of bother at school and knew that none of the kids would stand up tae him because of me. In the end ah gave up and let him in. At least ah knew how tae keep him oot o' the jail. Ah just couldn't keep him oot the road o' a bullet." There were tears at the edge of his eyes as he told the tale.

"What about his mother?"

"She buggered off when he wis four. Never bothered wi' him. She'll probably be back fur the funeral tae blame me and this time she'll be right."

"And what about you? How did you end up in this game? You're not daft, Malcolm. Your brains could have got you out if you had tried."

"When you're raised in Govan, it's better tae hide yir abilities if you've got a brain. School's never a way oot o' a place like Govan, the numbers are against you."

Tom Russell thought that it was a sad thing for anyone to say but even more so because he knew that McGavigan's statement was probably true. Life in Govan was hard and only the strong would survive. McGavigan's strength and intelligence had turned him into the leader of his troop of primates but he would never win any respect from ordinary people, only fear.

They finished their tea and Russell offered to drop the gang lord at the snooker hall door, but he declined.

"Don't let me doon," McGavigan said as he walked away. It was a sentence laced with the threat of a man who was reasserting his role; the civility of a mug of tea had evaporated and normal relations were being re-established.

***

As her boss walked away with the distraught father, Alex turned her attention to the witnesses. There were two men in their early twenties who claimed to have seen nothing during the incident. They said they were cleaning the car as it sat in front of the office and that they hadn't seen the episode. Alex thought that they were probably both part of McGavigan's less legitimate pursuits and decided there was no point in trying to extract any information from them; they wouldn't talk to the 'polis'.

The driver of the car was a different matter. He was a small, thin man in his early thirties. He had neatly trimmed light brown hair, hazel eyes that were wide in fear, a sharp aquiline nose above a thick moustache and a thin-lipped broad mouth. He was sitting in the office clutching a cup of sweet tea; a mature uniformed constable was sitting beside him trying to calm him down.

"Good afternoon, sir. I'm Detective Inspector Menzies, I'll be investigating this case. I was hoping I could have a few words with you about what happened here today."

"Ye...Yes, that'll be f... f...fine," he managed to say through chattering teeth.

"Can I start by asking your name, please sir?"

"Daw… Dawson, Stephen Dawson with a p…h."

"Right, Stephen, I would like you to try something for me. Close your eyes."

The terrified man did as he was told. Alex then took him through a series of breathing exercises that calmed his body's reaction to the shock he had suffered. After five minutes she had helped him to stop trembling and his breathing was now a little less laboured.

"OK Stephen, that's great. Now, can you tell me what happened?"

"I come here every week to get the car cleaned. It's a company car and I have to keep it clean or my boss goes nuts."

"What is it you do?"

"I sell photocopiers and printers."

"What time did you arrive at the car wash today?"

"It was about one-thirty, the news had just come on the radio. I listen to the radio as it helps to keep my brain working when I'm on the motorway; I do a lot of driving."

"So you pulled in and what happened?"

"As I'm a regular the guys know what I need. They had soaped the car and were working on the wheels when I noticed a motorbike pull up beside me. I could just make it out through the suds that were running down the window."

"You're sure it was a motorbike?"

"Yes, definitely."

"We must have got the wrong information," Alex said, to herself more than to the witness.

"I thought it was strange because why would you bring a motorbike to a car wash. Then I thought that it must be a courier until I realised there were two people on the bike. I could hear the engine was still running and then the guy at the back jumps off and lifts the faceplate of his helmet and shouts something into the office. The big man stepped out and then… and then…" His breathing started to become shallow again and Alex used the same technique to still it.

"The suds had cleared and I could see the guy in the helmet who took out a gun from his jacket pocket and shot the big man four times very quickly. I was so scared I didn't even move, not even to duck for cover. Then the guy who did the shooting bent down as if to pick something up but the one that was still on the bike dragged him up, he got back onto the bike and they sped away."

"What can you tell me about the shooter?"

"He was quite tall, about five eleven or six feet. He was wearing a black, puffy jacket and a pair of black trousers of some kind. The other one was wearing a black leather jacket, I think."

"What about the helmets they were wearing?"

"The man with the gun had a dark blue helmet with a black visor. The other one was wearing a white one, I think."

"What about the bike?"

"Red, a Suzuki. You could tell by the noise it was probably a big engine. Seven hundred and fifty CCs, minimum."

"That's brilliant."

"I'm a MotoGP fan," he explained needlessly.

"Stephen, that is excellent. We'll need you to make a statement at the station."

"Will I need to testify in court?"

"It's possible, if we can find the culprit."

He began to shake again as the fear gripped him once more. "Wh…what about m… my car?"

"We'll need to take it in to have a look, in case there is any evidence we can get from it. If not you'll have it back as soon as possible."

"Oh... oh... man. My b...boss will be p... pissed at me."

Alex felt sorry for the poor man, whose life was suddenly filled with violence, detectives and the possibility of a court appearance. "I'll give him a ring if it helps."

"W...would you? Th... th... that would be g... great," he said with relief.

Alex asked him for the details and he gave her a leaflet with his company's phone number. She asked the uniformed officer if he could look after Dawson by taking him to the station for his statement and then to his doctor for some tranquillisers. The PC didn't look too happy at being asked to babysit but acquiesced to the detective's request.

Alex rang the number on the leaflet and spoke to Stephen Dawson's boss, whose only worry was if the car was unharmed in the shooting. Alex reassured him that it was fine and added, "Stephen's unharmed too but he's a bit shaken up. He'll need to come to the station to give us a statement and he won't be in for a couple of days."

"What? Oh yes, of course," Dawson's boss said, but there was little real concern for his employee.

Alex kept her disgust to herself and hung up.

The formalities of organising transportation for Alan McGavigan's body for the short journey to the mortuary were completed by the time Alex left the little office. Noel Hawthorn had been called to another scene, a traffic accident in Pollokshields. Alex had hoped to catch a private word but it would have to wait. There was little else she could do at the scene so she left Sean O'Reilly and his team to finish their sweep while she headed back to the station.

CHAPTER 13

Russell could almost taste the anxiety that was permeating the station when he arrived back. There wasn't a copper in the city who didn't remember the fear that had gripped the citizens of Glasgow the last time the two gangs went on a killing spree. Three shootings in public places, two fatal fires and a vicious stabbing in the space of six months were all too recent to be anything other than fresh in their psyches. These were the times that the police were under the closest scrutiny and it put everyone on edge.

"The ACC wants to see you, sir," Alex said when Russell walked into the incident room.

Muldoon had taken over the office of DI Mackie and it looked like he was going to be there for the duration.

"Tom, take a seat."

Russell sat in an old rickety chair opposite Muldoon.

"What was that all about?"

"Sir?"

"McGavigan, where is he?"

"We've come to an arrangement."

"What kind of arrangement?" the ACC asked suspiciously.

"I've convinced him to give me a week to find his son's killer, in return I won't charge him with assault."

"I don't know if I approve of you making deals with gangsters, detective superintendent. Particularly one who may be responsible for creating this mess in the first place. Do you know how many witnesses there were to that assault? What's the Fiscal going to say?"

"To be honest, sir, I don't give a shit. I think there's more to this than meets the eye. I don't believe that McGavigan had Gregg Wright killed and I've got a feeling that Wright knows it. There's a chance that someone in Wright's organisation is trying to provoke a war."

"What proof do you have?"

"None. It's my gut telling me along with everything I've learned about the situation from Superintendent Morton; he believes that no one benefits from this." He began counting off his reasons on his fingers. "One, the territorial dispute appeared to have been resolved at the end of the last spate of deaths; two, Gregg Wright had no official role in his father's gang; and three, McGavigan is scared of someone else moving in if the two of them weaken each other to the point that they become easy pickings. None of it makes any sense, unless there are other factors in play."

"So what's your theory?"

"I think Billy McCarron fancies himself as the new emperor or that he's working with someone else to erode the McGavigan and Wright gangs to allow new masters to move in."

"For what purpose?"

"Power; money; terror – all the usual reasons these bastards use to justify their actions. McCarron's a psychopath. Look at his record. He was convicted of torturing a twelve-year-old boy when he was just fourteen. He loves the violence and would certainly do anything if it meant he could fulfil his warrior fantasies. He's not happy that Wright didn't finish McGavigan off and now he's been stirring things up to put Wright and McGavigan at each other's throats again."

Muldoon paused and then sighed, "You'd better be right or you've let a killer loose on the streets when you could have him banged up."

"I know, but I believe McGavigan when he says that he knew nothing about Gregg Wright's murder and if that's true, something other than the usual gangland tit-for-tat is in play."

"I'll let you run with this Tom, but this is your career on the line if you're wrong."

"Yes, sir. I understand that."

He also understood that there was no way that ACC Muldoon was going to take the blame for any more deaths and Tom Russell had just offered himself up as the perfect scapegoat.

***

When the meeting with the ACC was finished and Russell returned to the main office, he told Alex about his conversation with McGavigan and then she briefed him on Stephen Dawson's statement.

"Pretty good for somebody that was scared shitless," Russell said when she was finished.

"I don't know whether we'll ever get him into a court, mind you."

"I know. Mac?"

"Sir," Rankine raised his head from a pile of reports.

"I want you to check the CCTV for a Suzuki motorbike with two people on board. DI Russell will give you all the details."

"Aye, nae problem, sir."

"How did you get on with the search for Gregg Wright's bits on the side?"

"Ah found a couple of rich married wummin who were keen to keep it quiet. Their husbands don't seem to know or are too scared to have done anythin' about it. They seem to be just bored women who were attracted to the glamour of a gangster faemily."

"Don't treat it as a priority but keep digging. Phone round the dodgy private eyes when you get a chance, see if any of them followed a woman to a liaison with our victim. They bastards have to be useful for something."

"Will do, sir."

"Any news about Jennifer Wright?" Russell asked Alex.

"Still no sign, sir. We're still doing door-to-door in the towns around the Campsies. Nothing from the airports, railway or bus stations either."

"She's the biggest mystery of them all. If it's gang related, why take her? They don't normally involve wives in their macho bollocks. Even if they weren't expecting her to be there when they got a hold of Wright, why not dump her with her husband?"

"I know, that's something I've been thinking a lot about. The only alternative is that she's involved but I can't imagine her organising the murder and dismemberment of anyone, at least judging by all we've been told about her."

"This is a complete shambles. I have no idea how we can get the answers and the ACC's basically told me that I've got a week to save my career."

"We need to speak to Peter Wright. I know he'll deny any involvement but I think if someone's gone behind his back we'll be able to pick up on it," Alex reassured him.

"OK, let's go speak to the grieving father and his mob."

Before they could move Ann-Marie Craigan arrived in the office with Kelly close on her heels. She told Russell and Alex all that had happened with Evans, which prompted a large grin from Russell.

"You were absolutely correct to lift him, sergeant. We'll let him sweat overnight and see if his memory is a little better in the morning."

"A pleasure, sir." She returned the smile and walked to her desk to begin the paperwork.

"We're off to see Wright, you know how to get in touch if there's any news," Russell announced as he left the incident room with his DI.

They spent the journey running through what they knew and also where the huge gaps in their knowledge were. Russell asked Alex to watch how Wright reacted and between them they would be able to decipher the body language.

The younger Peter Wright ran his business from a taxi office close to St George's Cross. There was a small shop front where the drivers sat awaiting fares and in the back a small call centre with three people who were waiting to take telephone requests for cabs and then relay them to the drivers out on the streets. Next to the call centre was an office where the smoking laws didn't seem to apply. The painted Anaglypta wallpaper was stained with years of nicotine and the parquet floor was equally filthy. When Alex and Russell were shown into the room by one of the telephonists, Peter Wright sat behind a desk, smoke snaking from a cigar that rested in an ashtray on a cheap desk. More Rangers FC memorabilia decorated the walls and there was a line of filing cabinets along one wall. On a couple of low seats next to the window, a pair of Wright's heavies lounged like recently fed lions. The fact that neither of them was McCarron was already a significant one that Russell and Alex both noted. He was normally never far from the gangster's side.

"Caught him yet?" Wright asked when they walked in.

"No, but we're here to talk about another couple of crimes."

"Whit crime wid that be?"

"Alan McGavigan was gunned down in Kinning Park early this afternoon."

"Ah don't know what this city is comin' tae. A murder a day." Although his two goons laughed, Wright's words were delivered with a straight face.

"We both heard you make a direct threat against Mr McGavigan. That obviously makes you our prime suspect."

"Think whit ye like, but it's goat nothin' tae dae wi' me." There was genuine force behind his words, making Alex believe that he was convinced he was telling the truth.

"And what about Paddy Niven?"

He shook his head. "Nope, nothin's changed on that one either. It wisnae me. How many times dae ye want me tae say it?"

"Paddy was just a small-time crook who had links to McGavigan's crew. I told you yesterday that he was found beaten in a lane in town but we now know he died from a heart attack. Now I know how much you wanted to find out who killed Gregg, so once again I come back to you as a prime suspect. You see how this is going?"

"He died o' a heart attack. Fuck, ah don't know whit ah'm supposed tae dae aboot that. Ur ye bein' even thicker than usual, Russell? I. Had. Nothing. To. Do. With. Any. Deaths." He poked his finger in Russell's direction, emphasising every word.

"Don't give us your pish, Wright. You had one of your hand-maidens go find Paddy Niven, rough him up so he would tell you who killed your son. The problem was Paddy didn't know who it was and your boys got a little over exuberant. Paddy died, they panicked and dumped him in the middle of the city. From what I hear you're having real problems with discipline, Pedro. The empire might be about to crumble round your ears and I doubt you're happy with that." The two lieutenants made to move towards Russell but Wright raised a hand and they stopped like the obedient animals they were.

"What happens within ma organisation is ma concern but you are blowing this oot yir arse. There's nae crumblin' and ah'm well in control of whit goes oan."

"It's not only your concern. Not if it means people are dying because you can't prevent your sidekicks thinking it's the Wild fucking West. Where's Billy McCarron?"

Wright looked to be surprised and concerned at Russell's change of direction. "Whit?"

"McCarron, where is he? He's normally close enough to you when you're at work that you could piss on him."

"He's no' well."

"I'm sure. Well, you better hope that he's not away selling you out to a competitor. It could get really messy for you then."

Alex could tell that Russell's words were giving Wright pause for thought. "What d'ye mean?"

"A wee birdy told me that McCarron has been causing you a lot of problems recently. I've heard that he would quite like to move up the food chain by one means or another and that he's been talking to some parties from outside the city to see if he could secure their support for a wee coup d'état. One

147

that would leave you on the outside looking in or maybe just pushing up daisies."

"Ye can spin a tale, Russell, ah'll gie ye that." Wright's bravado couldn't hide the doubt that Russell had placed in his mind. Alex understood that Russell had exaggerated the facts to play on Wright's fears and it had worked.

"Look, I'm giving you fair warning so that I don't have to mop up the blood but if you don't want to listen it's up to you. It's your funeral, maybe even literally."

"Get oot ma office, ya prick."

"No worries. I'll speak to you soon, or then again maybe not."

The two detectives left the room and left Wright seething in their wake.

Back in the car, Russell was sporting a massive grin. "That was entertaining."

"He's definitely worried by what McCarron is up to," Alex suggested.

"And I've just fed his paranoia. I don't think he knew that McCarron was planning to take out Alan McGavigan. It'll be interesting to see what the next few days bring."

It was six o'clock before they arrived back at the station. There was a message from the mortuary to say that the PM would be at eight o'clock and that McGavigan's body would be available for viewing for identification purposes one hour earlier. Russell told Alex to head for home and that he would cover the PM with DS Craigan. Alex left him arranging to meet McGavigan senior at the mortuary. She was glad it was not a journey she would be taking.

***

Alan McGavigan's post mortem finished just after ten o'clock. When Tom Russell walked into his flat he was pleasantly surprised to find that his brother was in the cramped kitchen making supper. He had called Eddie to tell him that he would be late home but hadn't expected his brother to do anything about it. The narrow space looked like a troop of messy chimps had been running rampant in it, but taking shape in the middle of it all was a meal of pork chops, potatoes, vegetables and an apple crumble for pudding.

"I hope the food is worth this mess," he said by way of greeting.

"Ah'll clean it up. Ah thought it was the least ah could dae tae say thanks."

"Thank you."

They sat at Tom's dining table, which was just about big enough to accommodate their meals. Eddie asked about the case and Tom replied with vague generalities. When the last of the apple crumble and custard had been consumed, Eddie made coffee.

Eddie reached to turn on the television but his brother stopped him.

"Wait, I've got to talk to you about your little problem."

"Oh, aye?" he replied as he sat down.

"I spoke to a mate of mine in the Met. Dragovic is not a guy you should have crossed. This is one evil bastard and I'm genuinely worried that if he finds you, you're going to be in real danger."

"What d'ye mean?"

Tom proceeded to tell Eddie exactly what Dragovic was capable of and as the story unfolded the colour gradually faded from his face.

"Shit, aw fur a game of cards."

"I can't protect you twenty-four hours a day. You need to come up with something and fast."

"Aye, ah know ye're right. Ah'll get a haud o' that guy ah wis tellin' ye aboot the morra."

He finished his coffee in silence and, as promised, cleaned up the kitchen. The two of them watched TV until midnight when Tom went to bed with a range of dark thoughts about what could happen to his brother if he failed to clear his debts.

CHAPTER 14

The briefing the following morning began with the details of the latest killing. ACC Muldoon was hovering like a scavenging vulture ready to pounce on the smallest mistake but Russell did his best to ignore the senior officer's presence. A second incident board had been erected, from which Russell went through the crime-scene photographs and the eye-witness account from Stephen Dawson.

"No real surprises from the PM. Alan McGavigan was killed by gunshot wounds from a .38 calibre gun. One pierced the bottom of his lung, another his liver. The doc reckoned that death was almost instantaneous. Any word on ballistics?" Russell asked.

Ann-Marie Craigan answered, "The lab boys reckon the bullets were fired from a Glock semi-automatic. No record of it ever having been used in any other crime, nor is it registered to anyone, I'm afraid."

"Why am I not surprised? Any luck with CCTV?"

It was Mac Rankine's turn to supply some information. "We goat an image from a camera and we're trying to trace the bike's route through the city. Ah'll gie ye a shout when it's complete, sir."

"Well that's something. DS Weaver, how is the file search going?"

"It's getting very interesting indeed, sir. It looks like Gregg Wright's fortune wasn't as huge as he liked to make out. The lawyers were in a bit of a flap yesterday because we got a couple of boxes that had been mislabelled. Wright was up to his ears in mortgages and loans; they were so big that he was beginning to struggle to meet the repayments. There were a few meetings behind closed doors between the lawyers and Jason Garner while we were there and there seemed to be plenty of shouting. We're hoping the Fiscal might force the issue of full access to the files because there's a possibility of fraud as well as everything else that's going on."

"Maybe this has nothing to do with Peter Wright's gang after all," Russell said.

"I think we should interview Garner again. I think he knows more than he's let on to us. He must have had some idea that the company was in financial difficulty," Alex said.

"I hate all that financial bullshit, it's full of jargon to bamboozle the likes of me," Russell replied.

"The forensic accountants are beginning to make sense of it. I could get them to give you a briefing if it would help," Weaver offered.

"No, I'd rather have my eyes pierced with red hot needles. You seem to have a handle on it Frank, I'll leave it with you and you can translate for us mere mortals." Russell grinned, happy to have dodged that particular boring bullet. "Keep on it and we'll have another wee chat with Mr Garner."

"Yes, sir."

"Somebody please tell me we've found Wright's wife."

"Not yet, but we did turn up something in the property portfolio. As part of the buyout of Briar, Wright picked up an old farm half a mile from Bardowie Loch. Judging by the records it's not had anyone working it in a few months. Empty barns sound like a perfect place to dismember a body," DS Weaver offered.

"OK that's good, get someone to check it out. It's a lead of sorts, which is better than what we've had so far."

"DS Weaver, can you assign someone to have a closer look at the links between Wright and that wee prick Evans?"

"Will do, sir."

Russell ran through the rest of the tasks for the day and once again asked to be kept informed. He told Alex that they would be paying a visit to Jason Garner and would see where that led. Muldoon insisted that Lindsay Morton should be involved in the investigation into Alan McGavigan's murder. Russell couldn't argue, as he was the one proposing that the two crimes might not be related after all and Morton's expertise in the gangland politics would be invaluable. He suggested that DS Miller act as a liaison between the two teams and Muldoon agreed.

For all the difficulties they faced, there was the first sense that the team was beginning to get to grips with the various threads of the investigation and that progress would soon be made towards resolving it.

**

When they arrived back at the G. Wright Group headquarters the place seemed strangely muted. Alex noticed that the staff on the third floor seemed to be quieter and looked more worried than on their previous visit. They were shown into a boardroom where there were brown cardboard boxes filled with files covering every available surface. There were two forensic accountants as well as Frank Weaver and a DC who was introduced as Maureen MacDonald. Jason Garner was standing anxiously watching proceedings and beside him stood a balding man in a well-tailored suit.

"Mr Garner, we would like to have a word with you."

"Yes. This is our legal adviser, Joshua Stein. Joshua, this is Detective Superintendent Russell and his colleague Detective Inspector Menzies."

"Detectives," the lawyer acknowledged as he shook their hands. "When are you going to finish this?" he asked, indicating the files.

"It will take as long as it takes, sir. This is a murder investigation after all. I'm sure your valuable time could be used elsewhere, if you would just let us have full, unfettered access," Russell replied.

"You missed your calling detective; with lines like that you should be doing a turn in the comedy clubs," Stein replied with a smarmy smile.

"Well, I'm sure it must be helping your billable hours for this month. Always happy to help an officer of the court." Stein had succeeded in creating animosity with Russell. Alex knew he might well regret it.

"DS Weaver, I would like you to ensure that every box of files that the company has be brought here. Mr Stein can tell you which files in each box are within our remit." Russell knew that the original remit only required complete boxes of files that were relevant. He had just added a whole lot of extra work for the lawyer.

"Yes, sir."

"Oh, and make sure that every file we are denied access to is recorded, in case we need to have a closer look at them later in the investigation. Thanks for your help, Mr Stein. Mr Garner, can we have a word in private please?"

As she walked away Alex could almost see the steam coming from Stein's ears. He had learned that Tom Russell was not a man to cross lightly.

In his office, Garner looked a lot more stressed as the continuing investigation took its toll on him. His skin was grey, his eyes rimmed with red and there was an agitation to him that the detectives hadn't seen on their previous visit.

"Mr Garner, our investigation has discovered that Mr Wright's affairs weren't as healthy as they first appeared. How much do you know about the true state of the company finances?"

"I knew that certain parts of the business weren't performing as well as others but it looks like it was worse than Mr Wright told me."

"In what way?" Alex asked.

"Many parts of the business are mortgaged against other parts, which means that we basically have a house of cards. One part fails and the rest will be in danger of following it. The property business is the one that is really struggling at the moment and we have more mortgages on it than any other company in the group."

"What about his father?"

"What do you mean?"

"We've heard that certain companies within the group have been used to filter funds from his father's illegal business."

He shook his head firmly, "I know nothing about that."

Russell took over again and said, "What about the Scottish Council for the Defence of Family Life?"

"Who?"

"Your boss was making political donations to a right-wing organisation whose members aren't shy when it comes to using violence to get what they want. They're led by a guy called Hugh Evans."

"I know nothing about the donations but Mr Evans was at Mr Wright's birthday party last year."

"So they were friends?"

Garner smiled. "Mr Wright didn't have friends, he had resources, people who could be useful to him. Three quarters of the people in the room that night were probably meeting him for the first time."

Russell's phone rang. He looked at the display and said, "Sorry, I need to take this."

"DS Craigan," he said into the handset as he stepped out of the room.

"Sir, I'm out at that farm DS Weaver mentioned in the briefing. I think you need to come and see what we've found."

"Jennifer Wright?"

"No, sir, but we do think something happened here, there's blood."

"Is Sean O'Reilly there?"

"I've just called him, he's on his way."

"We're about finished here, we'll be with you in half an hour."

"Do you need directions?"

"Send the address to my phone. I'll find it."

"Yes, sir."

The call ended and Russell walked back into Garner's office.

"Thanks Mr Garner, I'm sorry but we'll have to call a halt to our meeting, some important new evidence has come up. If there's anything else you can think of that will help us to catch Mr Wright's killer, please don't hesitate to call. Alex, we need to be going."

They departed the office with Garner looking forlorn. His world was tumbling around his ears and he seemed to be incapable of holding it together.

***

The farm complex looked across the valley where Bardowie Loch nestled hidden from view by some trees and the rolling undulations of the landscape. It was probably only half a mile as the crow flies but a car journey would be around a mile and a bit.

The farmhouse door and all the windows in the building were boarded up. In the yard there was no sign of machinery or the normal detritus of a farmer's working life. A large tree, bare of leaves, was populated by a rookery of noisy birds that cawed into the breeze as small snowflakes fell. The house that was once the home for a working family was painted white, as was the largest barn. Both were trimmed with black; on the barn the darkness came not from paint but from scorch marks. The police activity was centred inside the old byre where the smell of departed cattle was combined with the smoky odour of charcoal.

DS Craigan stood to one side with the nervous DC Kelly, who had accompanied her to the scene. In the middle of the floor, Sean O'Reilly was joined by one of his junior technicians. The younger man was taking photographs while Sean directed him, barking instructions with his usual prickly demeanour. Alex was struck by the contrast in the Dubliner when he was at work compared with the jocular, light-hearted man he was in a social arena.

"Sean, what have we got?" Russell called.

"Ah, sure we've found a crime scene. Blood, and it's human."

"What else can you tell me?"

"I don't think anyone was killed here but I reckon it's where the dismemberment took place."

"Tell me more."

"There's not enough blood for the kind of killing wound that was found at the post mortem. There would have been arterial spray and a much larger pool of blood if the victim's throat had been slit here. If you look here you can see where the axe has damaged the concrete floor." The two detectives stepped forward to where O'Reilly shone a torch at a patch of the floor. Amongst the red-brown stain of dried blood there was a group of small indentations in the concrete that certainly looked like they could have been made by an axe blade.

"Thoughts, people?" Russell said to his officers.

"The killer must have been close enough to Wright to know about this place," DS Craigan suggested.

"Unless the killer had been following him or used the Range Rover's GPS to bring him here," DC Kelly said cautiously, as if expecting to be shot down by Russell.

"That's a possibility, detective constable. Alex?"

"I don't think this was a spur of the moment decision. The killer or killers had to have planned this whole thing very carefully. They knew about the Wrights leaving on holiday, which gave them a two-week window where no one would miss them. They also knew about this place and its proximity to the loch."

"That could put Dr Wright back in the frame. We still can't find her. Sean, is there enough blood for two bodies to have been chopped up?'

"Mmm… I doubt it. The way the blood has pooled and the size of the pools make me think not."

"If it was Dr Wright, she needed an accomplice. Maybe a lover; Briar for example," Russell offered.

"She would have found it easy to keep it secret, no one would suspect her of it, but in truth I think it would be out of character for her," Craigan said.

"The downside is who would have wanted to be involved with her and who would interest her?" Alex countered.

"I like Briar for this either way. The money he lost and the fact he used to own this place makes him a very good candidate."

"I think you're right. Time for a little bit of digging deeper into Mr Briar."

CHAPTER 15

Back at the station, Russell stood pondering the two incident boards. There were lines going in all directions linking the various suspects and possible motives. Practically all of those motives were associated with the two gangs although Briar did stand out as the one person who had multiple reasons for wanting his erstwhile partner dead. Russell added little notes of his own and moved some of the photographs around as if trying to establish a pattern.

His thoughts were interrupted by his mobile phone.

"Hello, Detective Superintendent Tom Russell speaking."

"Sir, it's Sergeant Berwick at Helen Street. I've got a call from a DI Amaechi on the other line. She said she's from Special Branch and that she would like to speak to you."

Russell was surprised but said, "Sure, put her through."

"She said it's confidential and asked if you could take it somewhere away from the main office."

"OK, get her number and I'll ring her back."

The desk sergeant did as he was asked and Russell went to see Muldoon. When he told the ACC what he required, Muldoon agreed but with the caveat that he was kept informed if Russell could get agreement from the officer.

When Muldoon had gone, Russell dialled the number the sergeant had provided.

"DI Sade Amaechi," a refined London female voice said.

"DI Amaechi, it's Detective Superintendent Russell. You wanted to speak to me."

"Yes, sir. My super asked me to give you a call. Your team has been looking at the Scottish Council for the Defence of Family Life, is that correct?"

"Yes. We're investigating a murder and the name came up as having a connection to the victim. It's leader Evans is in custody after he assaulted one of my officers when she went to question him."

"You have to let him go and stop your investigation, immediately."

"I'm sorry?"

"I think you heard me, sir."

"Let him go, just like that?" Russell was raging at the interference in his investigation coming from people four hundred miles away.

"Sir, this is coming from the top of our organisation. You have to cease looking at this group immediately."

"Can you tell me why?"

"I've been authorised to tell you that we know that Evans and his group have nothing to do with this murder and that you have to back off."

"And you know this how, exactly?"

"I'm afraid you'll need to trust me when I say that we are one hundred per cent sure that continuing this part of your investigation will be a waste of time and resources. Holding

Evans is also counter productive at this time but I cannot tell you the full details. I hope you understand."

Russell was frustrated that the spies were playing their paranoid games. He didn't think that he would get anywhere but he decided to push it.

"Detective inspector, it was me who tipped off your lot about Evans and his band of little brown shirts. This is the single most important murder investigation we have in Scotland and maybe even in the UK at the moment. I think I deserve the common courtesy of an explanation."

"One moment." There was a period of hold music while Russell waited for the woman to return to the phone. He knew that she would be checking with her superiors to establish if she could tell him any more about what they were up to.

"Superintendent Russell?"

"Yes?"

"Sir, I've been told to tell you that we have an asset within Evans's organisation. Your investigation could jeopardise our operative and with it the six months of work we have already done. We believe that there are bigger fish than Evans behind this group. We need to be able to trace those links and we can't afford to have you impede our way to that goal. This is not a request, you must cease your investigation immediately."

Russell knew there was no point in arguing, they would simply go above his head and get the result they wanted. His personal animosity to Evans was irrelevant in the context.

"I understand."

"Sir, this is simply a courtesy to you due to your diligence in notifying us about this organisation. No one, not even your senior officers, can know what I have just told you. If anyone asks, tell them to contact your chief constable. The Official Secrets Act covers this conversation. Do you understand?"

Although it was phrased as a question there was little doubt that the conversation was basically at an end and that Special Branch would have Russell hung out to dry if word of their operative was to be discovered by anyone else.

"I understand. One thing, inspector, if and when you take down Evans, I would really like to be there."

"I'll take note of that, sir. Thank you for your understanding and cooperation."

When the call was over, Russell sat back in the chair and stared at the ceiling. A slow perception dawned on him that the spooks had just done him a favour by removing one thread from the investigation, but it was little comfort.

He walked out of the room and back to the office where Muldoon was waiting.

"What was all that about, Tom?" the ACC asked concerned by Russell's scowl.

"We've been ordered to back off Evans."

"Why?"

"Special Branch can assure us that neither he nor his cronies had anything to do with Gregg Wright's death."

"How do they know that?"

"Need to know and apparently we don't need to."

"One of those."

"I'm afraid so."

Muldoon had had enough dealings with Scotland Yard to know that their hands had just been tied with a knot that wouldn't be untied. They were a law unto themselves.

"I'll leave you to it."

"Thanks, sir."

Russell shouted on Ann-Marie Craigan.

"Sir?" she said as she popped her head from behind a computer screen.

"Kick Evans loose."

"Sir? What about the assault charge?"

"That's an order, detective sergeant."

"Sir, you've not even questioned him yet."

"That's an order, sergeant!"

"Fine but I am doing this under protest," Craigan fired her reply before storming off in the direction of the holding cells.

Alex had overheard the conversation. "One less suspect?"

"Yeah." Russell put his own ire away and decided to turn his attention to other targets. "Where does it leave us?"

"McCarron and Briar as one and two. McGavigan, Doctor Wright and her son as possibles," she summarised.

"Let's get McCarron in. DS Miller?" he shouted to the other end of the office.

"Yes, sir," the DS replied.

"Has Superintendent Morton had any luck with Billy McCarron?"

"No, sir. McCarron wasn't at his house and the team staking out the Wrights' taxi firm haven't reported seeing him."

"Let me know if they find him. I want to be involved in questioning him."

"Yes, sir. I think the super knows but I'll pass the word."

"Right, Alex, it looks like Mr Briar will be our target for the day. Time to take him out of his comfort zone."

***

Two uniformed officers were despatched to bring Briar in for questioning. He was left in the interview room for three quarters of an hour before Russell and his DI arrived to interview him. Russell had decided to let the businessman stew to see if it would loosen his tongue any.

"What's this all about?" Briar said indignantly when they walked in.

"I'm sorry, Mr Briar, we had something urgent come up."

"I've been waiting here for forty-five minutes. I've got more important things to do than sit about in a shitty police station."

"There's no need for the attitude Mr Briar, this murder investigation is complicated and there are many things that demand my time." Alex thought her boss sounded like a scolding headmaster.

Russell's tone made Briar appear to shrink down further into his seat. "I'm sorry, I didn't mean…" he spluttered.

"Apology accepted. Now we have a few supplementary questions to our earlier interview. Alex?" Russell sat back and folded his arms.

Alex was surprised at Russell's insistence that she run the interview but she was happy to oblige. "Mr Briar, one of the properties that was allocated to you before your partnership with Mr Wright dissolved was a farm in East Dunbartonshire."

"Yes," he replied guardedly.

"Tell me about it."

"It was a repossession. We got it cheap but we couldn't get it to sell on. Gregg was thinking of looking at creating a farm park thing but he was struggling for investors and it was empty the last I knew."

"So you knew that it was both empty and isolated enough that someone going there would be undisturbed?"

"Yes, but what's this to do with me? Undisturbed to do what?" There was no mistaking the genuine fear that was sweeping over him as the colour drained from his face.

Russell took over. "We have evidence that a crime took place at that farm. Here's what we think could have happened. Gregg Wright destroyed both your marriage and your business life. Over time you grew more and more enraged by what had occurred and you hatched a plan to get rid of him. You discovered he was going on holiday; you saw your opportunity to get rid of him and no one would miss him for a couple of weeks. You decided to kill him at the deserted farm and then dump his body in a nearby loch. The only thing we need to know is what have you done with Dr Wright?"

"What are you talking about? Are you nuts? I didn't kill him and I have no idea where Jennifer is." Briar was shouting, his face twisted with fury and terror.

"Mr Briar, our forensics team is working on the scene and we will find something to connect you to the farm. Then things will get tough for you. It's better that you tell us the truth now."

"There's nothing to tell. I can't deny that I'm happy the bastard is dead but I didn't kill him. That's it, I want a lawyer." He started to shake and fat tears brimmed at the corner of his eyes.

Russell got up and led Alex out of the interview room.

"Check with Sean, but unless he's found DNA or fingerprints I doubt that Mr Briar is our killer."

"Not unless he's a great performer," Alex agreed.

"Stranger things have happened I suppose."

"What do you want to do with him?"

"Let him contact a lawyer and when he or she turns up, let him go. We can always pull him in again if needed."

"That's going to piss off the lawyer," Alex said with a knowing grin.

"It's billable hours," Russell kept his face straight but Alex knew that he was well aware of what the lawyer would say.

Alex went back into the interview room and told Briar that his lawyer would be called. She asked him for the contact details and left him to his thoughts.

When they were back in the incident room Russell did a check of all the possible threads. As it was Friday and there were no new leads, he told Alex to head home when she had called the lawyer. He would be there until well into the evening, studying the board and trying to unravel the connections.

***

Russell arrived home at nine thirty, his eyes red and irritated by a combination of tiredness and the stuffy atmosphere in the main office. The incident board had failed to reveal the magic connection that would break the case and he had driven home with his mind too exhausted to really function.

There was no sign of his brother, which was on one hand a relief but on the other a concern.

He decided that a shower might revive him a little and walked into the bedroom. He knew immediately that there was something not quite right. He lived a simple life and apart from his bed and set of drawers there was nothing else in the room. He paused and studied the area before he worked out what was missing. There was a space on the drawer unit where his father's watch box normally rested. His dad had left the timepiece to him in his will after his death six years previously. It was a gold Rolex Oyster made in the mid-sixties and Russell had insured it for eight thousand pounds. He wore it on special occasions but for him its main value was in the connection it provided to memories of his father. Eddie had been jealous of the gift but their father had been very specific that he would not get the wristwatch as he knew what would happen if he did.

When Eddie was eighteen he left school with some qualifications to his name but he wasn't interested in going to college or university. He persuaded his father to lend him five thousand pounds to set up a shop that would sell and repair skateboards. He was going into partnership with a guy he met who claimed to know the business. Unfortunately Eddie didn't bother checking the man out and within a month Eddie found himself with no money and a shop that had no stock. The partner had absconded with the cash and left Eddie with the debt. Their father had bailed out his son but vowed that he would never give him anything he hadn't earned ever again.

When the will was read out, Tom inherited the watch but the rest of their father's estate was given to charity. After the reading Eddie wasn't happy and railed against his father, calling him for everything.

Now he had taken the watch to try to get himself out of yet another self-inflicted predicament. Russell let out a weary sigh and dialled the local police station.

Twenty minutes later a pair of female constables named Farrell and Coyle arrived to take the details. When they realised who the victim was they both appeared to be a little nervous about handling the theft.

"I know who did it. It was my brother, Eddie Russell. I want him found and arrested."

"Are you sure, sir?" PC Farrell asked.

"Yes. He has betrayed me and he needs to be taught a lesson."

The PCs called the theft in and asked for a DC to attend. The next hour was spent waiting for the detective. When he arrived, Russell's full statement was taken and then the four police officers sat in his living room drinking tea. As the visitors were about to leave they heard the noise of a key scraping in the lock of the front door.

"That'll be him," Russell said.

Eddie walked into the living room and knew immediately that he was in trouble.

"Tam, whit's gaun' oan?"

"Why did you take the watch, Eddie?" Russell asked, making no attempt to disguise his anger and disappointment.

Eddie thought about denying the accusation but then realised there was no point. "Ah… you know how desperate ah am. Tom whit else wis ah tae dae?"

"What did you do, pawn it?"

"Naw, ah took it tae a jewellers if ye must know."

"Where's the money?"

"Well…"

"Eddie, where's the money?"

"Look ah only goat four grand fur it. Ah needed a way to make up the rest o' the cash."

"And?"

"Ah pit it oan a hoarse. Evens favourite it wis tae win."

"Eddie you are a fuckin' idiot. DC Leven, do your duty." There was no ire left in his voice, only passive sadness.

The detective constable stepped forward and informed Eddie of his rights.

"Tom, ah wis gonnae explain. Ah'll pay ye back, honest. Don't dae this, please." Eddie's plaintive voice and tear-filled eyes had no effect on his brother's resolve.

"Are you absolutely sure this is what you want to do, sir?" Detective Constable Leven asked nervously.

"Yes, absolutely. Get him out of my sight."

The prisoner was led away by the detective and the two uniformed officers followed them out of the flat.

Tom Russell was not the kind of man who put much store in material things but he sat and wept tears of overwhelming grief for the symbolism of the lost connection to his father. Having Eddie arrested wasn't about the watch, it was the result of his betrayal and his total disregard for the thoughts and feelings of other people. Russell knew his brother was a selfish person but this was beyond what even Tom thought he was capable of.

Although his dad had been a stiff man who found it hard to show any love to his family, he was a principled man; someone who believed in hard work, education and caring for others. He had instilled all of those virtues in his eldest son but he had no success with Eddie. Despite all that his father had tried to teach him, there was a devil in Eddie that believed there was always an easier way. No amount of gentle cajoling could bring Eddie round and Tom wondered if maybe his father had been too soft on his youngest son. A spell in prison may prove to be the best thing that could happen to his brother; a way to make him realise that his family was not his personal safety net when he messed up his life time and again.

A cup of tea later, Russell went to bed. For once his thoughts weren't filled with the case, but the night was no less restless as a result.

CHAPTER 16

Alex enjoyed the drive in to the station on the Saturday morning. She had begun the day by scraping a thick layer of ice from the window of her car but the sun was shining, the sky was bright blue and she was going on a date that night. Noel had called her the previous evening to make plans and they had spent nearly an hour just talking. It had been fun and she didn't feel any of the wariness that had plagued her since she had booted Andrew out of her life.

As she reached the station door Russell joined her.

"Good morning, sir."

"It may be morning, Alex, but there is fuck all good about it."

She was slightly taken aback by the vitriolic response. She knew how much her boss allowed his emotions to show – particularly when the case was as complicated and potentially explosive as this one was – but this was something deeper and darker.

'Everything OK?" she asked cautiously.

"Sorry, Alex. Family troubles." He cut short any further enquiry by walking to the tea machine.

There were a few bleary-eyed detectives already in the incident room when the two senior detectives walked in.

As Russell headed for his desk, a uniformed sergeant said, "Sir, ACC Muldoon called to say he won't be in today."

"That's a relief. Urgent round of golf or a visit to B&Q?" he asked sarcastically.

"Eh... he said he had to go to some team-building exercise for the new single force."

"Bollocks, a jolly for senior officers that probably involves a round of golf and some expensive food," Russell muttered under his breath, though it was still audible to Alex.

"We'll give it five minutes and then we'll get this meeting started."

It was ten minutes before everyone was assembled.

"OK, people, talk to me. Tell me we're making progress, please."

"Late last night me and George at CCTV monitorin' found that Calvin Wright did drive tae Glesga on the night his parents disappeared. We caught his Audi on the cameras on the M8," DS Rankine responded.

As he spoke Russell moved Calvin Wright's photograph to the top of the incident board. "Interesting. I knew that wee bastard was up to something. We'll deal with him later. Can somebody tell me where his mother is?"

DS Weaver had an answer. "Nothing yet but we've got a full list of addresses of the Wrights' houses. They've got four spread across the country, would you believe? One in Hertfordshire, one in St Andrews and a holiday home near Loch Lomond as well as the house in Milngavie. We're organising local uniforms to visit each of them to see if she's there or if there's any sign that someone has been there in the past few days."

"Why did that take so long, Frank?" Russell asked with annoyance.

"Sorry sir but the properties are listed under different companies. We only discovered that they were using these residences when we cross-checked the addresses."

"Right, get that checked as soon as possible. Make sure the other forces involved know how important this is."

"Will do."

"DS Miller, any word from the other investigation about the whereabouts of McCarron?"

"He's definitely not at any of his usual haunts. Superintendent Morton's team has circulated his photograph to all UK forces, ports, airports, car hire franchises and the transport police. They've also sent his car registration with the photograph."

"What's McCarron's game? If he committed the murders why isn't he here to stir Wright up? I don't get it. Anyway, let me know if anyone gets their hands on him."

"Of course, sir."

"Has anybody got anything else they want to share?"

There were negative responses and shakes of the head from the team.

"You know what to do. Get to it."

Before they dispersed, Russell grabbed Paul Kelly and Ann-Marie Craigan and told them to go to pick up Calvin Wright with orders to delay the arrival of the lawyer for as long as they possibly could.

***

Tom Russell was watching the interview process on the video feed and had detailed Alex and DS Craigan to conduct the interview. He had decided to see how the youngest member of the Wright clan reacted to being in the room alone with two women again.

"Mr Wright, we meet again," Alex said when she walked into the room.

"Alex, always a pleasure, and you've brought the lovely Irish lady."

"Mr Wright, I would appreciate it if you address me as Detective Inspector and my colleague as Detective Sergeant."

"Whatever you say, Alex. I mean inspector. Shouldn't we wait for Mr Jenkins? He's very fussy about what I say to the police and I wouldn't want to upset him." His condescending grin was back.

"He's on his way but we're just chatting."

"Yes, inspector, I'm sure we are."

"It's a very nice car you've got."

"It is, would you like to see the inside of it, maybe the roof from the back seat, eh inspector?" he asked with a lascivious leer.

Alex ignored his adolescent hormonal attempt at a pass. "How many people do you allow to drive it?"

"Just me. I wouldn't let anyone else near it. It's my fanny magnet."

"There's no' a magnet big enough to compensate for your failings, son," Craigan commented.

"Maybe you would like to take me for a test drive, sergeant?"

"I prefer men whose balls have dropped, not wee boys," she returned.

"Ha, that's good. I like you, you're not overwhelmed by my wealth."

Alex decided it was time to get to the meat of why they had brought him in. "You're not really a very good liar are you Calvin?"

"I don't know how you could say that, inspector."

"Well, how about when we asked you for your whereabouts on the evening of your parents' disappearance, you told us that you were either with a young woman or out drinking in Edinburgh. Is that about right?"

"Yes, I told you that's all I ever do."

"It's strange then that your car was seen on the M8 heading for Glasgow approximately four hours before your mother and father were due to leave for their holiday."

"What? Who said that?"

"The cameras we have the length of the motorway said it and the funny thing about them is, they never lie."

"Oh shit. I better wait for Jenkins."

He folded his arms and it was obvious that they would get no more out of him until his solicitor arrived. The two detectives walked out and left him with a burly uniformed constable who stood glowering at him.

"He's an arrogant wee shite isn't he?" Russell asked rhetorically when the three detectives came together in the incident room.

"He thinks he's God's gift to women," Craigan said with obvious revulsion.

"We'll see what happens when his brief gets here. The Lothian boys confirmed they found the stash, so I think we'll hold on to Mr Wright for a time no matter what lies he cooks up."

Twenty minutes later Jenkins arrived. Russell apologised for the misunderstanding about what time Calvin Wright was to be brought in but the lawyer was far from impressed and he knew a lie when he heard one. After all, he was used to telling them.

Russell asked Alex to be the one to watch the video while he led the interview with DS Craigan.

"Calvin Wright, you certainly live up to your family name, I'll give you that much."

"Is there a question coming any time soon, superintendent?" Jenkins asked.

"Why were you in Glasgow on the night that your parents were due to go on holiday?'

"My client's private life is just that, private."

"Up until the point he lies to us when we're investigating a murder. Now let me speak to the organ grinder." He focused his gaze on Calvin Wright. "If you refuse to tell us where you were we must assume that you have something to hide. As your inheritance from your father's estate will be substantial, you can understand why we would be interested in your reason for travelling back to Glasgow late at night, just hours before your father was killed and your mother went missing."

Jenkins whispered in his client's ear.

"I didn't murder anyone. I came back through to see my grandfather."

"Which one?"

"Peter," he mumbled reluctantly.

"What was so urgent?"

"Family stuff."

"I'll need a bit more than that. I'm pretty sure your grandfather would give you an alibi, but with his reputation you can imagine that I would be a little sceptical of him as a character witness."

"I can't tell you. He'd kill me."

"Fine. I'll get my sergeant here to process you and we'll take you into custody on suspicion of being involved in the murder of your parents." Russell stood up.

"Superintendent Russell, this is harassment," Jenkins protested.

"I'm sorry, Mr Jenkins, but you and your client have left me with no option." Russell reached for the door.

"Wait, I'll tell you," the teenager said, his face blanched by the thought of time in a jail cell. He might play on his family name but he was from a very different background and he didn't see prison as just an occupational hazard.

"Mr Wright, I must advise you to be very careful about what you say."

"Shut up, Jenkins. It's not you or old Peter that's facing jail."

Russell settled back down into his seat. "A very sensible reaction, young man. Tell me what your granddad wouldn't want me to know," he said with a fatherly smile.

The shaken youth hesitated before he said, "I was collecting the pot from him."

Russell laughed. "Talk about the family business. Let me get this straight, you are buying drugs from your grandfather?"

"He gives me it at half price. He told me that I could keep the profits so I can build a business of my own."

"Regular Lord Sugar your granddad. Encouraging young entrepreneurs. So did he give you the drugs directly?"

"No. I had to meet that thug that works for him – McCarron I think his name is. He gave them to me."

"Did he now?"

"Aye and he wasn't too pleased about it."

Russell leaned in to the narrow table. "Tell me more."

"When I told him how much Peter said I could have, he started moaning. He said he was sick of spoiled little brats getting everything handed to them on a plate and that I was just like my father. I told him to fuck off and take it up with my dad and my granddad if he didn't like it."

"And how did he react to that?"

"He said that he might just do that."

"This gets even more interesting. Do you think he was planning to go to see your father?"

Wright shrugged.

"For the sake of the tape can you please answer."

"I don't know, maybe."

"Where did this meeting take place?"

"At the taxi offices."

Just as Russell was about to complete the interview there was a gentle knock at the door. He gestured with his head to Craigan to indicate she was to answer it. She came back a moment later and bent down to whisper into the ear of her boss. "McCarron was picked up at the Stranraer ferry terminal an hour ago. The Dumfries and Galloway boys are bringing him up, they should be here within the hour."

Russell nodded and turned back to Wright and his lawyer.

"Our colleagues in Lothian and Borders would like a word with you regarding the marijuana that was found in your flat. We'll give you a comfy wee cell to occupy while you wait for them."

"Detective superintendent this is outrageous, my client volunteered that information."

"I'm sorry, Mr Jenkins, it's out of my hands. Our colleagues in Edinburgh can be very fussy. They shouldn't be too long, I think."

Jenkins and Wright continued to protest as the two detectives left the interview room. When they were clear of the door Russell turned to the DS. "Give L and B a ring and tell them we've got a drug dealer they might be interested in talking to. Make sure they know about his connections." He cracked a broad smile and Ann-Marie Craigan laughed as she replied, "With pleasure, sir."

***

Ninety minutes later, Russell was back in the same room. This time he was accompanied by Alex Menzies and they were facing an agitated Billy McCarron. He fidgeted in his seat, brought his nails to his mouth and ran his hands through his hair in a dance of obvious fear.

The detectives who had brought him to Glasgow said that he had been anxious to stay out of view when the car had reached the outskirts of the city and that he had crouched down in the back seat until they were at the station door. Russell had thanked them for their help and told them to grab a cup of coffee before they began their journey back.

McCarron was a tall, thin man but there was a wiry strength about him that came from his years as an amateur boxer. His face showed the damage those years had inflicted on him; all around his eyes were scars of varying lengths and widths, his nose was crooked where a break had never been reset and his ears were flattened by both the wayward punches and the helmet that he had worn to protect his head. Elaborate tattoos crept from his collar and cuffs like some parasitical plant on a tree. He was dressed in a blue tracksuit that was never going to keep out the worst of the Scottish winter.

"Billy boy, ye're looking a little flustered," Russell said when he entered and immediately lapsed into a broad Glaswegian dialect. Alex had seen him do it a number of times but she still found it strange.

"Fuck off, Russell ya prick."

"Now that's no' very nice is it? Here's me showin' some concern fur yir sorry arse and aw you cin dae is curse at me."

"Get tae the point and stoap fannyin' aboot."

"Billy, Billy, fur a man that's scared fur his life, ye're no' daein' yirsel any favours. So why wur ye oan yir way across the sea tae Ulster?"

"A sunshine brek," he replied sarcastically.

"Of course, where else dae ye go in the middle of winter when ye want a bit o' sun. Now let's get doon tae the real reason we're here. Ah'll ask ye again, why Ulster?"

"Cos ah wis tryin' tae get away fae this shit heap o' a city."

"Hopin' to better yirsel on the Emerald Isle wi' the help o' yir auld pals in the UDA?"

"Piss off."

"Now, could it be that yir oan the run cos ye killed Gregg Wright in the hope it wid provoke a wee gang war?"

"No way, ah didnae kill Gregg. It wisnae me but some bastard made Peter think it wis. If he gets his hauns oan me, ah've hud it. Some bastard hud it in fur me."

"It's terrible, you're such a likeable guy. As well as Gregg there's Alan McGavigan. If his da catches ye, ye're even further in the shit. Am ah right?"

"Whit ur ye talkin' aboot?"

"The four bullets ye put in tae McGavigan junior. Have ye forgotten?"

"Ah've nae idea whit you're bletherin' on aboot. Ye're talkin' shite."

"Billy, you're in enough trouble without lyin' tae me. Any chance ye've goat of bein' placed in protective custody ur diminishin' by the second. Maybe we'll turn ye loose, ah'm pretty sure Peter and McGavigan will know ye're back on the streets within minutes. It could be an interesting race tae see who gets tae ye first. Fancy a wee bet, Alex?"

"My money would be on Wright, sir."

"Ah don't know Malky's very motivated."

"Naw, don't dae that," McCarron said, panicked by the thought of what might happen to him.

"So dae ye want tae tell me the truth afore yir lawyer gets here?"

The gangster looked suddenly resigned to his fate. "Ah don't need a lawyer. Ah'll tell ye whit ah did but it wis jist me. Ah'm no droppin' anybody else in the shite so don't bother askin'."

Surprised at his refusal of a lawyer, Russell said,

"Ah'm aw ears."

"When ah heard that Gregg hud been murdered, ah thought that McGavigan hud tae be the wan that did it. Ah went tae Peter and he told me that youse had said that it might no be McGavigan. Peter told me tae pick up some wee tramp that wis supposed tae huv the inside track on McGavigan's mob. Ah picked the auld bastard up and took him tae ask him some questions. Ah tried some persuasive techniques…"

"Ye mean ye tortured him. Ah saw his boady," Russell said with a hint of menace.

"He said that there wis naebody in the McGavigan crew that could huv done it, so ah applied some mair pressure and the auld prick up and dies oan me."

The friendly bantering tone that Russell had used disappeared in an instant as McCarron dismissed Paddy Niven's death as an inconvenience. "That 'auld prick' was a harmless old man and a friend of mine."

"Look, ah didnae mean tae kill him."

"His heart gave out; he was already in the final stages of liver cancer."

"How wis ah tae know that? Anyway, ah went back tae Peter and told 'im whit the auld yin hud said. Ah told him ah thought that McGavigan wis behind Gregg's death and that we hud tae dae somethin' aboot it. Peter wisnae sure, so ah decided tae take things intae ma ain hauns."

"You decided to kill McGavigan junior."

"Well the Bible says 'an eye fur an eye'. He killed Peter's son, ah killed his."

"Your quotin' o' scripture is aw well and good but McGavigan maintains he had nothing tae dae wi' it. Aw our intelligence tells us he didnae dae it and no one can work out why he would want the violence to escalate again. You, however, would love it aw tae kick off again and you decided to take your chance to get the guns out again, like some outlaw in the Wild West. Is that who you think ye are, Billy the Kid striding through Lincoln County killing anybody that gets in your way?"

"Whit the fuck ur ye talkin' aboot?"

"Sorry, that was a bit too intellectual for the likes of you. Did you kill Alan McGavigan, that's what I want to know?"

"Aye and ah'll sign a confession sayin' that but youse need tae protect me."

"Aye, of course we do. That's what the public purse is for, protecting scumbags from other scumbags. I've still got a mind to let you go out onto the streets and see who wins that race to get to you first."

"Whit? Ye cannae dae that, ah've confessed. Ah don't even know why Peter is efter me, ah thought ah wis daein' it fur him."

"He thinks you killed Gregg in an attempt to move yourself one step closer to the crown. He thinks that you're after his job now, so it's a double betrayal as far as he's concerned."

"Where the fuck did he get that idea?"

Russell paused as if thinking. "Me, I think." McCarron made an attempt to lunge at Russell but the detective casually pushed his chair back and walked out of the room with Alex. They left McCarron cursing him and could hear him the length of the corridor.

Back in the incident room Russell said, "DS Miller, would you contact Detective Superintendent Morton and tell him we've got McCarron here if he wants to come over for a chat. Take McCarron's confession and organise to have him transferred to Helen Street. He probably should avoid the general prison population, at least until he's sentenced."

"Yes, sir," Miller said. She was delighted to be so involved at this stage in the case.

"Well, that's not a bad day's work. Muldoon should be happy that we've cleared up two of the murders," Russell said to Alex when they were settled with a cup of tea each at their desks.

"Just not the one that started it."

"No."

"Do you believe him about Gregg Wright?"

"I do, there's no point in him admitting to what he did while denying that he killed Wright," Russell said.

"That's why you didn't ask him where Dr Wright is?"

"I didn't see any point, to be honest."

"What next?"

"We need to keep looking at Wright's business life or who he was shagging."

Paul Kelly rushed into the office clutching a piece of paper in one hand and his mobile phone in the other. "Sir, Ma'am, the uniforms that went to check the Wrights' holiday cabin up at Loch Lomond say it looks like there might have been someone there recently. They're wondering what they should do." He proffered the phone.

"Hello, this is Detective Superintendent Russell. Who am I speaking to?"

"It's Sergeant Brodie, sir."

"Sergeant, I want you to wait outside the house. We'll be there in about forty-five minutes."

"Aye, sir. Nae problem, it's jist me an' young Joyce."

"Thanks, we'll see you soon." He gave the phone back to Kelly.

"Right, Loch Lomond it is. You don't need to come, Alex. I know you've got a hot date tonight."

Alex flushed in embarrassment, "Eh… how did you…"

"My keen-edged detecting skills honed over many years," he said with a deadpan look.

"Noel told you, didn't he?"

"No, he was quizzing me about you and I put two and two together. As I said, keenly honed detecting skills. Are you coming?"

"I might as well. If there's nothing there we'll be back within a couple of hours, if we find something the date will be cancelled anyway because Noel will need to be there."

"Perfect logic, detective inspector."

***

After a quick diversion to the Wright house to pick up the keys for the couple's holiday cabin from Clarissa McAdam, the two detectives set off for the famous loch, driving up the A82 in the fading light.

"Everything OK with you?" Alex asked after they had been on the road for ten minutes or so.

"No, not really. I had my brother arrested last night."

"What?" Alex exclaimed.

"He stole a watch that my father had given me. He pawned it and then gambled the money on a fuckin' nag."

"Why?"

Russell laid out his brother's sorry tale, giving Alex an insight to the difference between the two men and the chasm that had now appeared that may never close. Russell's despondency at the loss of the watch was clear and it proved a springboard for her to learn more about him on a forty-five minute journey than she had in their previous six months together. He told her a lot about his father, how much he admired him for raising the two boys after their mother had died when they were just young children. He worked hard as a supervisor at a textile mill in Paisley while the brothers were with their Aunt Cathy during the day. When the mill closed in the early eighties he had found work as a security guard but his pride had taken a dent. Russell was very emotional as he told Alex of his father's pride at his son's success in graduating from university. Although he had hoped for something different for him, Stuart Russell continued to be proud of his eldest son's achievements from the moment he graduated from Tulliallan Police College.

"He said to me that day after the ceremony, 'Justice should be blind, son. Look to a man's deeds to take the measure of him, not the size of his wallet'. It was his way of trying to make sure I didn't become the kind of policeman he hated. I've tried to live up to that ideal every day I come to do my job."

Alex reflected on how, for a very similar reason, her father had failed to understand why she had joined the force. When Andrew was gone, it gave father and daughter time to close the space that had appeared when she took the decision to join the ranks of the police. Russell's father had been a very special man and she could see the same nobility, strength and wisdom in her boss.

Russell then told the story of how Eddie could never quite bring himself to follow the same lifestyle.

When he told her about Dragovic, it was easy for her to appreciate the danger facing Eddie, and by extension his brother.

"Are you going to leave him in jail?"

"You bet. He's probably going to be safer in there anyway but I really want him to understand just how much he's let himself down."

"Do you think it'll work?"

"I have no idea, Alex. I can only hope that the message will sink in."

They had reached the village of Inverbeg on the west bank of the loch. The sheet of paper that Kelly had supplied told them that the Wright home was up a track on the northern side of the village. The road was pitch black but Alex spotted the entrance and Russell had to hit the brakes sharply in order to make the turn.

He steered the car up the single track for about four hundred yards before the foliage around them opened up to reveal a substantial log cabin. There was a bay for two cars at the bottom of the garden where a marked police car was already sitting. A burly sergeant stepped out of his vehicle and failed to remove all the crumbs of a piece of cake from his uniform shirt.

"Sir, sorry sir, we were having a wee bite tae eat."

"That's OK sergeant, I've sat waiting on detectives at one time and know that it can be tedious," Russell said as he smiled and extended his hand. A young female officer exited the car from the other side and introduced herself as PC Joyce Mills. She looked like she was just out of school and Alex wondered if she had ever looked so young when she joined the force.

"So, Sergeant Brodie, what have you got for us?"

"We had a look through the windae and ah couldnae say jist exactly why but it disnae look as if it's been lying empty aw winter. There's also a wee bit a tyre track on the grun that wid have been washed away in aw the rain we've hud if it wisnae recent."

"Good work, sergeant, constable. DI Menzies and I will take a look at the house, the two of you can finish your tea."

"Thanks, sir. If ye need us fur anything at aw just shout."

Russell retrieved a powerful torch from the boot of his car and illuminated their way up the stepped path to the front door of the house. On the lintel above the door were written the words, 'By yon bonnie banks'.

"The Wrights do like their quotes, don't they?" Russell remarked as he inserted the correct key into the door after two wrong guesses as to which one to use.

Alex fumbled on the wall before she found the light switch. The overheard light and lamps lit up to show a stunning room. All the surfaces were made from polished aged pine. Little nooks were carved into the wood and they were lit to highlight exquisite pieces of sculpture. An open fireplace dominated one wall with a pile of logs beside it arranged in a pyramid. There was a breakfast bar between the living room and an expansive kitchen. Directly opposite the front door was a stair with rugged, rough-cut wooden treads.

Alex knew what the sergeant had meant when he stated his belief that someone had been here recently. There was something intangible but someone had been in the house, she could feel it. Russell began to vocalise the clues. "There's a cup lying on the sink, the dust has been disturbed and you can still smell the smoke from the fire. It doesn't smell like a house that has been lying cold and empty since October."

Alex looked closely at the surface of the breakfast bar where plates, cups and the arms of the occupant had all made impressions on a thin film of dust. They worked the rooms methodically but there was no obvious sign of violence.

There were two bedrooms and a bathroom but no sign that Dr Jennifer Wright was still in residence.

"What do you think?" Russell asked.

"Someone's been here but I'm not sure it's her. Why don't we have a wee look around outside?"

They stepped out into the chill night air. When the room light was off and before he switched on the torch again, Russell paused and looked up. The stars of the galaxy were arrayed above them in numbers that were never visible in the light-polluted city.

"I love this," he said with childlike wonder.

Alex also looked up and said, "I know what you mean, it is like looking at a different sky."

He waited a few more minutes, drinking in the sight, enjoying the tranquility. When he was ready he said, "Anyway, back to work."

The beam of the torch worked its way around the right of the house and then to the back garden. As they walked towards the left of the house the beam highlighted an outbuilding.

"A shed or something," Russell observed.

"Worth a look I suppose."

They reached the large double door and Russell juggled with the keys before he found the one that opened the padlock. It popped open easily and he eased it out from the clasp that held the doors together.

As the two detectives each swung a door wide, the pungent smell of sawdust hit them, but there was another, darker aroma mixed with it. It took Russell a few seconds to bring the light around to focus on the interior. To the left, there was a huge pile of logs laid out to dry after being cut. On the right was a selection of garden tools, which included a shovel, a fork, a hoe and an axe, all arranged neatly on hooks on the wall. In the centre, apparently tied to a chair, was the decomposing body of a naked woman. There was an illusion of life still being present but it came from the hundreds of blowfly maggots that wriggled in a macabre dance, feeding frenetically on the decomposing flesh and squirming in a pool of dried blood that had formed at her feet.

CHAPTER 17

Russell found the perfect expression to capture the full awfulness what they were looking at. "Bloody hell."

Alex turned away and gulped in a breath of freezing, fresh air to alleviate the hot wave of nausea that engulfed her.

After checking that his colleague was going to be all right, Russell said, "We'd better get the team up here as soon as possible."

He found the number for Frank Weaver and initiated the call.

"Sir?"

"Frank, I'm at Gregg Wright's place near Loch Lomond. We've found a body that I presume is Jennifer Wright. We're going to need a full forensics team; the on-call pathologist and you better let the Fiscal know as well. Frank, there's not a lot of parking space, so if they can fit in one or two of the support unit minibuses that would probably be better."

"Yes, sir."

"We'll retire to the local pub for something to eat and we'll see you when you arrive."

When the call was finished he walked back to join Alex and the uniformed officers at the cars.

"Are you up to another look?" Russell asked his DI.

"Yes, sir. I was just shocked, it wasn't what I was expecting."

The two suited up before walking back to the shed hoping to learn a little more about what they had found. When they looked a little closer at the walls they could see traces of blood spatter which also appeared on the back of the doors. Even when they edged close to the body it was impossible to say for certain that it was Jennifer Wright.

"Looks like we'll need to wait to learn more. Come on, we'll retreat to the pub," Russell said, leading Alex back to the car.

The big sergeant seemed to have lost some colour after Alex had told him what they had found and the inexperienced constable looked reluctant to talk as the detectives removed their white overalls.

"Sergeant, we need you to secure the scene. I want all of the grounds covered with tape anywhere there is an opening."

"Yes, sir. We've never hud onythin' like this afore up here."

"I know. I wouldn't go up near the body if you don't need to, it's a pretty gruesome sight. DI Menzies and I will go and wait in the village until the crime scene team arrive."

"There's a guid inn in the village. Ask fur Moira and tell her ah sent ye."

"Thanks. Anything crops up in the interim, here's my number." He handed Brodie his card.

"We'll take the car down to the village and leave it there to allow the SOCOs some space."

They arrived at the enticing lights of the pub within two minutes. A wall of heat welcomed them as they walked into the inn. A stout woman with a round face and a cheery grin greeted them as they approached the well-stocked bar.

"What can I do for you folks?"

"Are you Moira?"

"That's me."

"Sergeant Brodie pointed us in your direction. We're looking for some good hot food to warm us up."

"Take a seat and I'll get you a menu. Can I get you a drink first?"

They both ordered a cola and then found a table close to the roaring log fire.

"Cosy," Alex remarked.

"It's just what I needed after that horror show."

Moira delivered their drinks and the menus. "I can recommend the Cullen Skink and then there's the Chicken Balmoral for a main course if that would interest you."

"Sounds good to me," Russell said.

"I'll have the Cullen Skink and then a Caesar Salad if you have such a thing," Alex replied.

"With chicken?" the woman asked.

"No, thanks." Alex had no intention of eating meat after what she had just witnessed.

"Excellent, I'll get chef to work."

She breezed away, seemingly happy and content with what she did for a living. At that moment, Alex envied the fact that the bar owner's night wasn't going to be filled with visions of terror created in the mind of a monster.

"Well, I think we can eliminate Jennifer Wright from our suspect list," Alex said.

"Unless she fell out with her accomplice, but that seems unlikely when you look at the crime scene."

"I don't understand, why dismember and dump Wright but bring his wife here?"

Russell sighed, "I have no idea but I think I'll concentrate on dinner and forget about the house of horrors until Sean and his team get here."

Moira arrived with cutlery and shortly after that with the warming soup, aromatic with smoked haddock, accompanied by a chunk of fresh bread.

The detectives sat in silence but Alex struggled to eat more than a couple of mouthfuls as the nausea returned. They were both lost in their own thoughts about the direction the case was now taking. Russell thought the food was excellent and it helped to divert his thoughts for a while but soon he and Menzies would have to go back to the shed and the all the awfulness it contained.

***

Russell contacted Weaver to tell him to bring the team to the pub car park in the first instance.

It took an hour and a half before the first of the crime scene personnel began to arrive. Frank Weaver had filled a minibus with Sean O'Reilly and four of his team, two detectives, Dr Gupta, three cases of technicians' equipment and two portable lights. The generator for the lights was attached at the back of the bus.

As the occupants poured out, Weaver leaned out the driver's window and said, "Who said a man can't pack, eh?" A few of the travellers looked a little green around the gills as they tried to overcome the effects of travel sickness.

"Where's Noel?" Russell asked.

"He'll be here in five minutes or so. There wasn't enough room for him, his kit and the Fiscal Depute, so they're coming up together."

Russell called Brodie and told him to move his car from the scene so the SOCOs could get to work. Meanwhile, white protective suits were donned and the team prepared to get to grips with the scene of another murder.

As they were ready to leave, Noel arrived with the Assistant Fiscal.

Noel's habitual smile beamed brightly as he said to Alex, "Not quite the Saturday night we had planned."

"No." Despite her displeasure at him for telling Russell about their date, she couldn't help but bounce the smile back at him.

"This is a bit different from the city streets. It's nice to get out in the country."

"You won't think that when you see the body," she shuddered as the image crept back into her mind.

"This is Fiscal Depute Waterson. Sheryl, this is DI Alex Menzies." Noel introduced a thin, willowy woman in her late thirties. She provided a contrast to the sharp, business-like image that her boss liked to project. She was dressed in a muted brown tweed jacket over a cream blouse and a darker brown wool skirt. She wore flat shoes, narrow spectacles and an old-fashioned brooch, all of which combined to give her a vaguely academic air.

"It's a pleasure to meet you, inspector." She was polite and quietly spoken.

"Please call me Alex."

"Why thank you, Alex. Of course you are welcome to call me Sheryl. I believe you may have found Jennifer Wright's body."

"It looks that way but it may take some time to confirm it. The poor woman's in a pretty bad way. Are you new to the Fiscal's office?"

"Yes, I transferred from the office in Edinburgh two weeks ago. It's been very busy, I've hardly had time to catch my breath."

"That's Glasgow for you."

Russell joined them and introductions were completed while Noel and Ms Waterson prepared for their visit to the scene.

As a group they made their way from the pub, along the main road and up the track to the Wright cabin. Sean and his team were already erecting the huge lights in front of the shed when they arrived. The black garden was suddenly filled with blue-white light and everything was thrown into contrast of light and shade, but even with the lights focused on it, there was a unique darkness that came from the corpse of the woman, murdered and abandoned by a mind that knew little of light.

The forensic team, the pathologist, the detectives and the Fiscal formed a little semi-circle at the opened doors of the woodshed.

Sean O'Reilly stepped forward with the forensic entomologist who began to remove the larvae of the many blowflies that had settled on the woman's body in the days after her death. The entomologist's name was Martin Murray, a scrawny man who said little and only seemed happy in the company of the insects.

"What d'ye think, Martin?" O'Reilly asked him.

He caught one of the maggots in a pair of tweezers and held it up like a trophy. "Calliphoridae larvae, definitely not less than three days old, so the victim has been dead at least four days but due to the cold weather it may be a little longer." His voice was soft and slightly effeminate.

"Which puts it at sometime around or before Monday," Russell said more for his own benefit than to illuminate those beside him.

"Around when Wright's body was discovered, so if it is his wife, she was kept alive for five days after they were abducted and five days after her husband was murdered, is that correct?" Sheryl Waterson asked.

"Yes," Alex responded.

"Why? A sexual motive?"

"That would be my first guess," she said.

Murray continued to lift the insects from the body, picking them carefully from the flesh and the stained red hair before placing them in plastic containers. He would use them to learn more about the condition of the cadaver they had been feasting on. As he worked removing the insect larvae from her body the woman was slowly revealed. In places the flesh was gone where the maggots had been particularly voracious, exposing yellow-white bone or purple organs. When he was finished with his task, it was the turn of Rajesh Gupta to take over.

The pathologist studied the body closely, taking his time to scrutinise each part and directing Noel on the photographs the investigation would need.

"The victim is in her late forties. From what I can see she's been subjected to some vicious torture, there are signs of burns, her genitals have been attacked with a sharp instrument of some kind and she has multiple stab wounds along her breasts and stomach. I think her death may have been caused by blood loss but obviously I won't be able to say for sure until the post mortem and we get lab tests done.

Poor lady," he finished sadly.

He seemed to be genuinely moved by the plight of the woman. For Alex it came as a pleasant change from the inhuman detachment that Hogan displayed, even when he was over the body of a child.

"Late forties would fit with Dr Wright," Frank Weaver said.

"I know we have to get it confirmed but I think everyone believes that this is Jennifer Wright. Now we have work out what happened that night and in the ten days since," Russell said firmly, trying to keep everyone focused on what needed to be done.

"What if we got this completely wrong? What if Wright was the collateral damage and his wife was the real target?" Alex postulated.

"Possibly. It was easy to get sucked in by Wright's connections and all that they imply, but why the dismemberment?"

"The only one who might want them both dead and have the rage that these crimes show is Calvin Wright," Alex suggested.

"Do you really think he has enough balls to do something like this?" Russell expressed his own doubts.

"I really don't know, sir."

Dr Gupta continued to work, recording as much of the scene as he could; the simplest thing could prove to be important in bringing a killer to justice and Gupta was very motivated to see that whoever had committed this murder was caught. The temperature was dropping rapidly and Alex found her teeth were chattering as she stood rubbing her arms trying to keep the blood flowing. While the pathologist completed his role, Sean's team of SOCOs had retreated to the relative warmth of the house. The search was on for fingerprints and trace evidence in the dust of the cabin.

Just as Alex thought hypothermia was going to set in the doctor announced that he was finished with the body. It was ten o'clock and everyone was exhausted. Sean decided that his team would return the following morning to complete the forensic sweep of the shed and the grounds. It took an hour for all the equipment to be packed away and the personnel to remove their protective clothing and load everything back into the minibus.

"I can give you a lift back if Sheryl doesn't mind slumming with old grumpy," Noel said to Alex when they were back at the pub.

Russell beamed a knowing smile. "Well, the poor soul must have been sick of the sound of your voice on the way up."

"I don't mind either way," Waterson said helpfully.

"Mr Hawthorn and DI Menzies have a lot to discuss, you're welcome to join me," Russell stated with a mischievous twinkle in his eye.

The Fiscal Depute appeared to take the hint. "I understand."

Alex felt like swinging for Russell, who took great joy in her discomfort, but she couldn't help but feel elated that she would get at least a little of the night in Noel's company.

On the journey south, Noel seemed to be in talkative mood and as he chatted he began to fill in a little about how he had made the journey from Haringey to his post as police photographer in Glasgow.

"I studied for a BA in photography at the London College of Communication, where I met Tricia. She was gorgeous and funny; she was also studying film so we had a lot in common. I fell for her, big time, and for the last two years of my degree course we lived together. When I finished the degree I had no idea which way I wanted my career to go. I loved taking pictures and processing them but none of the commercial photography jobs that were available really appealed to me. Then I spotted a job with the Met as a forensic photographer, I applied and was surprised when they offered me the job. I thought a lot about it and then decided to take it. Tricia was not happy. For eighteen months she nipped away at me, telling me I was wasting my talent and that I should be doing more with my life. I tried but I just couldn't make her understand the importance of what I was doing, I wasn't interested in the shallow world of fashion photography or indulging myself with some wanky artistic crap that may or may not sell. She walked out on me. I was devastated because I thought I really loved her. I wallowed in drink and self-pity for about a year then I spotted the advertisement for this job in Glasgow. It was less money but I thought, 'What the hell, I could do with a fresh start' and the rest, as they say, is history."

"Did you ever see her again?"

"I met her once when I was down visiting my parents. She was nice enough; she was working with some independent TV company doing documentaries. She seemed happy, I was pleased for her, but I had realised a long time ago that she was quite a shallow person and that material things and status were the only really important parts of her life. That's just not me, man." He indicated his scruffy jeans and the battered interior of his *classic* Mercedes.

Alex laughed. "So no one since you came to Glasgow."

"There have been a few passing fancies but I've not found anything worth holding on to. Yet."

"Is that what I am, a passing fancy?" she teased.

"I don't know yet but it'll be fun finding out." His eyes were alight as he flashed his smile at her.

"Do you want me to drop you at the station to pick up your car?" he asked her.

"It's late, why don't we got to my place for a cuppa?"

"As long as you've got a good strong, proper tea."

"Is there any other kind?"

They continued to chat until they had parked as close to Alex's flat as they could.

"You better bring your bag, you don't want it in the car overnight," Alex said with a glint in her eye of a different kind.

"Really?"

"These Xbox all-nighters can be a killer. Don't worry, I've got a spare toothbrush."

He nearly tripped in his rush to get out of the car.

CHAPTER 18

Alex woke to the warm touch and distinctive smell of another human being for the first time in over six months. Noel's muscular arm, the colour of autumn chestnuts, lay across her body. She rolled on to her side to look at him; he stirred and grinned sleepily when he saw her face.

"Good morning," she said.

"Who won the Xbox games?"

"I think it was a draw."

"Sure was fun. Fancy a decider?" he suggested

She moved in and kissed him, his arm slipped below the duvet and they lost themselves in each other once again.

***

Russell was already in the office with another ten or so detectives by the time Alex walked in.

"Busy night?" he asked casually.

Alex ignored him and made a cup of tea to kick start her day.

"PM is in an hour. Dental records have confirmed that it's Jennifer Wright, they decided against anyone trying to identify the remains due to the decomposition and the insects. Expect a big turnout again, the brass aren't happy."

"No, I don't imagine they will be. Have the newspapers got it yet?"

"It might be in the later editions but it's been on BBC news this morning. Speculation running faster than facts as usual."

"Sean on his way back up?"

"I don't know, he's not checked in yet. We'll leave the briefing until after the post mortem, we'll know more by then."

"Sir, you might want to see this," Ann-Marie Craigan called from the other end of the office, where a TV had been set up to allow the officers to keep an eye on what was being said by the media companies. It was tuned to the Sky news channel and the female newsreader was interviewing a grey, middle-aged man in an equally grey suit that was at least one size too small for him.

"... so it is your belief that Strathclyde Police have failed in the investigation into Gregg Wright's death?" the interviewer asked.

The camera cut to the man, a graphic appeared telling the viewer that his name was George Crichton and that he was a security consultant.

"Well, it's obvious that this investigation has been a disaster from day one. We've had three subsequent deaths now and it is my belief that if the senior investigating officer had a grip on his team at least one of those deaths could have been prevented."

Russell exploded with rage, "I'll kill that useless bastard. Are there any of our lot on there?"

"No, sir," said an apprehensive Craigan.

"Get me the fuckin' media officer on the fuckin' phone now."

The interviewer asked another question. "In what way have the investigating team failed?"

"Well, it was obvious from the start that there is a gangland element to these crimes but they seem to have been reluctant to address it. Maybe they find it too difficult to take on the real criminals."

"Never mind the media officer, get me a fuckin' gun. That useless bawbag couldnae find his arse wi' two hauns and a map."

"Sir, what's up?" Alex asked.

"That tosser is none other than the abominable Crichton, a brown-noser who climbed the promotion ladder by the ability to talk shite and reached the rank of chief super without ever once showing a degree of competence. He caused me to lose a conviction back in 2006 just before he took 'voluntary' retirement. He is truly one of the worst cops I ever worked with and now he's on national TV criticising me."

"Sir, the media officer is on the phone." Craigan offered Russell the handset.

"Tom, I know what you're going to say," Helen Paterson said before Russell could launch a tirade at her.

"Helen, that guy was a completely lousy cop. Why haven't we got someone on there to speak for us?"

"They blind-sided us. We refused to talk about an on-going investigation on air and asked them not to run the piece but it's a Sunday morning and they love to fill airtime with gas bags."

"I don't give a shit. I would be annoyed if it was someone who knew what he was talking about but this clown, bloody hell."

"Tom, I promise I'll deal with it. Don't let it distract you from what you need to do and for God's sake don't respond in the press."

"Fine." He hung up the phone.

"This is just what we need. The press'll be all over this like flies on shite."

"Helen knows what she's about, sir. She will deal with it."

"She'd better. Put that shite off," he grumbled and indicated the television where Crichton was still pontificating on the failings of the Strathclyde force.

Russell went back to his desk and lifted his own phone. "Davie, it's Tom."

"How you doing?"

"I'm fine. I'm looking for a favour. Do you remember George Crichton?"

"Big Yeti?"

"That's him. He's been on television this morning bad-mouthing me and my team."

"You don't need to say any more. If he's got so much as a faulty bulb, we'll pull him over."

"Good man, Davie. How's Charlotte and the kids?"

"Aye, they're fine. Good luck with case."

"Thanks, we need to go for a beer sometime." He finished the call and looked up to see Alex scowling at him.

"Who was that?"

"Davie Sutherland over at Traffic."

"What have you done?"

"I'm just making sure that Crichton knows you shouldn't shit where you once ate."

"Sir!"

"Don't worry, it's no as if I've put a contract out on him. Although I am tempted." He smiled innocently and Alex found herself reciprocating.

"We'd better think about heading to the mortuary."

"Here we go again."

***

The viewing room was nearly as crowded as it had been when Gregg Wright was on the table. Russell was disappointed to see Jacqui Kerr in attendance; he had been hoping that Sheryl Waterson would have followed up from the previous evening. He had spoken about Waterson on the journey over to the south side of the city.

"She's pleasant, understanding of the difficulties of our job and she appears to be very competent. She won't last long with Kerr," he had observed cynically.

ACC Muldoon approached the two detectives when they arrived.

"Golf course busy sir?" Russell asked.

"Pardon?"

"Was the team-building course busy sir?"

"Oh yes, yes. I had to come away early when I heard about Dr Wright."

"She was not a pretty sight, that's for sure."

"What's your thoughts on this?"

"I want to hear what the docs say but I'm beginning to think that the McGavigans and the Wright clan are a sideshow in all of this."

"I don't know whether to feel relieved or worried by that thought, Tom."

'Time will tell, sir."

On the other side of the glass, doctors MacNeil and Gupta arrived in the autopsy room. They were joined by one of the technicians and Noel Hawthorn bearing his camera. Alex flushed like a schoolgirl when she saw him and at the corner of her eye she noticed Russell casting a glance in her direction.

"Ladies and gentlemen, if you're ready we'll get started," Dr MacNeil announced.

The assembled collection of senior officers, detectives and the Procurator Fiscal either sat down to face the television screen or stood at the glass to watch the proceedings.

MacNeil began by cataloguing the condition of the body and the damage caused by the insect larvae. On areas where Jennifer Wright's skin was still intact, samples were taken using adhesive tape, which were placed in evidence bags. She also combed through what was left of the woman's hair and placed any detritus into separate bags.

Brian, the technician, then began to gently wash the corpse. The water ran away with ripples of red and brown towards the drain in the table. To an outsider he seemed to be treating the body with extreme deference but some of that care came from the need to preserve evidence, which was equally important as treating the deceased with some dignity.

When the technician was finished Doctor MacNeil stepped in again.

"The victim has suffered a number of shallow cuts to her arms and legs. These appear to have been administered over a period of several days as some of them had begun to heal before she died."

"Torture," Russell said.

"It certainly looks that way, superintendent."

She then turned her focus to the woman's genital area. She took internal swabs from Jennifer Wright's vagina and womb before saying, "The vagina has been subjected to penetration at least three times with a sharp instrument, possibly the same knife as was used to perform the other cuts. Again, two of those wounds show signs of healing."

"God save us," Muldoon said.

The Y incision was followed by the removal of the ribcage as the inspection of the organs began. MacNeil reported on further damage caused by the maggots in the days since Wright had been murdered. She removed the heart and observed, "The heart has been punctured with a sharp instrument. The wound was inflicted perimortem and it is most likely the cause of death."

There was stillness inside the viewing room as they absorbed the details and imagined the horrors that Jennifer Wright suffered in her final days.

When the formalities were complete, Jacqui Kerr approached Russell and said, "Billy McCarron."

"What about him?"

"You're only charging him with the murder of McGavigan and the culpable homicide of Niven?"

"That's correct, because that's what he's confessed to."

"What about Gregg Wright?"

"He denies involvement and there is nothing substantial that would link him to the killing."

"Find it." She moved as if she was going to step away but Russell stopped her.

"Wait a minute. We have no physical evidence that points that way and the more we look at it, the more it looks like these murders were committed by someone who knew the Wrights far more intimately than McCarron did. Why would he confess his involvement in two deaths and then deny a third?"

"I don't care what it looks like to you. He has motive and his gang connections make him a perfect fit. There are some people who think this investigation has not been well managed and that your incompetence has cost people their lives."

He laughed. "You're taking your line from a failed cop who has become a talking head on television? I'm not wasting resources trying to find evidence to pin this on McCarron just to make your life easier."

"I will take this discussion up with the chief constable."

"Take it up with whoever you like, but you'll still be wrong."

She stormed away in the direction of Muldoon.

"Having fun?" Lindsay Morton grinned as he approached Russell, who had been joined by Alex.

"I'm having a great day."

"I heard about Crichton, what a dick."

"But he's stirred up a whole pot of trouble. It doesn't matter how hopeless he was, he's on the telly, he must be an expert."

"McCarron insists he's not involved and if you look at what happened to Jennifer Wright and look at the way her husband was disposed of, it just doesn't gel with McCarron, no matter how much of a nutter he is."

"That was personal," Alex said, indicating the table where Brian was finishing the stitching of the Y incision on the woman's body.

Morton agreed with her assessment. "You're right, that's not how the world of gangs works. They have their own twisted ethics and women are normally non-combatants as far as they are concerned."

"We'd better be going, we've got a briefing in half an hour," Russell said.

"If you need anything you know where I am."

"Thanks, Lindsay."

***

Russell bent Alex's ear all the way back to Milngavie station, complaining about both Kerr and Crichton in a litany of swear words and remarks that disparaged the relative abilities of them both. She was glad when they pulled into the car park and he had to turn his thoughts to the briefing.

The team was assembled although Ann-Marie Craigan was a notable absentee as she was with the forensic team in Inverbeg.

Russell posted the grim photographs of what they had found in the woodshed. The majority of the detectives in the room had been hardened by their exposure to what human beings were capable of but the pictures and the superintendent's description of the horrific abuse Jennifer Wright had suffered were enough to move most of them. This was a truly hideous crime and when Russell asked for their thoughts there was a period of silence before anyone spoke.

DS Rankine was the first to respond. "Whit did the lassie dae that made somebody think she deserved that?" His question hung in the air, unanswerable.

Frank Weaver sought some clarification. "Was there any sign of sexual assault?"

"The doctor has taken swabs but with the damage that had been done to her it was impossible for her to say one way or the other. We'll need to wait on the results from the lab."

"Let's have a look at the timeline." Russell drew a horizontal line on the board and put a mark at the left side of it.

"The Wrights are due to leave for a skiing holiday on the 9th. At least one assailant gets hold of them before they can reach the airport. The chances are that Gregg Wright was killed immediately, possibly in his car. The body is driven to the farm where it's dismembered, wrapped in polythene and then dumped in the loch. The Wrights' car is taken to Peathill Wood where it is set on fire, probably to destroy evidence. That same day Dr Wright is driven to their Loch Lomond home where she is tortured for four or five days, subjected to degradation and then is finally murdered and left. Wright's body is found around the same time as she was murdered. Is that about right?"

Alex had been pondering the sequence as Russell posted up each individual moment of the timeline. "Looks right to me. I think that it's probable that the discovery of Gregg Wright's body was the trigger for the killer to finish off Dr Wright."

"Do you think that they made Jennifer Wright watch while they dismembered her husband's body?" Weaver asked.

"I think it's probable, but the alternative is that the body was dropped at the farm, one assailant does the deed, then drives in a second car to Bardowie Loch and then on to Peathill Wood to pick up the accomplice and Dr Wright," Russell said.

"Are we convinced that this is a team?" Alex asked.

"It has to be."

"Does that rule out Calvin Wright? His only alibi is McCarron and even that is only partial," Alex said.

"What time did he drive back through to Edinburgh?"

"About four in the morning according to the cameras," Rankine replied.

Frank Weaver expressed his thoughts. "I don't see how it could be him. Jennifer Wright was subjected to continual daily abuse. He would have to drive for two hours each way every day if it was him."

"If he hated her enough, maybe, but it's unlikely. I know it's a pain Mac, but check the CCTV for the days following the original abduction please and any alternative routes he might have used to get to the loch," Russell ordered.

"It'll take a while."

"I know, but we have to be thorough."

"If it's not connected to Gregg Wright we have to look a lot closer at his wife," Alex said.

"What about the father, are we sure that he was in the States?" Russell's suspicions were too horrible to contemplate but he had to be sure.

"Definitely, sir. We had to phone his hotel to tell him about his daughter's death. He can't get a flight until tomorrow."

"Who else might be involved?"

"Extremists against the genetic work she did?" Weaver suggested.

"An ex-employee?" Rankine said.

DC Kelly found his voice. "What about that scandal that McDougall hinted at?"

"Someone from her past came back to haunt her. Mmm, an interesting idea Paul. I think we need to speak to Dr McDougall tomorrow." Russell was happy to see the young man begin to have some confidence in his ideas.

"There's probably not a lot we can do for the rest of the day, so go home, get refreshed and get ready for a whole new set of problems tomorrow."

***

Russell was feeling the aches and pains of the long days he had had to put in over the week. It was well past midnight before he got back to the flat the previous night and he felt that his brain needed an early night to allow him to better tackle the problems he would face when the investigation resumed the following morning.

He was so distracted that he didn't notice the two men step from the shadows and take position on either side of him.

"You Eddie Russell's brother?" a Slavic accent asked.

"What's it to you?"

Before he could react the man on the right turned and punched Russell in the midriff. The air was forced from his lungs and his legs folded like a cheap pasting table.

"Where is your brother?"

"In jail," Russell replied desperately trying to gulp in oxygen.

"You lie." A kick plunged into Russell's ribs like a mallet.

"No. He stole a watch... He's in jail... I put him there," he managed through gritted teeth.

"Why you do that to your brother?"

"Because, like you, he's a bit of an arsehole."

They each took turns to swing their boot at him and he heard a rib snap.

"Tell him he has two days to find money. If not we kill you. We are at Holiday Inn Express Hotel."

Another farewell kick from each of them – one of them to his head – and they were gone.

Russell lay for about five minutes as blood dripped from his mouth and every breath felt like daggers thrust into his lungs. Gingerly, he managed to stand and fumble in his pocket to get the key for the door to the close. Every step was excruciating as he climbed to his home. When he was safely ensconced in the flat, he made sure that every lock on the door was secured and the chain firmly set in place.

He went to his bathroom cabinet and took out two paracetamol, two aspirin and two ibuprofen. He edged his way to the kitchen where he kept a bottle of 18-year-old Highland Park. It was an expensive bottle of whisky but he wasn't interested in the taste as he poured a large glass and downed it along with the painkillers. He made his way to bed and initially found it difficult to sleep but eventually the alcohol and the pills helped to take the pain away and he dreamt of angry bears.

CHAPTER 19

When his clock radio woke him on Monday morning, Tom Russell had temporarily forgotten about his broken ribs and bruised face. When he reached to turn off the alarm, he remembered very quickly. Pain seemed to shoot from every part of his body.

"Oh, shit," he muttered to himself.

During the process of rising from his bed, washing and pulling on his clothes, he felt like someone had put him in a blender. When he looked in the mirror, more of his face was bruised than was not. He had a breakfast of coffee and pain-killers as he sat in anguish on his sofa.

He decided that there was no way he would be able to drive and called Alex.

"Sir?"

"Alex, can you pick me up?"

"Sure, what's up? That fancy car of yours on the blink?" she asked playfully.

"No, I'll explain when you get here."

"I'll be there in twenty."

He thanked her and sat hoping that the painkiller cocktail would still have some effect without the aid of the whisky.

Alex rang the doorbell just after the twenty-minute mark. Russell buzzed her in and then unlocked his door.

When she saw him, she gasped, "God, Tom, what the hell happened?"

"Unhappy messengers looking for my brother."

"You need to get to the hospital."

"No, I don't. All they'll do is give me painkillers and I can do that myself. We need to get to Hayworth and find out what MacDougall knows."

"What's this all about?"

"My brother's Serbian pal is keen to get his eight grand back. He sent a couple of his friends to find Eddie but when I told them he was in jail, they decided that maybe I wasn't being entirely honest. Eddie's got two days to find the cash or something worse will happen to yours truly."

"You need to let somebody else deal with this."

"I will deal with it my way. End of discussion."

Alex was going to argue but knew that she would be talking to herself. She helped Russell to put on his jacket and coat and they walked slowly to her car.

He groaned as he bent to get into the seat and she tried once again to persuade him to go to the hospital but her attempt at convincing him was in vain.

Every pothole she hit on the road brought a complaint from her boss about her driving and her decrepit car. She let him grumble on until they reached the Hayworth car park. Getting out of the car proved even more difficult than getting in had been for Russell. He tried to straighten up and walk normally but Alex thought it wouldn't make a lot of difference to how people regarded his gait, as his face looked like some psychedelic painting due to the vibrant range of colours it was displaying.

"Oh, are you all right?" Harriet, the receptionist, said with concern when she saw Russell.

"I'm fine, just a rough weekend."

"OK then," she replied doubtfully.

"Is Dr McDougall available?"

"I'm sorry, he just called in sick. Is this about Dr Wright's murder?"

"Possibly. How…" Russell was gripped suddenly by a vice of pain and his knees nearly folded for a second time in twelve hours.

"Sit down, sir. I'll deal with this."

"Sorry," he said softly as Alex led him to a row of comfortable reception chairs. She made sure he was settled in one of them before returning to the desk to speak to Harriet.

"Are you sure he's going to be OK?"

"I'll get him to a doctor when we're done here. How long have you worked here?"

"About nine years."

"When Superintendent Russell spoke to Doctor McDougall he hinted that there might have been a bit of a scandal a few years back, do you know what that was about?"

"Eh… we're not supposed to talk about that."

"Harriet, this could be really important and might help us to find who killed the doctor."

She considered her response before saying, "I suppose you are the police. Wait a moment."

She rang a colleague and asked them to look after the desk. When the woman arrived she cast a suspicious glance at Russell. Harriet led Alex into a small room close to the reception; leaving Russell slumped in agony on the chair.

When Harriet had closed the door and both women were seated she said, "Do you really think this could have something to do with Dr Wright's murder?"

"We don't know for sure but we have to explore all the possibilities."

"I don't know all the details, it's a bit like Chinese whispers, you learn a little about it bit by bit after you join the company. Apparently Sir Nigel and Dr Wright were conducting unauthorised experiments. It got covered up by the authorities because it would have caused a huge stink if it ever got out."

"What kind of experiments?"

"I don't know exactly what they were doing but they were apparently using children."

"Children? Where was this?"

"A place in Ayrshire. Kilduncan or Kildougan House, something like that."

"Do you have any idea where it was?"

"I'm not one hundred per cent sure but I think it's near Dalry."

"Is there anything else you can tell me?"

"Not really, that's all I know."

"Thanks Harriet, you've been a great help. If Doctor McDougall comes back in, can you ask him to contact either Superintendent Russell or myself?" She handed the woman her card.

"I will do. What happened to the doctor?" Alex then repeated the phrase she had used on numerous occasions to divert a curious member of the public or press. "I'm afraid we can't give you details of an ongoing investigation, but thanks again for all your help." When they walked back into the reception area, under the bruises Russell looked vampire white.

"I'd better get him to the hospital. Goodbye."

Harriet went back to her seat but continued to keep an eye on the detectives.

Alex grabbed Russell's arm, which provoked a worrying groan. She helped him to his feet and led him out to the car. She refused to listen to his arguments as she drove him to the Western Infirmary for a check-up. On the way she told him what Harriet had said about the house in Ayrshire.

"And she had no clue as to what happened?" he responded through a haze of pain and medication.

"No, it's like some Victorian family secret that the downstairs had some vague idea about but were never told the full story."

"We'll check it when we get back. Aargh… watch they bloody potholes."

Two hours later, the doctor in Accident and Emergency confirmed that Russell had two broken ribs and a hairline fracture on the bridge of his nose. He told him that he needed to rest for at least three days to give his body time to recover but Russell dismissed his advice and asked him to prescribe some stronger painkillers that wouldn't inhibit his ability to do his job.

"I must insist, Mr Russell."

"Insist all you want but I've got a murderer to catch," Russell growled.

"I can give you a small amount now but you will have to go to your GP to get the full prescription."

"Fine."

The doctor tried one last time to persuade Russell to rest but Russell's stubborn streak was asserting itself strongly. He gave the detective the prescription and shook his head.

Alex apologised to the doctor and then drove her boss to a pharmacist in Byres Road. She left him in the car and went in to pick up the tablets. When she got back to the car, Russell ripped the pills from their packaging and swallowed them without a drink of water.

"Right, back to the station and we'll do a search for this Kildougan or whatever it's called."

***

There were expressions of shock from a number of the officers in the incident room when they saw the state of the detective superintendent as he walked in. He dismissed it as a mugging but as the day went on there would be a lot of gossip in the break room as to what had happened. Over time the idea that he had been beaten up by an irate husband became the favourite and one of the DCs set up a sweepstake on what the truth was. Russell knew nothing of the speculation, which for those involved was definitely for the best.

He eased himself into his chair and switched on his computer as Alex joined him. She took the keyboard to ensure that the process was a little quicker than the pain-racked, two-finger attempt at typing Russell would manage.

The search quickly established that there was a Kilduncan House, but it was in Fife. When Alex typed in the search for Kildougan there was not a single hit.

"Try Kildougal," Russell suggested, but once again they were thwarted.

Alex then typed Kildonald House and was rewarded with several pages of hits. They patiently read each entry until, half-way down the second page, they found what they were looking for. On the North Ayrshire Council website they found a property for sale close to Dalry.

Kildonald House. 19th-century red sandstone mansion. Eight bedrooms. Three large public rooms. Kitchen. Three bathrooms. Outbuildings. 3 hectares of grounds. In need of restoration/redevelopment. Ideal opportunity for spacious family home or conversion to flats. Contact property department for details.

"That must be the place."

"Give them a ring and we'll see if we can find someone who might know what happened there."

Alex rang the number on the website. She gave a short explanation of what they needed and after being passed through four different departments finally landed at a woman in the social work department called Bridgit O'Donnell.

"Hi, my name is Detective Inspector Alex Menzies from Strathclyde Police. I'm calling about Kildonald House and I was told that you might be able to help me."

"What's it in connection with?" she replied cautiously. Relationships between the police and some social workers could be strained and Alex was hoping that Ms O'Donnell didn't see her as the enemy.

"It may have some connection to a case we are currently working on."

"That old place has been closed for years."

"Do you know any of its history?"

"Not really, it was shut down before I started here, I used to be with Renfrewshire Council. I think there's a man in Dalry who keeps an eye on the place for us. He used to work as the caretaker, so he might be able to help you."

"That's great, do you have a number for him?"

"One moment please."

Alex sat and listened to hold music while Russell drummed impatiently with his fingers on the desk.

When she returned to the phone the social worker gave Alex both the name and telephone number of the man who was responsible for the maintenance of Kildonald House. Alex thanked her and Bridgit wished her luck with the investigation before they said goodbye.

"Well?" Russell asked.

"I've got the name and number of a guy who used to work there. Hopefully, he'll be able to tell us what happened."

"Give him a ring then."

Alex dialled the number she had been given but there was no reply.

"No answer, I'll try again in an hour."

"I suppose it might give the painkillers some time to work."

Alex retreated to her own desk and started her computer. She was ploughing through her e-mail when DS Rankine walked in.

"No sign o' Calvin Wright on the CCTV for the nights after his parents' abduction," he told Russell.

"OK Mac, that probably excludes him unless he's one of a pair. Give L&B a ring and find out what they've done with him. If he's out and about ask them if there's any chance they can keep an eye on him, see who he contacts. Tell them they can send us the bill if they like."

"Who can send us a bill and what the hell happened to you?" Muldoon asked as he walked into the office.

"A mugging outside my flat. We're just trying to make sure that Calvin Wright isn't involved as one member of a team. I still think his inheritance would be a major motive. I was going to ask L&B if they could keep an eye on him."

"OK, if you think it's worth it. Have you reported the mugging?"

"No, sir."

"Don't you think you should, Tom?"

"I will do, sir, but I didn't really see who it was so it's probably a waste of time," Russell was on the defensive as the last thing he needed was the ACC nannying him and stopping him doing his job.

"Any further updates?"

Alex gave Muldoon a quick run down of all they had learned about the Kildonald House connection.

"And you think there's something there?"

"We think it's worth looking at; we're thinking about the possibility of Dr Wright as the primary target rather than Gregg. There's a hint of something about this Kildonald House that has a cover-up written all over it and that might just give us a motive."

"OK. Keep me updated. I'll be in the office."

When Muldoon was gone, Alex said, "Are you going to report the attack?"

Russell dismissed the idea. "No, what's the point? The Serb'll just send more thugs. I promise I'll find a way to deal with it myself."

Alex sighed and returned her attention to her e-mails until the hour was up.

When she called the number for a second time, an elderly man answered, "Hello?"

"Mr Hamilton?"

"Aye, wha's this?"

"Mr Hamilton, my name is Detective Inspector Alex Menzies. I was hoping to speak to you about Kildonald House."

"Oh… I wondered when this day wid come."

"I'm sorry?" Alex said, taken aback by his reaction.

"I've been waiting' fur wan o' your lot tae ask me aboot that place since it shut."

"We're investigating a recent case and we think there may be a connection."

"It's that Wright wummin, isn't it?"

"Well…"

"Ur ye in Glesga?"

"Yes."

"Ye best come doon and we'll talk. Ah'll meet ye at Kildonald in an 'oor if that's OK wi' you?"

"That's fine, I'll be there with my colleague."

When she told Russell what the man had said, he responded with, "What the hell went on down there?"

"We'll soon find out."

***

They drove through the Clyde Tunnel and then found their way on to the A77, the road that took them into Ayrshire and towards their destination. Alex presumed that Russell must be feeling a little better as there were a lot fewer complaints coming from the passenger seat.

Alex's phone guided her to the address of Kildonald House, about a mile outside the town of Dalry, not far from the railway line that ran down from Glasgow to the coastal town of Largs.

There was a short tree-lined drive that led from the main road to the house. The listing on the website had been a little less than honest when it indicated that the property required some restoration. It may once have been a fine large family home but now the red sandstone structure lacked a complete roof, there were windows missing and there was a general level of dilapidation that would require a lot of time and money to repair.

The paint was cracked and peeling on the substantial front door and close to it stood a short, stocky man with a ruddy complexion. A tweed cap was perched on the back of his head and at the front, his pate was shining through what was left of his white hair. His round face was weathered and wrinkled by a life lived outdoors and a pair of thick glasses hung precariously at the end of his bulbous nose. He was wearing a thick green Aran jumper under a pair of blue dungarees with solid workman's boots on his feet.

He walked towards the car and offered a chunky, leathery hand to each of the detectives in turn.

"I'm DI Alex Menzies and this is my senior officer, Detective Superintendent Russell." She shook his hand.

As he shook Russell's hand, Jock Hamilton commented on his appearance. "Ah hope the other chiel looks worse than you."

"Unfortunately not," Russell replied morosely.

"Mr Hamilton, you said you were expecting a call from us," Alex prompted.

"Aye hen, it wisnae a shock. Ah thought the truth would catch up wi' us sometime. Ah'll show ye roon if ye want, and tell ye the story?"

"Yes, that would be great, thank you."

He led them on a tour of the exterior and began his narrative. "This place wis built in the early part o' the last century by a textile mill owner fae Paisley. It wis in his faemily until the sixties an' then they couldnae look efter it properly as they ran oot o' cash. The cooncil took it o'er and it wis used as a ootdoor centre fur the school weans but then they ran oot o' money tae fund it in the eighties. Cutbacks, ken? Anyway, it was empty fur a few years when a women's shelter applied tae use it as a halfway hoose in 1989. It wis a temporary thing until the cooncil could find a place fur the pair lassie's tae live safely permanently."

"These were women that had been physically abused?" Russell asked.

"Aye, a lot o' them hud weans as well. This place hud been running aboot three years when they started tae struggle. They goat some cooncil money but they wur always reliant oan charity donations to keep the heatin' oan and the folk fed."

"When was this?"

"Early nineties, ah think. Anyway, wan o' the cooncillors knew this Hayworth guy and Hayworth offered tae fund the place if they would allow them tae dae a study oan the kids."

"What kind of study?"

"Some genetic thing. They said that they were studyin' how clever folk wur and whether the talents wur passed fae parents tae their weans. Whether they wur good at maths or art, that kind o' thing. At least that's whit they told the mothers and the folk fae the charity."

"But that's not what happened?" Alex asked.

"Naw. Come oan, ah'll show ye where they worked."

They walked away from the main house towards a collection of outbuildings at the far end of the garden. There were two or three sheds and a bigger L-shaped building constructed of the same sandstone as the house. Once upon a time it may have been stables or a garage but there had been so many alterations done to it over the years it was difficult to know its original purpose.

"This wis their lab," he told the detectives as he opened the lock in a large door. The interior was dark and it took a few moments for Alex's eyes to adjust. It had a musty coldness about it and the smell of damp decay hung in the air like a permanent ghost. There were a couple of filing cabinets, their empty drawers lying open. An old hospital bed minus a mattress could be seen at the far end of the room, a solitary reminder of what had occurred in the building.

"They took maist o' the equipment away wi' them efter the fire."

"What fire?" Russell asked.

"There was a big blaze in the main hoose. Wan o' the kids went mental wan night and set fire tae the curtains in the room. They went up in seconds and we hud tae evacuate the buildin' sharpish. By the time the fire brigade goat here it wis too late, we hud loast the whole tap flair."

"Do you think it anything to do with the what was going on in here?"

"Well, that's the bit ah don't know fur sure but the weans were different efter Hayworth and his lot arrived. Some o' them seemed restless and wur always oan the go. There wur others that didnae want tae dae anythin', they wid jist sit aboot, and then there wur others that seemed tae want tae fight wi' the world. Ah think they wur gi'ein' the bairns somethin' that changed the way they behaved."

"Did you see them giving the children anything?"

"Naw but ah saw the effects. Wee Jamie – he wis a nice kid afore they arrived. Shy but always smilin'. But then he became really sullen and aggressive. Know what ah mean? He wis the wan that told me that when they went tae the 'doactor's hoose' they would get a special drink."

"And Jennifer Wright was part of this group?"

"Aye there wis her an' another wummin assistant. She wis still ca'd Hayworth back then, goat merrit tae that gangster's laddie when she wis here. She's a right weird fish. She treated the kids as if they wur just lab rats. There wis nae warmth in her at aw."

"You think that they were conducting illegal experiments on the children?" Alex asked.

"Ah dinnae ken fur sure but ah think it's poassible."

"You guessed that we wanted to speak to you about Mrs Wright, why?"

"Ah just thought that if ye muck aboot wi somebody's life the way they did that it might come back an' bite them oan the arse."

"Was the kid who started the fire prosecuted?" Russell asked.

"Naw, here's the thing, it wis aw covered up. They said it wis an accident and didnae want anybody else findin' oot. If that's no' suspicious ah don't ken whit is."

"Do you remember the name of the boy?"

"Ben or somethin'. Sorry hen, ah cannae remember the laddie's name at aw."

"Do you remember the names of the people who worked here?" Alex was hoping that they would be able to piece together the full story.

"The Hayworths' assistant wis a nice lassie but ah'm buggered if ah can think whit her name wis. Then there wis Sally Merchant, she wis in charge of the shelter. She'd be able tae tell ye who else worked here."

"What about the women and children?"

"Sorry, there wur a lot o' them came through here. Ah couldnae be sure other than wee Jamie, he wis ma favourite."

"OK, Mr Hamilton, thanks for your help. Is it OK if we have a look around?" Russell was keen to get a sense of the place without the little man hovering around.

"Sure, son. Ah'll be at the hoose."

He left the two detectives in the middle of the old lab.

"What do you think?" Russell asked Alex as he kicked some dust.

"It's shocking if they were conducting some bizarre experiments but why would it take nearly twenty years for someone to take revenge?"

"Maybe some trigger. Illness or the death of a mother, I don't know, Alex. I'd be guessing."

"It's definitely worth digging into, isn't it?"

"Without a doubt."

They looked through some of the other rooms in the building but they were equally deserted and barren of anything that might help the case.

Back at the main house they said goodbye to Jock Hamilton and began the journey back to Glasgow.

**

Alex finally persuaded Russell to go home and rest, despite his insistence that he was fine. When she showed him a mirror, he could see that under the bruises, his skin was pale and the pain that racked him was contorting his face. His broken look persuaded him of the sense of resting.

She walked him up to the flat and mothered him a little by making sure he took some more of the pain medication. He thanked her and then ordered her to go. When she was gone he walked to the kitchen, reached tentatively for the whisky bottle that was on the top shelf and poured himself another large measure. He sat on his sofa, hoping that the agony would subside again with the help of both the medical and distilled painkillers.

His phone rang and he groaned. He had left it in his coat pocket and would have to get up to answer it. He was tempted to ignore it but professionalism won out.

"Russell."

"You're not sounding too hot, Mr Russell."

"McGavigan?"

"Aye. I'm just phoning to say thanks."

Russell was immediately suspicious. "For what?"

"Picking up McCarron. The media say he killed Alan."

"It looks that way."

"What about Wright's boy?"

"He's denying it. He thought it was you."

"He's wrong."

"Is there anybody in your crew that would have gone out on his own? One with maybe a history of sexual violence?"

"No way. Ah widnae tolerate any of they perverts anyway. Why?"

"It's just a question."

"Where's McCarron, Barlinnie?"

"Malky, let us deal with it. If anything happens to him you know where I'll come first."

"Ah never said anything. If what ah hear is true it's Wright's tossers that are more likely to take action. He went against orders and that's a big no-no. Wright'll feel he needs to enforce discipline before any of the others get ideas."

"Thanks for the tip."

"How come you sound so rough?"

"Let's just say I had a disagreement with someone. Well, two someones to be accurate."

Russell could hear the smile as McGavigan replied, "Sounds like you took a kickin'."

"It's great chatting with you but is there anything else? I could be doing with getting to my bed."

"You and I are never gonnae be pals but I wanted you to know that I'm glad you got McCarron for Alan's sake and that I don't need to start anything that would have got worse. If there's anything I can do, let me know."

"Give up the drugs trade, walk to the station and confess to all your crimes. It would make my life a lot better," Russell replied quickly.

"Ha, you're funny, Russell. Ah'll gie ye that."

The detective was about to hang up when an idea occurred to him.

"There might be something you can do. There's a couple of Serbs in town to cause some trouble. It would be good if they were taken out of the picture in a way that didn't have me overworked in the aftermath. I don't want any violence, just a way to stop them causing any further bother."

"They the 'someones' you mentioned earlier?"

"Could be."

"Let me think. Nae violence?"

"No violence."

"You don't make it easy, dae ye? I'll see what I can do."

When the call was over, Russell wondered if he had just done his own deal with the devil.

Exhausted and still in pain, he was ready to have an early night when the phone rang again with another number he didn't recognise.

"Russell," he said with irritation.

"Tam," his brother replied.

"Eddie."

"Tam, ah've learned ma lesson, honest. Ah'm really sorry fur whit ah've done, ah promise. Please say ye'll drap the charges."

"Eddie, you stole from me. You took the one connection I had to dad, sold it and then lost the money on a fuckin' horse. And to top it all off, I got a kicking from your Serbian pals because they couldn't find you."

"Fuck, man. Ah'm really sorry but ye cannae leave me in here, please Tam. Ah'm yir brother."

"You should have remembered that brotherhood is a two-way relationship before you nicked my watch." He pressed the button to end the call.

He scrolled through his contacts to find the number of Phil Davis, a defence lawyer he knew and trusted.

"Hi Tom, how are you?"

"Not bad, Phil. I need a favour." He then detailed all that had happened since Eddie had crashed back into his life.

"And you want me to defend him?"

"Yes, I don't want him left with some legal-aid bottom feeder."

"And you're going to pay for the defence of someone who stole from you?" the lawyer asked incredulously.

"Despite the fact he's a diddy, he's still my brother."

"No problem, Tom. I'll get on it."

"Cheers."

When the call was over, Tom Russell switched off his phone and walked to his bed, clutching his ribs and another couple of painkillers.

CHAPTER 20

When she had dropped off Russell – and after a short period of begging her car to restart – Alex finally made her way to the station.

The incident room was still crowded and she could see that many of the officers were looking haggard by the efforts they were exerting in the pursuit of the killer. She decided that a short briefing about Kildonald House was required.

She called the team to the incident board and listed the salient points from the day so far. It was clear that they needed a new focus for their energies. She asked for and got three volunteers to help her trace some of the background information on the charity involved and who had been at Kildonald House as a member of staff or as one of their protected clients. The rest of the team went back to studying the witness statements and calls from the public.

The Kildonald House team consisted of Ann-Marie Craigan, Mac Rankine and Paul Kelly. They surrounded Alex's desk as she began to lay out a strategy with their thoughts to help guide her.

"The first thing I think we need to do is get a list of staff and clients from Hayworth GS. They must have records of the staff going back to the very early days."

"I can do that," Rankine offered.

"If they're reluctant, contact the Fiscal's office and get a warrant. I don't know what it is about this but I think there's a good chance that what happened at Kildonald House has a bearing on what is happening today. We need that information," Alex emphasised.

"No problem," Rankine replied.

"Paul, I want you to contact the fire service and ask them for details of the fire at Kildonald. If Jock Hamilton is right, there was a cover-up and that is something that makes me very suspicious. I want to know what the fire investigators were told at the time."

"Will do."

"Ann-Marie, we need to have a look at the charity. What happened to the people who worked or volunteered there? What did they know about what went on in the laboratory? I doubt we'll get details of the women who were sheltered there but it's important that we get as much information on the people as we can."

"What was the charity called?"

"The Ayrshire Haven."

"What do we know about it?"

"Not a lot. That's what you'll need to find out. Shout out if there's anything you want to ask or if you've got something that might prove useful. All clear on what you've got to do?"

After nods of agreement the little group dispersed to their various desks, while Alex went out for a quick bite to eat before settling in for a long stint at the computer.

She returned to her desk with a sandwich and a cup of tea. She logged in to the old desktop, which churned and rumbled while she had time to finish her sandwich. Eventually, it was ready for her to do some background research on the science of behavioural genetics. From what she could gather, it had been a field of study for many years but only in the last twenty or so, with the mapping of the human genome, had it become significant. Although the geneticists had narrowed some of the markers for mental illness, there was little to say that particular behavioural traits were purely genetic. There was a school of thought that the ability to identify a gene for violence or general criminality could lead to a 'treatment' that could remove anti-social behaviour from society. Others were still held the belief that nurture was more likely to lead to criminal behaviour than the meeting of a sperm and an egg. Alex could understand both arguments, as some people could move away from their life of crime when their social conditions improved. Equally, she had seen people who seemed to be controlled by an evil they could never escape no matter their upbringing.

Jennifer Wright's son had said how obsessed she was by her area of study. Would that obsession have driven her to unethical practices? Did those practices lead to her terrible end?

As she mused on these thoughts, Mac Rankine was the first to offer new information.

"Inspector, Hayworth HR have sent through the list o' employees, going back to the beginnin' of the company."

"Brilliant, I'm glad they co-operated. Do you have the names of the female employees around 1994?"

"Three women between 1992 and 1995, other than the victim, that is."

"E-mail the names to me and I'll take it from there. If there's nothing else you need to finish, then you're welcome to go, Mac. Thanks for your help."

"Cheers."

It was half past five and much of the team were beginning to pack up.

The list of three names arrived and Alex prepared herself for a longer shift. The first name was Samantha Cavendish. She was listed as an office manager and Alex thought it unlikely that she was the woman who had worked at Kildonald House, but she may have an insight into where the records were from that time, so she was put on the list of possible sources. Georgina Thomas was a student who worked for the company in the summers of 1994 and 1995. Finally, there was Amanda Irvine, a post-graduate researcher who worked with the company through 1994 into 1995. She looked to be the best candidate as the assistant at the refuge.

There was an address and a telephone number for each of the women and Alex chose the number for Irvine.

"Before ye start, ah don't want solar panels, tae answer yir survey or fur ye tae dae a PPI investigation fur me," an older man answered grumpily.

"No, sir. I'm not trying to sell you anything. My name is Detective Inspector Alex Menzies from the Glasgow Major Incident Team. I'm looking for Amanda Irvine."

"Whit? There's naebody here wi' that name."

"Maybe the person that was in the house before you?" she suggested.

"Naw." He hung up abruptly.

Frustrated, Alex called the number for Georgina Thomas, but the woman who answered was no more helpful, although she was a little more polite about it. Resigned to a long search, she called Samantha Cavendish's number.

"Peter Cavendish," a man answered.

Alex introduced herself once more and was happy to hear that Samantha still lived at that address and that she was at home.

When she was handed the phone, the woman said nervously, "Detective Inspector, is there something wrong?"

"No, I'm hoping you'll be able to help me. I believe you worked for Hayworth Genetic Solutions for a time?"

"Oh, that was nearly twenty years ago."

"I understand that, but it may be that there is a link to the murder of Jennifer Wright."

"Really? I saw it on the television but I didn't think that it would have anything to do with the company, at least not back when I worked with them."

"It's one of many lines of enquiry that we are pursuing. During the period you were working for them, do you remember that they had a laboratory in Ayrshire at a place called Kildonald House?"

"Yes, they used it for some research on kids."

"Do you know what happened to the records for that time?"

"I'm not sure. I think Jennifer was responsible for them. They were never returned to the main office, I know that much."

"Was that unusual?"

She considered before replying, "It was, yes, because research tends to lead to further study but there was never any further development of what they had done there; at least in the time that I was at the firm."

"So you don't know the details of the research?"

"No, I'm afraid not. It was all very hush-hush but that's the way it is with genetics. A big break could make the company very rich and there's always a big fear of industrial espionage so they are very careful who knows what."

"There was a research assistant on that project, I believe."

"That's correct, Amanda Irvine."

"I don't suppose you would know how I could get hold of her?"

"She was head-hunted by a big university in the United States when she got her doctorate. She was quite brilliant, maybe even more so than Jennifer."

"Do you know why the project was stopped?"

"There was some scandal about a fire but again I don't know exactly what happened, I'm sorry."

"Thank you, Samantha. You've been a big help."

When the call was over, Alex turned back to her computer and began another hunt, this time for Amanda Irvine.

Her initial search based on Irvine's name didn't produce anything that she felt confident would lead to the woman she was looking for. She tried again this time with the criteria 'Scottish genetics doctor' but once again the answers were inadequate. Then she thought that Amanda Irvine may have become a professor and tried with 'Scottish genetics professor' in the search box.

Half way down the list of results was a Wikipedia listing for Professor Amanda Rodriguez. Alex clicked on the link and knew she had found the correct Amanda. Her listing told of her educational background at Glasgow University and the fact she was a Professor Of Human Genetics at the University of California at Sacramento – the university that Sir Nigel Hayworth had been visiting.

"Bingo," Alex said in relief.

"Ma'am?" Kelly asked with a confused look on his face.

"It's OK, Paul. I'm only talking to myself," she replied.

Alex calculated that it would be just after nine o'clock in the morning in California. There was a good chance that the professor would be in the university and that she might be able to speak to her. She would have to clear an international call with someone and as Russell was indisposed she dialled the ACC's number.

"DI Menzies, do you have news for me?"

"Not exactly, sir, but I think we might have a lead on Dr Wright's past that may prove useful."

"Excellent. And?"

"I need to call California."

"California? Who's there?"

She spelled out what she knew about Kildonald House and the fact that Professor Rodriguez may be able to help with the details.

"Why do you think this is important?"

"The violence that was inflicted on Dr Wright was personal; the kind of violence that was festering in the killer for some time. I think Kildonald House might be the key."

"Fine, but please keep it short." Muldoon hung up.

Before Alex could dial the number for the professor, Paul Kelly approached her desk. "I've managed to get the report from the fire service."

Alex put the phone down and sat back in her chair to listen to what he had to say.

"The fire occurred in February of 1995. It was ruled as accidental by the investigators. The staff told them that there had been a power cut that night and that they had lit candles in the rooms. One of those candles was placed too close to the curtains. There was nothing to indicate anything other than what the staff had said and the building was renowned for electrical problems due to its age and the fact they struggled to pay the electricity bill from time to time."

"So either it was perfectly innocent or they covered up what the kid had done. Interesting. OK Paul, good work. I'll see you tomorrow."

Alex looked up the international dialling code for the U.S. and then called the university. She was passed from one receptionist to another and then to a personal assistant before Professor Rodriguez finally answered the phone.

"Detective?" Her accent was predominantly Californian with only a small trace of her Scottish roots.

"Professor, I'm sorry to bother you but I need to speak to you about your time at Hayworth GS."

There was a brief pause before she replied, "I'd rather not."

"It's extremely important as it may have some bearing on what happened to Jennifer Wright."

"I'm sorry about her death but I can't see how anything that happened then would have anything to do with it."

"It's an area we're exploring due to the very personal nature of attack that the doctor suffered. Now, can you please tell me about the research you were conducting at Kildonald House?"

"It's not a part of my career I look back on with any pride. Please, I require your discretion or it could have a very negative effect on my career."

"Professor, a woman was brutally murdered. Doesn't that mean anything to you?"

"I'm sorry. Will you try to keep my involvement out of the press?"

"I'll do my best."

Alex heard the woman sigh. "When I joined Hayworth, I thought that I was part of a ground-breaking company who would be pushing the boundaries of science with work that would make a real difference in people's lives. Sir Nigel was the leading light in the field in the UK. His daughter was gaining a reputation for herself and they had picked me from a list of over twenty of the brightest people in the country. I was thrilled." She paused as if reflecting back on the younger, more idealistic version of herself.

"The work at Kildonald House was all about identifying the genes for aggression and criminal activity. Jennifer was on a crusade; she believed that if she could identify those genes, then she could cure the world of crime. She and her father came up with the idea of using the Kildonald children as the perfect specimens, as it was obvious their fathers were all violent men. Her father told the people who ran the charity that the work was all about intelligence and how it may be possible to increase a child's ability to learn. I don't think the charity knew exactly what was going on but they needed the money."

"This work was unethical?" Alex asked.

"Very. It wasn't just the lies that the mothers and staff were told, it was the methodology used. Jennifer came up with this idea to try a variety of medical and hormonal drugs on the children. The idea was to see the effect it had on the children, to see if they would trigger a response. She was looking for something that would provoke the kind of behaviour that was associated with criminals. She thought if she could work out what triggered the gene, we would have a better understanding of how to combat it."

"Were these new drugs?"

"No, they were existing treatments for a variety of medical and psychological problems. I knew that the methodology was flawed and the science behind it was wrong but as I said, I was in awe of the pair of them, who was I to criticise? I did express some reservations at one meeting but she said that current methodology was too slow and that she believed this would lead to quicker, more useful results."

"What happened to the children?"

"The results were erratic. Some children would become withdrawn and sullen. Others on the same drug regimen would become hyperactive and impossible to control. About a year into the project, the woman in charge of the refuge, Sally Merchant her name was, came to Jennifer and expressed some concerns. Jennifer told her that it was teething problems and that we were getting closer to cracking the code. Her father increased the donation to Kildonald and Ms Merchant's complaints disappeared."

"This sounds more like Mengele than proper science," Alex said.

"You're right. As I said it was not a time in my career I look back on with any fondness. It made me decide that the commercial world wasn't for me and I retreated to academia when I got the chance."

"There was a fire, do you know the story behind it?"

"That was the end for the project. One lad, his name was James... oh, I can't remember the second name. Anyway, he had a severe reaction to one of the drugs. He became disruptive and violent. He bit a member of staff, slapped his mother and was constantly fighting with the other children. I begged Jennifer to stop the treatments she was giving him but she thought that he was the most important subject we had and was the one that might be the key to understanding the genetic markers for violent behaviour. She had no concern for the children as people; she only saw them as guinea pigs. The boy had a bad start in life and his father ended up in jail for killing another woman. Anyway, on the day of the fire he was particularly bad. He had punched a boy at school and was suspended. He was brought to the lab and I tried to give him a sedative but that just made him worse. He told me that he didn't want any more medicine and threw a jar at me before running out. He missed lunch and they were about to call the police but he came back later in the day. One of the other boys taunted him, told him he was crazy. He picked up a candle and set fire to the other boy's bed. The bed was next to the window and the curtains caught fire. The place was an inferno within minutes. Luckily, everyone got out of the house."

"Why was it covered up?"

"The Hayworths panicked and realised if their work with the children was exposed, their careers and mine were finished. There was a meeting that night while the firefighters were still trying to get the blaze under control. The Haven staff was told that they had to lie because they were going to be in trouble for their unethical dealings with the Hayworths. I'm not sure, but money may have been paid to ensure their silence." She sounded ashamed by her own part in the whole affair.

Alex felt that the story was depressing, but how could she connect it to the Wrights' murders?

"What happened to the records, were they destroyed?"

"No. I'm pretty sure that Jennifer was planning to hold on to them. She was sure that they were the basis for the eradication of those anti-social genes she was so desperate to find. In truth, she was so intent on making her mark and eclipsing her father's achievements that she would have done almost anything to prove her theories."

"And did she?"

"No. She's achieved some interesting developments in identifying genetic causes of mental illness but nothing truly astounding."

"Do you think the drugs you administered to those children could have a damaging long-term effect on them?"

"It's possible. The children she used as subjects were all in puberty; a time when there are a lot of chemical changes going on in the body, it's a distinct possibility that it caused problems."

"Thanks for your time, professor. I hope you think your career was worth the damage that your work caused," Alex said in revulsion.

"Once again I would appreciate it if you could keep me out of this if you can. Along with my colleagues, I have done a lot of good since then."

"I can't promise anything." Alex ended the call and threw down her pen.

"What's up?" Craigan asked.

"Jennifer Wright and her father used the kids at Kildonald like they were petri dishes; something to peer at and treat as if they were disposable. They were kids who had a bad start to life and the Hayworths made it worse."

"Do you think that could have got her killed?"

"I don't know for sure but – you won't hear me saying this often – I could understand if someone was driven to kill her."

"I've got a name for the Ayrshire Haven project, a Sally Merchant. She was in charge of the staff at Kildonald."

Alex nodded, "The professor mentioned her, anything else?"

"There were three full-time staff and a number of volunteers, the majority of whom were women who had survived spousal abuse. I'm still trying to get the names of the other staff. Do you want Merchant's details?"

"No, we'll trace her in the morning. We need to find the files on the experiments, they could tell us who the killers might be, but I don't think we'll get much more done tonight. Off you go and I'll see you in the morning."

Alex tried to call Tom Russell but there was no reply. Exhausted and feeling unclean after what she had been told, she felt that home was calling.

***

She was shivering from the bitter cold as she neared her flat. She was searching in her bag for her keys when a figure stepped in front of her. Instinctively she was about to swing for her attacker when she looked into the brown eyes of Noel Hawthorn.

"Noel, you gave me a fright. I nearly punched you."

"Am I forgiven?" he asked as he produced a single red rose from behind his back.

Alex gave him a light-hearted punch. "I suppose so. What are you doing here?"

"I thought you might like a surprise and someone to cook some dinner for you."

"That would be great. Come on."

They walked up to the flat and after a wonderful homemade curry, spent another passionate night together.

CHAPTER 21

Tom Russell's aches and pains had eased a little overnight and he was ready to face the day after a long, restful sleep. He still winced a little as he pulled on his clothes and his face was now showing the full spectrum of colours, but he definitely felt better. Alex called and offered him a lift to work but he felt confident that he could drive.

He arrived at the station at eight-thirty just as the incident room was filling up for the morning briefing. Alex arrived five minutes later and she was delegated to lead the meeting, which allowed Russell time to catch up on the significant developments of the previous evening.

As other avenues of the investigation began to dry up, the process of tracing those involved at Kildonald House became the priority for the team.

"Has Sean turned up those records anywhere?" Russell asked when Alex was finished.

"Not that I'm aware of."

"Get a warrant and ask him to have his document guys take a look at Hayworth's company records. You and I will take a trip to the Wright household to see if Jennifer Wright kept any of that stuff at home. Where do we stand with young Mr Calvin Wright?"

"Nae sign that he had been back in the west efter his faither's murder," Rankine said.

"Check if he had access to another vehicle, Mac. That wee bastard is the one that would gain the most from his parents' death and there's something about him that gets under my skin."

"Will do, sir."

"Ann-Marie can you keep looking for the Ayrshire Haven people, please? See if you can get any of them to talk."

"Yes, sir."

"The rest of you keep looking at the calls from the public, and McCarron needs checked out again."

"Sir, Detective Superintendent Morton is going to take a run at him today to see if he will give us anything about Wright's organisation. Do you want me to sit in?" DS Miller asked.

"Sounds like a plan, Shona. I doubt Lindsay will get much but you never know."

Tasks assigned, the meeting broke up with a strong feeling that there was still a lot to do before the case would reach a conclusion.

***

When she walked into the interview room, DS Shona Miller knew that Billy McCarron was in no mood to help the police with their enquiries. He sat with his arms folded and stared at her and Lindsay Morton, his face set.

"Billy, how are you?" Morton asked.

"Fan… fuckin'… tastic," he replied sarcastically.

"Need a smoke?"

"Aye, if there's wan goin'."

Morton offered him a cigarette and told him to stand under the window and blow the smoke out. The smoking ban could sometimes be an obstacle to cooperation for some of the people who sat on the wrong side of the interview table. Many detectives would allow a cigarette if it meant the suspects were less irritable; it was all part of the game of give and take they played to try to unearth the truth.

When he was finished, McCarron looked a little less angry with the world and Morton hoped he would be willing to be forthcoming about what he did for Peter Wright.

"Billy, what we need is some details on what's going on inside the Wright gang. It would help you with sentencing if you were to offer us some help."

"Fuck off, Morton. Ma life's no worth shit just noo, it wid be worth even less if ah start shootin' ma mooth aff."

Morton ignored the reply. "We don't need a full rundown on everything he gets up to, we know most of that already, but we do need to know who else might decide to take the law into their own hands and go after McGavigan."

"Whit dae you care?"

"Because I don't want to have a bloodbath in this city, if I can avoid it."

McCarron shook his head. "Wright will be lookin' tae bump me aff and ah don't doubt that it'll probably happen. Believe me, nae other fanny wid be stupid enough tae step oot o' line wance ah'm in the grave." He seemed strangely resigned to his fate.

Shona Miller asked, "What about Gregg Wright? Do you know who killed him?"

"Naw, and before ye ask again, it wisnae me. There's naebody oot there who knows who did and that means it probably wisnae wan o' yir usual suspects." He grinned. "That makes it a lot mair difficult fur you bastards, is that no' right? But yir no' makin' me take the faw fur it. Ah tellt ye whit ah done but there's nae way ah'm copping fur that jist tae make your life easier."

"What about the other guy on the bike when you killed Alan McGavigan?"

"Fuck off, ah've tellt ye ah'm nae grass. Ah've said aw ah've goat tae say."

"Fine, but we'll make sure the Fiscal asks for the maximum sentence," Morton said.

"Ah don't give a shit. There's a shank wi' ma name oan it an' the only way ah'm gettin' oot o' jail is in a boax. So whit the fuck does it matter?"

When the two detectives had left the room, Morton went to the custody sergeant and asked that a close eye be kept on McCarron. Morton felt the gangster was too resigned to his fate and might just decide to try to shorten the waiting period by taking his own life.

Miller reported to Russell, who wasn't in the least bit surprised at McCarron's recalcitrance; he was too deep in the culture of gangland to do what was best for him. Someone else would step up to replace him in Wright's gang and normal service would eventually be resumed.

***

Clarissa McAdam was not at all pleased to see Russell and Menzies roll up in front of the Wrights' home.

"What do you want now?" she asked curtly when they stepped out of the car.

"We need your help, Ms McAdam. There are files we need to find that may relate to the murder."

"Your technicians have been all over this house already. What more could there be?"

Alex smiled kindly. "That's where we need your help. The forensics team would not have been looking for these particular files. They date back to the early nineties and there is a chance that they are related to the murders."

"I suppose you'd better come in then," she told them with reluctance.

They were back in the sumptuous hallway when Russell asked, "Is there anywhere in the house, other than the office, that files could have been stored?"

McAdam made a show of thinking before she suggested, "There's a part of Dr Wright's wardrobe that I wasn't allowed to touch. The doctor told me that she would deal with it. I thought that it might contain jewellery or something valuable."

"Show us, please."

She led them upstairs to what they had thought was a guest bedroom the last time they were there.

"They slept in separate rooms?"

"Yes, of course," McAdam replied as if it should have been obvious.

"Why didn't you say that when were here last time?"

"I thought you knew."

"The master bedroom looks like a couple slept in it."

"Yes, I suppose it does, but that is for show. When there were guests in the house they would sleep in the same room but they mainly led separate lives and that included their bedroom arrangements. As I told you before, they were not a typical couple."

"You're not kidding," Alex said under her breath.

McAdam opened a sliding door that exposed the innards of the wardrobe. There was a line of feminine business suits in greys and blues, around ten white blouses and a couple of dresses. Four pairs of plain black low-heeled shoes were arranged on a rack and there were drawers built in to the back wall of the space.

The housekeeper then pushed aside the suits to reveal a panel that ran the height of the wall. It was slightly narrower than shoulder width but there was no handle or sign of a lock. Russell tried pushing it and then tapped it, which created a hollow sound.

"How do you get in?"

"I don't know. As I said, I was told it was off limits."

While Russell continued to try to get some kind of hold on the door, Alex began looking round the bedroom. There was a small set of drawers and a dressing table. She checked the drawers, which were filled with plain, functional underwear and simple T-shirts. There were also two bedside cabinets with a drawer in each. The one on the right of the bed was unlocked and contained nothing but applewood scented air but the other was locked.

"Ms McAdam, I am going to force this lock. We will pay for any damage. Can you get me a screwdriver please?"

"OK," the older woman said. She went downstairs and came back with a large flathead screwdriver with a bright yellow handle.

Alex levered the head of the tool into the space between the drawer and the frame and pushed. The lock was not too strong and the drawer popped open with little real effort. Inside there was a small black plastic remote with a red button and a green button.

"This might help, sir."

She pressed the green button and there was a click from the door as it swung open about an inch. Russell reached in and opened it further to show a row of shelves. At the top were a number of jewellery boxes containing diamond earrings and necklaces, many of them antique. Below that shelf, however, stood a series of filing boxes packed with documents in beige folders. Russell took out a box and brought it into the light of the room. It didn't take him long to establish that they had found what they were looking for.

"These are the Kildonald House files," he confirmed.

The two detectives removed the other boxes from their hiding space.

"We are going to take these to the station, Ms McAdam. Alex, could you create a receipt please?"

She did as she was asked and then, with Russell's help, spent the next fifteen minutes transferring the files to the back of his car. There was a daunting amount of reading ahead of them.

***

The incident room had morphed into some long-forgotten archive in some dusty basement; there were so many boxes of files on every surface. Paul Kelly and Ann-Marie Craigan were given the onerous task of cataloguing the records and entering them into the evidence log. When the first two boxes were recorded, Alex and Russell picked up a box each and began to read.

The boxes were dated from the early months of the project and were packed with early assessments of the subjects. Each file that Alex was given showed the sex, height, weight and age of each subject. All of the records were for children between thirteen and sixteen years of age. There were also measurements for their heart rate, blood pressure and a series of blood tests that only someone trained in medicine would understand. Each of the records had a unique number but there was no name recorded for any of the children.

"There are no names on any of these. She treated them like animals," Russell echoed Alex thoughts.

"Maybe she was trying to remain objective," Alex said, playing Devil's Advocate.

It became apparent very quickly that there was little to be gained from these files. They both expressed a hope that the rest of the boxes may reveal more of what went on.

DC Kelly and DS Rankine had finished the cataloguing of the boxes and took a set of files each and began to read through the mountains of paper.

"We're looking for the records of the effects on the children's behaviour. Give me a shout as soon as you see something that may be important," Russell told Rankine and Kelly.

In the second box that Alex had picked out there were thicker records, each of which dealt with a single child. They were diaries that recorded the drugs that were administered and the effect they had on all the physical markers. Blood tests were taken once a week and the children appeared to be subjected to one drug or cocktail of drugs for about two months before there was a period of sugar pills for about a month. The subject would then be given a new cocktail of drugs and the process would begin again.

As well as the physical records, psychological profiles began to appear.

Subject KH013 - May 23rd 1994

Subject displays signs of lethargy and disinterest. Does not want to attend school or take part in house activities. Recommend ending treatment FR236 with immediate effect.

JH

Some of the behavioural notes were more positive but Alex was alarmed at how many of the children were suffering from fear, anxiety, depression and outbursts of violent anger. She couldn't understand what the Hayworths hoped to prove with any of these bizarre experiments.

The boxes that contained the records of the children who were entered into the project towards its end included comparisons between those who were on the same regimen at the same time. The tone of the comments that were entered initialled JH became more enthusiastic.

Subject KH034 - October 25th 1994

Treatment GL839

This subject is showing greater aggression on this regimen than any other subject. Recommend blood tests and DNA analysis. This could be the breakthrough we've been looking for.

JH

Mac Rankine called out, "I think I've got something."
Russell joined Alex looking over the sergeant's shoulder.

Subject KH034 - February 8th 1995
Treatment GL839
Subject was extremely aggressive in exam. Threw
a flask at me and threatened to kill me. MUST
BE COMPLETELY REMOVED FROM THE
PROGRAMME IMMEDIATELY.

AI

"Paul, when was the exact date of the fire?"

Kelly looked back through his notes before saying,

"February 9th, 1995."

"Anyone like to take a bet that subject KH034 was the one that was tipped over the edge into setting fires?" Russell asked.

"And an unhealthy interest in fire can be the precursor to other violent behaviour," Alex noted.

Russell then asked, "Has anybody found a list of the kids' names?"

The detectives shook their heads.

"We need to find the key to who these kids were. There are still two or three boxes to go through, let's see if we can find it."

"Look at this," Alex said.

"What, you have you got the names?" Russell asked hopefully.

"No, it's a file on Gregg and Calvin Wright. She's catalogued elements of their behaviour over the years. Comparing her son to his father as if he was just another subject."

"She was mental," Rankine said.

"I've got to agree," Russell said, "but she didn't deserve to die like that so we need to find her killer."

"Yes, sir."

They went back to their desks and continued the search.

"Sir," Ann-Marie Craigan, who had been trying to contact the Ayrshire Haven's staff, approached Russell's desk.

"Ann-Marie?" Russell saw a concerned look on her face.

"Sir, I traced the names of the three permanent staff who worked with the women and children at Kildonald."

"And?"

"They're all dead. All killed in accidents in the past six months."

"What?" Alex said incredulously as the others also focused their attention on the detective sergeant.

"When I called the number in the records for Sally Merchant, I got her husband. She was killed in December in a hit and run accident in Ayr. He told me that she had lost two friends in the previous couple of months. When I did some polite probing he told me that Barbara Jones was killed in a house fire in November and a mugger in Carlisle killed Theresa Hendry last September. He told me that all of the women worked together at the Haven project. He thought it was just a terrible run of bad luck, a coincidence."

"I want the reports on all those incidents, Ann-Marie. There's no way these deaths can be happenstance."

"It looks like our killer might be on a revenge mission," Alex said.

"I think it's beginning to look that way. We need the children's names. Paul, you take over the Haven stuff while Ann-Marie rings round for those reports. Contact the social work department direct and make sure they understand that there may be other lives at stake."

"Yes, sir."

"Is Hayworth back in the country yet?" Russell said, referring to Jennifer Wright's father.

"Due in some time today I believe."

"Alex, give him a ring. If the killer is out to wipe out those responsible for the Kildonald House project, we have to warn him he might be the next target."

The atmosphere in the room was now sombre and contemplative as the number of people involved became a reality in the minds of the detectives. Ploughing through boring paperwork was not particularly glamorous but it was now the key to unravelling the case.

Alex rang the number they had on record for Sir Nigel Hayworth but there was no reply. She left a message asking him to ring her as soon as possible.

She returned to the box of files. Its contents were similar to all that had gone before and there was no sign of a key to the subjects' names.

It was Mac Rankine who made the next discovery. At the bottom of one of the boxes he had chosen, he found an old five-and-a-quarter-inch computer disc with a label marked in Jennifer Wright's handwriting.

KH Project - Subject records

He held it up and shouted on Russell.

"Brilliant, Mac, but have we got something that can read it and will it even still be readable?" Russell said morosely.

"The I.T. boys are bound to have something tucked in a room somewhere that will be able to read it."

"I hope you're right, Alex. Get it over to them and see what they can do for us."

CHAPTER 22

When Alex arrived at the forensic I.T. department in the city centre, she was treated like Indiana Jones arriving back from a trip with a precious artefact. The older members of staff were quick to tell nostalgic tales of computers past, while the younger ones were amazed to see such an ancient disc outwith the confines of a museum.

Roger Green, one of the more senior members of the team, was helping Alex with the data problem. He was a big man in every proportion with greying brown hair and a patient smile. Alex had worked with him before and he was always pleasant and helpful despite the huge volume of work that he and his team were dealing with. Alex had a feeling that he fancied her a little and she did flirt with him gently when she needed something done quickly.

Every investigation produced huge amounts of I.T. related equipment and data. They required specialist skills to extract the information that would lead to the capture and conviction of suspects and these guys were the best at what they did.

"This is an old one, we don't see too many of these nowadays," Green said with his West Country burr. He had been in

Scotland for over twenty-five years but he still sounded like he had just left Exeter.

"We need to get the information that it has stored on it if possible. What are the chances?" Alex asked with a winning smile.

"How was it stored?"

"In a cupboard at the back of a built-in wardrobe."

"If it was dry and well ventilated then there's a good chance we'll be able to get something from, it as long as the data wasn't written in a really obscure piece of software. I'll be back in a minute."

He walked away and returned five minutes later with a large packing case. As he opened the box there was further interest from some of his colleagues. He unpacked and assembled an old Dell desktop computer. The base was a dirty beige colour and with it was – compared with modern displays – a tiny screen. There was a space on the machine for each of the floppy disc sizes. The keyboard and the mouse both looked cumbersome compared to their modern counterparts. He plugged the bits together and booted the machine.

"How do you keep these things going?"

"We've got a huge archive of parts that we can cobble together if they break down. It's difficult because you use the older equipment less and less but there's always the odd time like this when we need it."

When the computer was ready the screen showed an older version of Windows that Alex had never used. However, Roger Green obviously knew his way around it as he put the disc in and began navigating around the screen with the mouse.

"Ahh… yes. Mmm… let me try…"

He continued muttering to himself as he worked to get to the data.

"It's an old spreadsheet format, SuperCalc. Let me work on it."

Alex left him to it and went to get a vile cup of tea from a machine in the corridor. She rang Russell and told him that there was a chance that they would get the evidence they needed from the disc, which was greeted with cautious optimism by her boss.

When she went back to the office, Green was wearing a large grin. "Here you go," he said, indicating the screen.

There was the usual grid layout of a spreadsheet that Alex had seen before. The column headings included 'Subject Identity Number', 'Subject Name' and 'Date Of Birth' and the key to identifying any possible suspects.

"That's great, can you print it?"

"Not from here, but there are things that I can do to get it there."

He walked to a cupboard and came back with a smaller floppy disc that he inserted into the machine. He saved the new version of the file to that disc and then ejected it. Alex followed him to another part of the office where there were two modern computers. Attached to one was an external three-and-a-half-inch floppy drive. He pushed the disc into it, busied himself on the computer and then saved the file back in another format. The external drive was then connected to the other machine and once again he worked on the file to get it into a format that Alex would be able to use on her computer in the incident room.

"That's it. I'll e-mail it to you and add a copy to the data we've collected for this case. Some of the functionality is gone but the data is complete."

"Thanks, Roger. You're a genius, I could kiss you."

Her comment elicited an embarrassed grin from the big man. "Always happy to help, it was nice to get something a bit different and it's always a pleasure to help you, Alex."

***

It was late afternoon before Alex returned to the incident room in Milngavie. Russell asked Ann-Marie Craigan to brief Alex about the reports on the other Kildonald-related deaths.

"Sally Merchant was killed by a vehicle in the street just outside her house. There were no witnesses, although one person did see a white van speeding away from the area but didn't get the plates. There was no CCTV and the case is still open. Theresa Hendry had moved to Carlisle after she left the Haven project. Local police believed that she was killed in a mugging gone wrong but once again, no CCTV and no witnesses. The case remains open. Barbara Jones lived alone in Kilbarchan. She was killed in a house fire that the local fire service and detectives believed was accidental."

"And wait till you hear this," Russell said.

"They thought that the fire was a result of a misplaced candle."

Alex allowed the information to sink in. "Well, we have a list of the kids involved in the experiments. There are nearly a hundred different names."

"How many were called James?"

"I'll check," Alex said as she turned to her computer.

"There are two, plus a Jim."

"Jock Hamilton said that Jamie became sullen and aggressive. What's the name of the KH034 subject?"

Alex turned to the screen and consulted the file. "James Gardiner," she announced.

"Let's have a closer look at Mr Gardiner, he's as good a starting point as any."

Alex began clicking and typing as she attempted to find out more about the possible suspect. There was no record for him at the DVLA as ever having applied for a driving licence. There was no criminal record either for anyone with his name and date of birth.

"Nothing obvious, it's going to take some more work."

"What about the social work department at the council?" Russell asked.

"I'll try Bridgit O'Donnell."

The social worker was less than pleased to hear from Alex at that late hour in the day.

"I was about to go home," she said.

"I'm sorry, but this is important. We're looking for a boy called James Gardiner who was at Kildonald House in the early nineties. Would there be a record for him somewhere in your archives?"

"That would be during the old Strathclyde Regional Council days. I honestly don't know, you would need to talk to our records department."

"Do you have a number for them?"

O'Donnell gave her the number and said, "You'll be lucky if there's anyone there at this time of day."

"That's OK. Thanks for your help."

"North Ayrshire Council, records department, Barry Colquhoun, chief records assistant, extension 728. How may I help you?"

"Mr Colquhoun, my name is Detective Inspector Alex Menzies and I am hoping you can help me with some information relating to Kildonald House in the early nineties."

"Detective Inspector, there are procedures that have to be followed when accessing our information." His officious tone wasn't what Alex was hoping to hear.

"I understand that but this is a murder investigation and it is at a very delicate stage. The information could be vital in finding a killer and possibly preventing further deaths."

"Firstly, you could be anyone pretending to be of the inspectorial persuasion. Secondly, I can't access confidential records for any Tom, Dick or Jane. Thirdly, I have a number of forms that have to be filled in if I'm to peruse my extensive databases on the search for the relevant missives. Fourthly, if you really are an officer of Her Majesty's constabulary, don't you require a warrant?" Alex had a vision of a little grey man dressed in beige who protected his records like they were his children.

"Mr Colquhoun, I understand your concerns. If you would like you can phone Assistant Chief Constable Muldoon, who will vouch for me and the reason I need the information."

"Well that might be possible but it will have to be quickly. I finish at six thirty."

Alex looked at her watch; it was already six twenty. She was about to give him the details when Russell said, "Give me the bloody phone." She handed him the handset.

"Mr Colquhoun, this is Detective Superintendent Thomas Russell. If you don't give us the information we require, I will call your local station and have you lifted for perverting the course of justice and I'll make sure you're thrown in a cell overnight with the biggest, hairiest, baddest fuckin' villain I can find," Russell shouted.

"Oh… there's no need for that. Of course I want to help the members of the constabulary."

Russell thrust the phone back at Alex. She gave James Gardiner's name and date of birth to the now petrified man on the other end of the phone.

"It might take me a few minutes."

"That's fine. Give me a ring back when you're ready." She finished the call by leaving her phone number.

"You are terrible sometimes," she said with a smile to Russell.

"No wonder, why does everyone have to act like an arse?" he replied.

They waited twenty minutes, with Russell growing increasingly annoyed at the delay.

When he called back, Colquhoun told Alex that Gardiner, his mother and his sister were found a council house in Dunlop. He had stayed with her until he was eighteen when he applied and got a council flat in Fairlie. He disappeared from their records three years later when he stopped paying rent and vacated the flat. Alex thanked Colquhoun for his help before relaying the information to Russell.

"Shit," he sighed.

"We'll need to wait until tomorr…"

Before she could finish the sentence, Russell's mobile phone rang and he held up a hand indicating she should stop speaking.

"Russell," he said with tetchy shortness. His painkillers had worn off, he hadn't been to his doctor for another prescription and with the combination of the continuous aches, his tiredness and a case that was getting ever more complicated, his temper was being stretched to breaking point.

"Sir, it's DS Weaver. Just to let you know that's us finished with Wright's business records."

"Anything interesting?"

"The forensic accountant said that he will need time to analyse what we've collected but he thinks that the cross-mortgaging means the whole group could collapse with the failure of just one of the businesses. There are also some interesting accounts in the Cayman Islands that will need to be investigated. The money shown in them doesn't seem to tie up with what the group was earning."

"His father's dirty cash?"

"It's definitely possible."

"That's great, Frank. Are the files going to the forensic accountants' office?'

"All the financial stuff, yes. We've got personnel files that will need closer scrutiny."

"OK, we'll see you shortly."

"One thing, sir. It might be nothing, but Jason Garner didn't turn up for work today and no one could get hold of him."

"Interest... Garner, Gardiner. It couldn't be."

"What?" Alex asked as she saw the expression on Russell's face change.

"Jason Garner, James Gardiner. Could it be the same person?"

"He'd be about the right age," she agreed.

"Frank, have you got Garner's personnel file?"

"It'll be buried in one of the boxes that we've got in the van."

"Get it here as soon as possible."

"Yes, sir."

The conversation over, Russell shouted, "Let's get these boxes piled up in a corner. We've got another batch coming in."

The remaining detectives began replacing the files in the boxes and stacking them neatly in the designated area.

When Weaver arrived, Russell led everyone out to the car park and helped to carry the new set of files up to the office. The personnel boxes were identified and Alex, Paul Kelly and Ann-Marie Craigan began to riffle through them looking for Garner's file.

After five minutes Paul Kelly shouted, "Got it."

He handed it to Russell who scanned it and said, "According to this he was born on 13th March, 1979."

Alex was already poised at her computer and entered the criteria of his name and date of birth into the database of the Scottish Registrars. There was a single entry.

"Jason Garner, born 13th March 1979, died 4th June 1980."

"He assumed a new identity?" Russell suggested.

"Unless our Garner was born outside Scotland."

"Let's go and ask him."

Alex noted Garner's home address and raced to catch up with Russell, who was already striding towards the car park.

CHAPTER 23

arner's flat was in the Cathcart district of the city, close to the national football stadium, Hampden. Russell parked in the shadow of the old ground and walked purposefully towards the address.

A two-minute walk brought them to the building. Gregg Wright's assistant lived on the ground floor, but Russell's repeated presses of the button on the controlled-entry panel brought no response. He began to try the other residents and it was after he tried a flat on the second floor that he got an answer.

"Hello," a young woman's voice was almost drowned out by the sound of a screaming baby.

"My name is Detective Superintendent Tom Russell. We need access to the close."

"Oh, what's up?"

"Please open the door."

"Wait a minute."

Russell cursed loudly.

A short time later a woman appeared at the door to the close with the screaming child in her arms. She opened it just enough to look out and say,

"Can I see your I.D. please?"

"There," Russell shouted as he brandished his warrant card.

"You can't be too careful these days," she said apologetically.

Alex reassured her while Russell moved towards the door of Garner's flat. He rattled the letterbox and waited. When there was no response he bent down and shouted into it. "Mr Garner, it's Superintendent Russell."

The only sound was the baby, who was now sobbing gently while the adults stood waiting.

"I don't suppose you have a key," he said to the woman.

"No, I don't think I even know the man that lives there. What's he done?"

"He may be injured, I will have to kick the door in. Can you please go back to your flat while we deal with this?"

She agreed eagerly and almost ran up the first flight of stairs, out of the detectives' sight.

"He may be in danger, agreed?" Russell checked his assessment with Alex.

"If he's been out of contact then yes, of course."

Russell began kicking at the lock and then regretted it as the pain arrows pierced him everywhere a Serbian boot had landed during his beating.

"Ow," he exclaimed while clutching his ribs.

"Here, let me."

Alex's time as a Tae-Kwon Do player came in useful as she used the full force of a kick to rip the door's lock from the frame. As the splinters flew, she was glad of the flat shoes she had chosen that morning.

Russell's pride had taken a dent, as he had to watch his younger colleague deal with the door but that was incidental as he turned his focus to the interior of the flat.

The short entrance hall had tiles on the floor and halfway up the wall. It was painted in a bright yellow and the style of the ceramics gave it a vaguely Spanish feel. The first door on the left led to a cool, blue and equally narrow bathroom. Opposite it there was a stark bedroom, painted white with a wardrobe, a bed and bedside cabinet. They moved along the hall to a T-junction. On the left was the kitchen and dining area but it was to the right that they turned their attention.

The living room door was closed but through the frosted glass the detectives could see that it was very dark. Russell reached for the door handle and very slowly pulled the door towards him. Alex was almost expecting the smell of decay but instead there was a pleasant aroma of a pine air freshener.

They edged into the room; thick brown curtains were drawn against the daylight. Alex walked across and slid them back to let the light stream in from the huge bay window.

It took a second for their eyes to adjust but as she turned back towards Russell she said, "Oh boy."

The main wall of the room resembled the incident board back at the station. There were photographs pinned up, each with a piece of red yarn attached that led to an index card. Those in turn had further connections shown in different colours to other cards. Each card carried particular details of the lives of the people in the pictures including their names, addresses and where they had worked down through the years but there was one constant, they had all been staff at Kildonald House. All the photographs were arranged in a column with Sir Nigel Hayworth at the top, followed by his daughter, running down to Barbara Jones at the bottom. With the exception of the noted knight, there were large red diagonal crosses covering each photograph.

"I think it's safe to say that we have the right man," Russell said.

"He'll be going after Sir Nigel next to complete his revenge."

"Definitely. Have you still got Hayworth's number?"

"It's on my phone." Alex dialled the number, hoping desperately that the geneticist would pick up, but there was no reply. She shook her head.

"Address?"

"At the station, I'll ring."

Ann-Marie Craigan answered and quickly retrieved the address.

"Tell her to send the A.R.U. to that house. Let's go, before it's too late."

Craigan confirmed to Alex that she would organise the Armed Response Unit and also send some extra detectives. Russell and Alex set off in the direction of Hayworth's home, concerned about what they may find.

***

Russell drove with siren blaring and lights flashing until they were two streets from the home of the geneticist, who lived in Giffnock. As Russell's car turned into the road he also killed his headlights.

The house was a grand blonde sandstone Victorian villa, set back from the main street on a small hill. There was a paved drive leading up to the front door. A silver Mercedes S-Class sat in front of the house. Alex could see a little light through the closed storm doors but all the curtains on the windows facing the street were closed and dark.

"Do we wait for the A.R.U.?" Alex asked as Russell parked the car across the entrance to the driveway.

"No, we can't risk it. Come on."

"Are you fit for this?" she asked with concern.

"I just need to be."

They exited the car and quietly shut the door. They walked cautiously up the drive and then a short set of stairs to the front door. As she reached for the storm door, Alex prayed that it had been oiled. The heavy painted wood swung back easily to reveal the inner door, which had not been closed properly. From deep in the house they could hear a man weeping and pleading.

Russell signalled with his hand encouraging Alex to proceed. She edged the inner door to a position that would allow them to enter the house. The plaintive sounds of an elderly man were coming from a room at the back of the house; pitiful and petrified, his terror was so strong Alex could almost feel it pulsating in her.

The hall was just broad enough for the two detectives to walk side-by-side. They continued to creep with snail-like speed towards the sound.

"Noooooo…" A shout came from a door on the right as Jason Garner came rushing out of a darkened room. He was brandishing a cleaver, which he swung towards Alex. His animalistic shout had given her some warning and she managed to get her right hand up to stop the blow coming down on her head but the corner of the blade nicked the trapezoid muscle on her shoulder. The blow caused the knife to spin out of Garner's hand. She let out a cry of her own but shifted her weight on to her assailant almost like a rugby tackle and they tumbled through the doorway into the darkened room.

A quizzical shout came from further back in the house, "Jason? Jason, what's wrong?"

Leo McDougall stepped into the hall brandishing a cordless nail gun. When he spotted Russell he brought it up and fired. The glass in the front door exploded outwards as the detective ducked below the deadly projectile. Before he could regain his balance, Russell found the gun being pointed at his head.

"Come out or I kill him," McDougall shouted in the direction of the room that Alex and Garner had fallen into. He pulled Russell to his feet and held him in front of him as he continued to aim the gun at the policeman's head.

Alex emerged with Garner close behind, her hands raised in a gesture of submission despite the pain she felt in her shoulder. Garner pushed her past the other two towards the noises of distress. McDougall swung Russell round and pushed him in the same direction.

When she walked into the small sitting room close to the rear of the house, the sight that greeted her was like something from a horror movie director's worst nightmare. Nigel Hayworth was nailed to the wall; his arms and legs splayed wide like an aged parody of Da Vinci's Vitruvian man. He was naked, and blood seeped from the holes where the nails had been driven through his wrists and ankles, as well as a multitude of small wounds on his torso that were reminiscent of those that had been found on his daughter. Despite the rigidity of the position he was crucified in, his skin and muscle tone reflected his age and they drooped pathetically. His face was streaked with rivulets of tears and mucus ran from his nose; the whites of his eyes were red, stained by his crying and terror. He continued to moan despite the fact that his mouth was covered with silver tape. In front of him, on a low coffee table, was an array of weapons that were obviously meant to be part of a long period of torture; they included nail clippers, scissors, knives and a corkscrew.

When he saw the two detectives at the mercy of his tormentors, his moans went up in volume.

"Shut up, you old bastard," McDougall screamed at him. There was no sign of the nervous, shy scientist Russell had met. Instead, McDougall was consumed by the passions of a demonic mania.

His victim's moan became a whimper.

"Sit," he told Alex and Russell, gesturing with his head towards two dining chairs.

"You! Tie them up," he commanded Garner.

Garner walked to a bag and removed some strong gaffer tape, which he used to bind the hands and feet of both officers to the legs of their respective chairs.

"You OK?" Russell said to Alex as Garner bound them.

"It's just a nick. You?"

"I've had better weeks."

Alex managed a weak smile in return.

"Shut up, the two of you."

"Leo, this doesn't have to end like this. There's an armed response unit on its way. If you don't surrender this can't end well for you." Russell, despite his own injuries, was able to sound both calm and measured.

"Shut it. I don't care any more." McDougall said, his face a picture of loathing and rage.

Alex could see from Garner's face that he still did care. There might be a little hope after all.

"I know what he did to you was wrong but this isn't going to undo that, is it?" Russell said.

"Ha. You don't have a clue what he did to us." He had been brandishing the nail gun like some outlaw in a cowboy movie but he now laid it down on the table and lifted an open razor.

"I like these," he said fondly as he exposed the blade. "They're very old-school Glasgow, don't you think?" He turned his attention to Hayworth, whose sobs increased in volume once again.

"Did you know that this old bastard and his bitch of a daughter used us like we were some chemistry experiment? They exposed us to a cocktail of drugs that left us mentally and physically scarred. And what's worse is they fucking knighted him for it."

"I know, I know but…"

McDougall exploded. "No! You don't know even the fuckin' half of it. You don't know about the nightmares we suffered or the uncontrollable moments of explosive anger that came from nowhere. You don't know about the four boys they used in their experiments that went on to commit suicide or what happened to the final group of boys. Does he, Sir Nige?"

He leaned forward and drew the razor across the old man's right nipple. There was a muted scream from Hayworth and both Alex and Russell shouted,

"No."

As the blood dripped to the floor, McDougall took up his narrative once more. "They decided that they thought they had a drug that might adjust our violent genes. They couldn't be bothered with the proper testing procedures; they thought they would try it on the poor wee boys without a voice. Tucked away in the country, where the world couldn't see."

He ran the blade of the razor around his victim's right shoulder joint and down into his armpit. The narrow line seeped an almost brown liquid as deoxygenated blood, diverted from its way back to the heart, traced an erratic path across the man's torso.

"That worked really well, didn't it Nigey-boy?" he laughed with a bitter madness.

"Do you know what happened to each and every one of the boys he used that crazy concoction on? Do you?" he shouted at the detectives.

"No," Russell said quietly.

"Every single one of us has been emasculated. Every single last one of us is sterile. A dozen jaffas, all fucking seedless." He cackled, his eyes wide and his teeth were bared.

"I'm sorry, Leo, I truly am," Russell said, trying to connect with the maniac.

"What are you sorry about? You weren't the sick, greedy bastard that decided that we were collateral damage on the way to scientific advancement and obscene profits. He was." This time the red line appeared on the slack stomach of the near unconscious figure.

At that moment Russell's phone rang.

"That'll be our colleagues; they'll be outside and that means the game's up."

"Maybe we should just give up, Leo," Garner said with quiet acceptance of their situation, his panic beginning to take hold.

"Ah poor wee Jamie. You've never quite had the stomach for this, have you, pal? Just like back at the house of horrors when you couldn't even bring yourself to set fire to the shit hole. I needed to persuade you that it was the right think to do, you just wanted to howl at the moon." McDougall shook his head at the scared figure who seemed to be visibly diminishing by the second.

"I can't give up now, not when we're so close to finishing this project. I can't let the others down. They've played their part but it was always going to be us that had to complete the task."

"What others?" Alex asked.

"There was a group of us who decided to take our revenge on the people who landed us in this position. The corrupt social workers were the first to go but those lads didn't have the stomach for the real stuff. The good stuff." He slashed the top of the scientist's left leg with a flourish, which elicited the smallest of groans from the broken man.

"They decided not to offer the real personal service that Jamie and I offer." He cracked another strained smile.

"What about Gregg Wright? He had no part in Kildonald House," Alex said.

"Did you ever meet the little shit? He was a special favour to Jamie for all the crap Wright laid on my pal since he started working for him. We had to get close to them somehow and he managed to get a job with the gangster's boy."

"And you got close to Jennifer? Why genetics?"

"I became obsessed with what they had done. I worked my way through uni with one thing in mind, I was going to get close enough to them to prove to everyone what they had done. But then when I couldn't give my wife kids, she left me. They had ruined my life with their crazy pseudo-science. His daughter had made a fortune out of what they did to us and she was going to inherit a fortune. My inheritance was violent genes, according to them; genes they wanted to rewrite, and look what they did. When my wife left I knew my revenge had to be more hands-on, you could say. And now the coup de grâce, a little emasculation of my own."

He stepped forward and lifted Hayworth's genitals. He was about to slice them off with the razor when a red dot appeared on his right temple. There was a loud crack and the red dot was replaced immediately by a black hole and the wall behind him was sprayed with his blood. At the same moment the back door was kicked in and police officers armed with assault rifles charged through the kitchen and into the room, where McDougall had slumped to the floor. Jason Garner was standing with his arms raised in surrender, his eyes wide with shock and fear, screaming loudly.

The bullet that had killed McDougall had shattered the back window on the way from a sniper's rifle. He lay at Hayworth's feet like a supplicant at the scene of a martyrdom.

When the A.R.U. were happy that the scene was secure, DS Craigan and DC Kelly were among the team of officers who raced into the house. Craigan ran towards Russell and Alex but Russell said, "Get him down."

The detective sergeant ran into the kitchen in search of something to lever the nails from the scientist's joints. She returned with a claw hammer. She asked a couple of the uniformed officers to help as she went to the victim's aid. One of them supported his weight, while the other began the painful process of removing the six-inch nails from his joints. Ann-Marie Craigan continued to talk softly to Hayworth, reassuring him while the two men worked to end his torture.

Meanwhile, Paul Kelly had removed the gaffer tape from his senior officers' limbs. Russell felt he had been rolled in a cement mixer with a bag of rocks, while Alex's shoulder was stinging with the effects of the cleaver's blade. Garner stood, his hands cuffed while an armoured female officer stood over him.

When they had lifted Nigel Hayworth from his position on the wall, they laid him delicately on the ground and called for the paramedics. Two green-suited men arrived with an oxygen tank and their medical bags to begin working on the old man. The room was now crowded with people and Russell said, "Get him out of here," indicating Garner.

Two officers hauled the silently weeping man away and Alex and Russell followed them out into the brisk night air that smelled of a sharp frost ahead. Russell drew a huge breath of it, relieved to be away from the iron-sweet smell of blood and terror.

"We need to find out who the others are," he said, accepting of the long night of talking that lay before them.

"Hopefully, he'll be cooperative. He looks as if his need for revenge has gone."

"What a fuckin' mess. All these bodies, all these lives ruined and for what?"

"I know, but that's what we do. Clean up the mess that other people cause and do what we can for the victims."

"There are an increasing number of days that I'm not sure I want to be a cleaner. You get that shoulder seen to," he ordered.

Alex went to an ambulance that was parked in the road outside the gates of the house. The paramedic patched her up and advised her that she would need to go to the hospital for a couple of stitches. She promised that she would go once she had finished work, which prompted a shake of the head from the young medic.

When she walked back towards the house, Russell was sitting on the steps.

"All sorted?"

"I need to go for stitches but I'll pop in on my way home."

"You should go."

"No, we'll get this finished. Come on, let's go grab a coffee before we chat to Mr Garner, or is it Gardiner?"

Russell stood up wearily and walked with her to his car.

CHAPTER 24

On the way back to the station, Russell had put on the radio and tuned it to a station playing gentle, soothing music. At the top of the hour the tunes were interrupted by a news bulletin. One item in particular caught Russell's attention.

"Two men were found shot dead in Glasgow earlier tonight. The police believe they were Serbian nationals and that they may have been involved in a drug deal that went wrong. A large cache of weapons was also discovered at the scene. Police are appealing for any witnesses to come forward."

Russell swore.

"What's up?"

"Nothing, just tired."

Alex hadn't really been paying attention to the radio broadcast. "Are you sure?"

"It's fine. I'll deal with it." He wore a fierce scowl all the way back to the station. He knew that his relationship with the gang leader had just been complicated and that there were going to be repercussions further on down the line. The last thing he needed was Professional Standards taking an interest in him and his idiot brother. McGavigan just couldn't resist the violent approach but Russell had no idea how he could pursue it without his involvement becoming public knowledge. The case would be handed to another superintendent in the MIT, so maybe Russell could minimise the damage depending which of the team it was but he could be heading for a career-ending confrontation. It was a problem for another day but he knew a day of reckoning would come.

It was not something he wanted Alex to know anything about that night but she was a smart copper and she would work it out without his help. He kept his dark thoughts to himself as he completed the drive, wondering if this was the last case he would work with her.

***

A cheer greeted Russell and Menzies when they walked back into the incident room. Many of the detectives had returned to the office when they heard about the possible arrest, just in case they were needed to help out in any way.

Garner sat disconsolately in the interview room, a silent uniformed constable his only companion. He had turned down the offer of a solicitor and didn't seem to care what was going to happen to him.

"Would you prefer Jason or Jamie?" Russell asked as he sat down.

"Jason. Jamie died a long time ago," he replied.

"Do you want to tell us what happened?"

Garner began to talk and everything came tumbling out at once. He started the story with his father, an ex-miner who had failed to find a place in the world after his pit closed. He had drifted from one poorly paid, low-skilled job to another and with every change his drinking increased. He had beaten his wife on a regular basis and she took it until the first time he hit Jamie. The boy was only twelve when he had stepped in to stop his father handing out to his wife his latest piece of resentment at the world. His father fractured the young boy's cheekbone and his mother took him to hospital, leaving the family home for the last time.

He spoke about his time at Kildonald; his mother's constant fear that his father would appear; his initial joy at sharing his life with other children before the Hayworths arrived. The mothers had been told that the medicine their children were given would help them with concentration and schoolwork but it was soon obvious that there was something else going on. He remembered how his friends had changed, their behaviour becoming changeable and unpredictable. When it was his turn he was frightened to go to the 'doctor's hoose' as the children referred to it. When a nice lady gave him a fruit drink, he thought that it wasn't as bad as he was expecting.

After three visits he began to feel different. A simple thing like losing a game of snakes and ladders would send him into a rage and he would hit out at people. His pal Lennie was suffering the same problem and one night he persuaded Jamie that they had to do something to stop the treatments, which were now increasingly painful, as they had moved from drinks or pills to injections. They thought of destroying the hut but Lennie reckoned they would just use another building. He said that Jamie should burn down the big house and then they would have to move them away. Jamie wasn't keen but then, after a particularly bad treatment, he had thrown something at the nurse and decided that Lennie was right. He set fire to the curtain with the candle and he was free of the house for good.

The freedom didn't extend to his sleep. When he had been away from the house for three months, the nightmares came. Flaming demons and a horned beast haunted his dreams every night until he became scared to even lay his head down on his pillow.

He hadn't seen Lennie since the night of the fire but then he bumped into him aged twenty-one. Lennie had gone to university and was about to graduate. Jamie was working in an office, still haunted by the occasional dream. They went for a drink and told each other similar stories of pain and horror. Lennie had met two other men who had been subjected to the experiments when they were kids and they had told him of their similar suffering. That was when the plot was hatched to get the information to convict the Hayworths. Jennifer was now married to Gregg Wright, and Lennie believed that he and Jamie should pursue two different paths to try to get close to her. Lennie would finish his degree and get a job with Hayworth Genetic Solutions. He was so persuasive and so driven that Jamie was willing to do anything, including following Lennie's example of changing his name. Lennie had become Leo once he left school and went to university. His birth name was Leonard Dickinson but his mother's maiden name was McDougall. He told his mother that he no longer wanted to be associated with his father and changed his name by deed poll to Leo McDougall. He helped Jamie become Jason Garner when he spotted a grave bearing the name and persuaded him to adopt a new persona.

They had continued to meet with the two other victims occasionally but then Leo discovered he was sterile and everything began to change. He suggested to the others that they got tested and their status was confirmed. Leo spent two more years tracing the other eight boys who were involved and each of them confirmed that they too had been sterilised by the drug. When his wife left him, Leo's anger was uncontrollable and he persuaded, cajoled and coerced the other three at the heart of the group to take direct action against those he believed to have ruined their lives.

Garner took an hour to tell them the full story with only the occasional question or prompting by the detectives. In many ways it was a distressing tale, which only got worse when he gave them the details of their final crimes.

"Leo killed Wright in his car and something in him seemed to snap. We were just going to dump the whole body at once but there was a bloodlust about him. He told me to chop him up, that it would look more like a gangland killing. Then he decided to take Jennifer to the holiday home near Loch Lomond. I wish I had never told him about that place. I wanted to kill her and get it over with but he said she had to suffer for what she had done to us. He tortured her for days and then left her to die."

Neither Russell nor Alex knew what to say, it was all too much to take in after the day they had endured.

Garner supplied the names of the other two men that had been involved in the hit and run, the mugging and the fatal fire. He was left to write a statement while Russell and his DI went back to the office. Russell called ACC Muldoon and told him all that had happened that day plus the details of Garner's confession.

"Sounds like a rough day, Tom. Get yourself home. And pass my thanks to the whole team."

"I will do, sir. Good night."

EPILOGUE

A small group of people stood in silent reverence as a cloud of condensed breaths rose from them to coalesce in the early morning snow that fell quietly around them. They were congregated around an open grave where a light brown coffin lay on wooden planks, while a priest read the funeral rites.

Tom Russell and Alex Menzies were two of the nine people surrounding the grave of Paddy Niven. Apart from the priest, there were three worthies from the Astral Bar and two people from the post office that he collected his benefits from. His estranged wife and two daughters hadn't appeared but at least his son was there, even if he was displaying little emotion. It was a bleak and pathetic way for any life to be remembered.

The priest finished the final part of the ceremony and Russell and Alex helped the body on its final journey. The coffin rested at the bottom and the casting of handfuls of brown soil completed the formalities.

The group dispersed with a brief word of thanks from Paddy's son. Alex and Russell headed to his car.

"I heard you dropped the charges against your brother," she said.

"Aye, I think he's learned his lesson. At least I hope he has, with him you never know. Have you heard how old Hayworth is doing?"

"Out of intensive care and on the mend but I think he's going to be facing a lot of questions when he's up to it. There are professional and criminal investigations under way from what I hear."

"I hope they throw the book at him, he was the real cause of all this."

"How are the bruises?"

"Just about gone. Your arm?"

"A wee but stiff but it should be OK with some physio."

As they reached for the car doors, Russell's phone rang.

"Russell." He listened to the caller.

"OK, text the address, we're on our way."

"A job?" Alex asked.

"A stabbing in Pollokshields."

"Here we go again."

THE END

ABOUT THE AUTHOR

Sinclair Macleod was born and raised in Glasgow. He worked in the railway industry for 23 years, the majority of which were in IT.

A lifelong love of mystery novels, including the classic American detectives of Hammett, Chandler and Ross Macdonald, inspired him to write his first novel, 'The Reluctant Detective' featuring Craig Campbell. There are two further Reluctant Detective novels, 'The Good Girl and 'The Killer Performer as well as the short story, The Island Murder.

The first Russell and Menzies novel is about a serial killer and is called 'Soulseeker'

Sinclair lives in Bishopbriggs, just outside his native city with his wife, Kim and daughter, Kirsten.

For more information go to

wwwsinclairmacleod.com

twitter: @sinclairmacleod

Lightning Source UK Ltd.
Milton Keynes UK
UKOW05f1509241116
288440UK00001B/10/P